the
summer
hideaway

ALSO BY JENNY HALE

Christmas Wishes and Mistletoe Kisses
Coming Home for Christmas
A Christmas to Remember
A Barefoot Summer
Summer by the Sea
Summer at Oyster Bay
All I Want for Christmas
The Summer House
We'll Always Have Christmas

the
summer
hideaway

JENNY HALE

bookouture

Published by Bookouture in 2018

An imprint of StoryFire Ltd.

Carmelite House
50 Victoria Embankment
London EC4Y 0DZ

www.bookouture.com

ISBN: 978-1-78681-713-6
ISBN: 978-1-78681-521-7
eBook ISBN: 978-1-78681-520-0

Previously published as *One Summer*

For Justin, my rock

Prologue

Alice Emerson plopped down in the sand, looking out at the restless ocean as it peeked over the sea oats. The blooms at the end of each thin stalk of wild, tall grass made them top-heavy, so they always seemed to be leaning. Each stem swayed on the dune in front of her, while she forced herself to keep her mind on the landscape instead of somewhere else. She closed her eyes briefly to allow her concentration to move from the sea oats themselves to the last time she'd seen them: bright green and swaying as if they were dancing in the coastal breeze, the sun on her face, stinging her nose and cheekbones, the smell of the sea all around her.

Alice leaned against the weathered clapboard wall of her gramps's bicycle shop, where she'd gone to sit and collect her thoughts, rushing outside to catch her breath, every inhalation in that building pulling her back into the life of her beloved grandfather. If she let herself, she could channel the smell of the chocolate chip cookies he'd bake whenever she asked, the natural wood floors that she'd run on, barefoot, as he chased her around, and the clean cotton of the crisp sheets she used to sleep cocooned in after a day of swimming, falling into bed and closing her eyes right away so she could still experience the swishing feeling from bobbing in the waves all day.

The building itself, having stood the test of time since its construction nearly a century ago, was stronger than she was, clearly. While it had withstood many storms, Alice was struggling to handle this one. She grabbed hold of the earth beneath her and lifted her hands, allowing the grains of sand to drop from her clenched fists, opening her fingers until the red of her nail polish emerged. Her shoulders ached and her mind was swimming with emotion, her only solace the lull of the tide and the screech of seagulls overhead.

"When you need to know the answers to life," Gramps had always told her, his bushy eyebrows pulling together the same way they had when Alice was worried about something and he wanted to help her, "you turn to the sea. It gives you the calm you need to filter through the static in your head, until you can hear the answers loud and clear."

Alice needed those answers right now. She needed him. Six months had slipped away already—six months without her beloved Gramps. She'd only just now been able to return to his old bicycle shop on the North Carolina coast. Originally constructed to house the people who'd built the protective sand dunes from Corolla to Ocracoke, and later inhabited by fishermen, the tiny building had seen its share of visitors. Alice was its most recent, but this time was her first visit alone, without Gramps. She'd waited for the sunshine of spring because that was how she wanted to see it again: bright and happy.

To Alice, this beach wasn't just for vacations, mini-golf, and paddle boarding. It was the place where Gramps had allowed her to stay up past her bedtime to hunt ghost crabs, where he'd told her the legends about Blackbeard the pirate's adventures on nearby Ocracoke Island; it was where she'd spent her days running through the foamy surf as it bubbled around her little toes just before Gramps scooped her up into the air. Alice had spent many summers here—just her and Gramps in his shop.

She tipped her head back to let the sunshine warm the cold that was filling her chest. It was getting late, even though the sun didn't want to *admit it. She stood up and stretched her back, wondering if it wasn't the sea that gave her the answers, but Gramps's presence. Alice didn't have any more idea of what to do now than she had when she'd gotten here.*

With a heavy sigh, she turned to face the shop that now sat nearly empty. It looked sad, broken like her heart. Gramps had given this place to her—for what? What was it without him? She had no idea what to do with it, but all she knew was that staying here was too difficult. Perhaps she could sell it, like she'd sold all his bikes, add the profits to the money that Gramps had so generously left for her, and follow her dreams on some big adventure. Was that what Gramps would have wanted for her?

One more time, she looked over her shoulder for answers, but none came. After that last glance at the ebbing tide that had comforted her for years, she opened the door on the back of the bicycle shop and went in to see what the future held.

Chapter One

"I can't believe he didn't show," Sasha said quietly from behind her double decker vanilla and strawberry ice cream cone, her pale blue spring manicure complementing the ice cream colors.

Alice and her best friend Sasha Miller sat together at an outdoor picnic table, Alice's gaze darting to the counter across from them where her five-year-old son Henry was waiting for his ice cream, before focusing on her friend.

Alice had known Sasha since they were seven years old. Sasha had moved in down the street from her and they'd met on the bus ride to school. All the seats had been taken except the spot beside Alice. Sasha had dropped down next to her that day and started talking as if they'd been together their whole little lives. To this day, Sasha could talk Alice through anything. And that was exactly why Alice had called her right after Matt hadn't shown up, when he'd texted that he would.

"He didn't even have the decency to face me. After two years together."

"You shouldn't have gone to meet him." Sasha rolled her eyes. "He doesn't deserve your presence."

"It would've been hard to see him again, but I was hoping to have some closure."

With a paper bag of Matt's things clasped tightly in her grip, Alice had waited for Matt at their favorite park, where they'd had their first date. She'd had to take in calming breaths the entire time to keep the tears from surfacing, focusing on the tinkling of her dangly earrings in the breeze to try to take her mind off of what he'd done. She'd worn those earrings just to spite him; they were the ones she'd bought after finding out he'd been unfaithful, the ones she'd decided matched her new overpriced highlights the best.

Alice hadn't been trying to win him back with her little makeover, but she did get a certain amount of satisfaction from knowing that she'd never let herself spend another evening crying over Matt again, depressed in her sweats, holding a pint of rocky road ice cream and an empty box of cookies. She had firmly made that decision.

It had taken that monumental event to bring her to her best.

"For Matt to show up and give you closure, it would mean that he was actually a good person, which he is not. He'd only disguised himself as one." Sasha took a bite off the top of her cone.

"I did get a little closure, though, leaving our park. There was something about walking away from it that made me feel stronger." Alice played with her bowl of ice cream, not really eating it. "And it made me feel better when I chucked the bag of his things in the trashcan." She grinned deviously before sobering. "I thought he could be The One," she said, shaking her head. "The sad thing is that *both* Henry and I loved him. If he'd been a better man, he could've had the two of us forever."

Alice tucked her curly blonde hair behind her ears before dragging the small spoon around the lump of overflowing ice cream in her bowl, to keep it from dripping down onto her fingers in the evening heat. She looked over at her son again. Henry could barely reach the counter, but he'd insisted they take a seat and let him get his on his own—he was a big boy, he'd said. He stood patiently, his fingers tapping the shiny surface that held the container of napkins and a tip jar that read, "We're all in college. Need we say more?"

Alice took a bite of the melting ice cream and swallowed, still angry at the situation. "I'm so awful at picking guys."

"No, you're not."

Sasha was just being kind. Alice had fallen for some real losers: one had claimed to be a traveling musician, but was more of a homeless party guy with a guitar; another had decided to follow his dreams and sail around the world. He just forgot to tell her that he'd financed a boat with their joint bank account. And there was Henry's father, the biggest loser of them all, a minor league baseball player who'd run off the very minute she'd told him she was pregnant, joining a European team and leaving the country and his son.

"It's not your fault that he decided to run around with his personal trainer behind your back. Who does that?" Sasha said, her eyes squinted in irritation, a frown on her face.

On that point, Sasha *was* right: it wasn't Alice's fault. But it *was* her fault that she'd let her guard down enough to waste two years on him and allow herself to be emotionally wounded by him. The hurt at being blindsided was only a tiny piece of it all—she could get over that. What she couldn't get over was the look on Henry's face when she had to tell him that Matt wasn't going to take him to hit baseballs anymore.

But she'd realized, after Matt's leaving, that she didn't need anyone to go through life with her; she could do it on her own. She could be the sole parent for Henry—after all, she knew better than anyone else what kind of person she wanted to raise him to be. She didn't need any help with that. She also didn't need any assistance with finding things that made her happy—she knew how to do that too. So from this point on, she wasn't going to allow another man to ruin what she and Henry had. Relationships introduced risk, and she wasn't willing to gamble anymore. She was too tired of wondering at the end of every relationship how they'd gotten there. Instead, she wanted to turn her energy to herself and Henry, and with her new inheritance, something new and wonderful could be right around the corner.

Chapter Two

Alice had let her ice cream completely melt, thinking about the wreckage of her love life. Sasha brought her back to reality, reaching down and tugging on Einstein's collar to keep him from running off. Alice, just realizing she'd dropped the leash, picked it back up. They'd been holding the puppy while Henry got his ice cream. He turned around and waved at them from the counter, a smile on his face under that old ratty baseball cap of his that he refused to take off.

"This puppy is so cute," Sasha said, stroking Einstein's head, clearly trying to get Alice's mind off of Matt. Einstein's deep chocolate eyes peered up at Sasha as he nudged her with his snout for more affection.

Einstein was the black Labrador Alice had bought Henry after she'd told him about Matt. Henry had had to go to baseball practice, and she'd made him go even though he'd said he didn't feel like playing ball that day. She wasn't going to let him wallow like she had. Matt didn't deserve Henry's energy. And Henry *always* felt like playing ball; he'd be just fine once he got those dusty cleats to home base and the bat in his grip as he circled it by his shoulder, waiting for the ball to sail into his view.

Even though they had no contact at all with Henry's father, Joel, Alice hadn't kept him a secret from Henry, putting old newspaper clippings of his dad's accomplishments in his room. It was all he'd left behind. Since the time Henry was little, he'd always shown an interest in baseball. She'd wondered if he was just genetically predisposed to love it like his father did, or if it was some way for Henry to have a connection to the man who'd been absent his whole life.

The day Matt had left, Henry had tied the laces of his cleats, looping the ends of them—they were stained orange from the clay on the fields—with tears streaming down his cheeks. That picture of him was now burned in Alice's memory.

She'd gotten Einstein for fifty dollars at the shelter after dropping Henry off at practice, and then surprised her son with him because seeing his sadness over losing Matt tore her heart out. She promised herself she'd do everything she could to bring back his smile to make up for it.

So now, after they'd had dinner, Alice and Sasha had decided to take Henry for an evening treat at a walk-up ice cream shop. Henry loved ice cream about as much as he loved baseball, and taking him had been on Alice's mind all day.

"Just think," Sasha said, her face blocking Alice's view of Henry for a second, "if you both could love a dirt bag like Matt, what would your love be like for someone amazing? He's out there."

Alice smiled, more out of kindness for her friend than agreement. The thing was, she'd devoted so much energy to finding Mr. Perfect, when really she didn't think he was actually out there anymore. She was starting to think that she'd wanted a dream: someone to be that perfect family man for Henry, someone to keep her company during those quiet times, someone to share her life with. But as she looked around at the people she knew, she didn't see that anywhere. She believed now that it was a fantasy that she'd created for herself as a young girl, and she needed to let it go. This was real life. She wasn't looking for Mr. Right anymore.

"What if he isn't out there, Sash?"

Sasha had always been the optimist of the two of them, whereas Alice was a realist. But there was a flicker of understanding mixed with fear behind those thrift store aviator sunglasses of hers, and Alice knew that, even though Sasha was a dreamer, she was plagued by the same question, having just gone through an awful divorce herself. The legal fees from the divorce alone had sucked Sasha's bank account nearly dry and she was living on her tiny nest egg until she could recoup that money.

More than fear lurked in Sasha's face this time, however, yet Alice couldn't place it. Her friend looked oddly worried. If Sasha didn't tell her what it was, Alice was definitely going to try to get her to open up about it at another time because, by the look on her friend's face, there was definitely something she wasn't sharing; something was wrong.

Henry came over with his ice cream: a vanilla cone with sprinkles for hair, two candy eyes and a licorice mouth. He held it out with a smile so they could see, as the sun filtered through the trees, casting its rays on his little face. Einstein stood at attention, his back end swinging from side to side while he nudged Henry's arm.

"I like it!" Alice said, the moment with Sasha gone. She gently petted under the dog's ears as Henry sat down. The blond hair that peeked out from under his baseball cap would become almost white in the summer, his skin tan from playing all day in the sun. The weather had been unusually warm already and they'd spent tons of time outside to escape the small apartment they lived in.

She didn't know what she'd been thinking, getting a puppy this size when they were in that small apartment, and she barely had enough time to take him for walks. Alice was a secretary at a dental office, and she didn't finish work until nearly six o'clock every night. Once she got Henry from daycare and arrived home, she wanted to spend time with him, helping him with his schoolwork and hearing about his day. But every time she found a chewed-up shoe or the puppy had an accident on the floor, she'd close her eyes and remember Henry's face when he'd seen her walk across that baseball field with Einstein the night she'd gotten him. She wanted the rest of his life to be just like that moment.

"Can I walk him in the grass?" Henry asked, holding his ice cream in one hand as he reached for the leash with his other. His baseball cap was on backwards, the sun still hitting his face and showing off his freckles. She noticed how long his legs were getting—he was gangly now, not a toddler anymore. It was as if she'd blinked and he'd become this well-spoken little boy.

"Do you think you can handle him?"

"Yeah. I'm strong," he said, with vanilla on his bottom lip from his bite of ice cream.

"Okay. I'm right here if you need me. Just call over."

Henry took Einstein, and the puppy happily trotted along beside him, alternating between jumping up to try to reach Henry's ice cream and stopping to sniff spots in the grass. Alice smiled, warmed by the sight, the sun still setting earlier than it would in the thick of summer and making a silhouette of Henry, Einstein, and the ice cream—like in one of those movies that made her come out of the darkness sighing with a big grin, while everyone else hustled on to the bathrooms with their empty drink cups and popcorn boxes.

"It's been two weeks since you went to your grandfather's bicycle shop and I haven't asked you yet if you're really okay," Sasha said, changing the subject. Thank goodness they'd moved on from Matt.

Sasha pulled her hair behind her shoulders, revealing the silver hoop earrings Alice had gotten her for her birthday.

Sasha leaned toward her. "You're more quiet than usual, all in your head somewhere. You okay?"

Alice nodded. What she didn't want to admit was that she was okay at this moment, on this day, but she didn't know if she was *really* all right. Perhaps going to Gramps's place might not have been the best timing, given the enormous disruption that Matt's leaving had caused for her and Henry. His infidelity had come out of nowhere, completely turning their lives upside down, right when she was starting to actually face life without Gramps.

Sasha had been the first friend Alice had called when all her emotions were at their height, and she had been right there by her side. But thinking back, Sasha—usually the one who could spin any situation into a positive—had been just as brokenhearted, and she hadn't been able to find anything reassuring to say. The more Alice thought about it, Sasha had been very quiet herself over the last few weeks, her demeanor different. She hadn't put it together until now, but as she looked at her friend, she knew something definitely wasn't right.

"Are *you* okay?" Alice said, instead of answering.

"Me? I'm fine!" Sasha said, a little too quickly, before turning the focus back to Alice, her bright red cheeks giving her away. "Matt's timing is impeccable… Couldn't he have at least waited for a better time to drop this bomb?"

Alice shrugged, letting her friend off the hook. This wasn't the time to talk about it, obviously. "I'd rather know now than carry on like nothing was wrong, I guess. I already feel like he's robbed me of my time."

Sasha offered a sympathetic pout. Alice had gone straight to Sasha's the night she'd found out that Gramps had died. While he'd been having a few health problems, they'd been nothing too major, and his death had come out of nowhere. He'd been working right up to the day, at his bicycle rental shop in the Outer Banks of North Carolina. It sat directly on the beach next to a busy fishing pier, full of tourists lining up at the binocular stations. He lived upstairs and ran the shop from the bottom floor. After work, he spent most of his free time fishing.

"Have you had any luck selling the bike shop?" Sasha asked, as if she could read Alice's mind. She waved to Henry. He was running along, laughing every time Einstein followed his lead. He yelled for them to look and both of them acknowledged him with their biggest smiles. Sasha pushed her sunglasses up on top of her head, and Alice could see the concern in her eyes as she concentrated on her.

"The realtor's had a few calls asking for specifics and she said there's been one person who's toured the property, but she hasn't heard back yet."

She watched Henry as she decided if she should actually entertain the thought that had been going around in her head since Matt left. Their breakup had brought back a memory of the boy she'd met one summer's day at Gramps's shop all those years ago, making her wish for something better. She and the boy had had ice cream that day, and she could still remember the smile on his face as he looked at her, holding his cone. It had gotten her thinking… The upheaval of losing Matt had completely changed her outlook on the bike shop. It wasn't so difficult to be there anymore; instead, it was calling her home—maybe she could settle down there and still, in a way, be close to Gramps.

Finally, she said, "I've been playing with an idea—it's crazy—but what if I moved there and opened some sort of shop in its place?" She had been thinking a lot about what it would be like to spend this summer at Gramps's beach house; the shop downstairs, the ocean out her window…

"I'd miss you!" Sasha pouted. "It might be nice to get away from everything, though," she relented. "I know I'd like to get away." She had that odd look on her face again, but she ironed it out, producing a smile for Alice's benefit. "Tell me more!"

"I've been thinking a lot about it," Alice said. "But the bike shop barely made Gramps any money. The shop was so small, he couldn't house much inventory, so the turnover was high, but it still didn't give him enough to really become comfortable financially. He never seemed to mind, but for Henry and me, I'd need something more to keep us afloat."

Sasha looked over Alice's head in thought. "So what could you fit more of in that little building, then?"

"It's prime beachfront property—something would work there. But I've been trying to answer that question and I can't think of anything making me as much as the sale of the land itself."

She'd decided to save the money from the sale until the right thing came along, but now she wondered if the right thing was sitting in front of her, and opening a business was in her future. She let her mind wander to the white clapboard siding of the building, the bells on the door that jingled as people opened it, the small front porch where she used to sit and drink ice-cold bottles of Coca-Cola, digging her toes into the natural sand walkway just beneath the steps while Gramps was busy with customers.

"But will the money make you happy? What will it get you? You have the chance to escape to a totally different life, leave everything behind. There's got to be something you could do with that place that would light your fire." Sasha caught a drip of strawberry ice cream on the side of her cone with her finger, that unusual look of concern surfacing again before she wiped it away. Whatever it was that was bothering her would be quite a conversation, Alice was certain now.

"Do you really think I could live and work at the beach?" she said, keeping the conversation on her, as Sasha clearly wanted her to do.

There was a tiny part of Alice that worried she couldn't do it. Creating a business from the ground up was quite an undertaking and she didn't have the expertise for it. She had wanted to go away to college with Sasha—they were both going to study marketing—but when she got pregnant with Henry, she'd decided to do a two-year degree and work at the dentist's office instead. Sasha had gone on and finished her studies, and Alice had always felt like she'd missed out.

"Why not?" Sasha gave her a stern look. "Don't sell yourself short," she said. "It's not all about the money and you know that, which is why you're considering doing something with the building. You own a piece of beachfront property and you have absolutely nothing holding you here in Richmond. Life is too short not to take risks."

"I'm worried about leaving my job," Alice said, looking down at her nearly untouched bowl of ice cream, which now resembled green soup, little flakes of dark chocolate floating in it.

"You hate your job."

"Yeah, but it pays my bills. And we get free spray tans every year at the hygienists' summer party. And there's also you. I'd have to leave you and I don't know if I could make it without you." Alice had never had a sister, but if she had, she'd have wanted her to be just like Sasha.

With a doting smile, Sasha stood up and gave Alice a squeeze. "It's so hot out here," she said, grabbing the long curls that fell down Alice's back, pulling them up into a ponytail like she'd done since they were kids. The breeze on Alice's neck immediately cooled her, but before she could really enjoy the release of heat, the strands came tumbling back down to her shoulders as Sasha picked up her bowl of green minty soup and chucked it into the trashcan. "I'm going to get you another ice cream and I want you to enjoy it!"

She knew she couldn't argue with her friend, so while Sasha was at the counter ordering another, Alice walked over to the grassy area where Henry was sitting under a tree, Einstein sprawled across his lap, chewing on Henry's ice cream cone.

"He wanted some," Henry said. "I was okay with sharing."

Alice giggled. "That's very nice of you," she said, putting her weight on a large tree root that made a perfect little bench for her. She stretched her legs out in front of her, the grass cool on her skin.

Einstein looked up at her and wagged his tail, his deep brown eyes loyal already.

Sasha came back over, carrying a small cone with mint chocolate chip. "You know, it hit me when I was ordering this: you could open up an ice cream shop in your grandfather's building! It's right by the pier. You'd have a ton of business."

Henry sat up on his knees, Einstein following his lead and standing, his ears perked, his tail midway between the ground and full-on wagging.

Alice didn't know a thing about ice cream or running an ice cream business. What would she even do in the off-season when the tourists had all left? Not to mention, she was still deciding whether it was smart to sink the small inheritance she'd gotten from Gramps into a new company, only to lose it all because she had no idea what she was doing.

Sasha gave Alice a dismissive look, as if she could see her deliberation. "Say what you will, but to some, that isn't so crazy."

"It isn't crazy to me," Henry said, his face so innocent, those blue eyes sparkling at the mere idea of it.

"You'd love to have ice cream every day, I'm sure."

Alice knocked off his hat and ruffled his hair playfully. He grabbed it and put it back on. Alice got up and took Einstein's leash, licking her ice cream down as it melted. She wasn't completely opposed to the idea and she decided to hold on to the notion of an ice cream shop. She didn't want to come to a decision right now anyway, so she turned the conversation toward Henry and the day he'd spent with her father.

"Come on," she said. "Let's get home so I can hear all about your fishing with Grandpa Frank." She tossed her keys to Sasha. "Will you drive so I can finish my ice cream?"

Chapter Three

"So tell me," Alice asked Henry as she tucked his blankets around him, his hair wet and combed to the side after his bath, "how many fish did you catch with Grandpa Frank?" She leaned down onto the other pillow on his bed, the lamplight casting a golden glow in his room. Above his bed, the planets whirled around on the ceiling from his nightlight and the soft clicking of the small machine was almost lulling.

"I caught seven!" he said, his eyebrows rising in excitement, his blue eyes aglitter. She hadn't seen him like that since the day his team, The Bobcats, won the little league championship, and she maintained a certain satisfaction from the fact that he'd gotten his love of fishing from her—one thing that didn't remind her every day of his father.

That little league game was the last one Matt had attended. It had started to drizzle outside, so Matt offered to keep score from the press box, and he invited Alice to climb up to get out of the rain. Henry made a home run that day, and Matt had called out over the loudspeaker, "Way to go, Henry!" Henry pumped his fists and pointed at his mother with that same smile on his face, making her laugh.

"Grandpa Frank caught twelve. How can he catch so many?" Henry said, as the memory of his game faded away.

Alice let out a small chuckle. She'd thought the same thing when she'd gone fishing with her own grandfather. "Grandpa Frank learned from his dad, my gramps. Your great-grandfather was amazing at fishing. He had trophies." She said the word "trophies" in a whisper to drive home how thrilling it was. Because, as a girl, she'd felt that excitement.

"You want some slack in the line," she remembered Gramps saying, the sparkle of the Atlantic behind him as he looked at her with that crease between his green eyes, his skin weathered from years of being in the sun. He would grab her line with his fingers still wet from securing the shrimp onto her hook, and pull just a little. They always fished with shrimp because he swore that shore fishing was better with real bait.

Alice had done all the things young girls do—tea parties, dress-up, playing with dolls—but there was something about fishing with Gramps that was more fun than any of those other things. The fondness of her memories could've been due to the fact that her mother had died too early and she'd spent so much time with the men in her family. Or perhaps it was the wind on her face, or the squawk of seagulls overhead, or the swooshing of the ocean, or the way Gramps told her "good job" with that wrinkle of his nose when she caught a fish—whatever it was, she couldn't get enough of it. So when he invited her to visit, she always jumped at the chance.

"I used to fish with my gramps from a big pier that stretched out into the ocean," she said, her memories inching into their conversation. She tucked Henry's blankets around him.

"I wish I could've tried that," he said, his eyelids getting heavy.

Gramps had told her once that he'd started fishing more after he'd lost Gran. Gran was a character that Alice had pieced together using old photos, family stories, and fuzzy memories. Alice had only been four when she'd passed away of heart problems. From what Alice knew of her, she was a free spirit, dancing and twirling around the kitchen while she dried dishes, always smiling. Alice could remember her shoes: flat, like ballet slippers, dark, and perfect with the shorts she liked to wear. If Alice worked really hard, she could see the pattern on the scarf that Gran used to tie her hair back in the coastal wind. But that was about it.

Alice had so many more memories with Gramps. She used to love the way he lined up the bicycles outside in a rainbow of color every morning, with the salty breeze blowing against their faces, warm as an oven despite the sun barely peeking over the horizon. When she used to visit him, they'd get up well before dawn, and as soon as those bikes were out, people would show up with their paper cups of coffee from the local shop and rent their bikes so they could take that first morning ride as the orange glow rose up over the ocean. The white sparkles on the waves were like fireworks, the air crystal clear before the day's humidity set in.

Henry inhaled deeply and wriggled like he always did when he was fighting sleep, but the busyness of his day was more than he could battle and sleep was winning over.

Alice quietly set the pile of books they'd read earlier onto the floor, as Henry slipped into dreamland. She stayed on the edge of his bed, thinking. Henry didn't remember visiting the Outer Banks where Gramps had had his bicycle shop. He'd been so small the last time they'd gone. He'd seen Gramps on Thanksgiving, and Henry always received a ten-dollar bill in his birthday card from him, but life had gotten in the way and they hadn't gone to see him like they should've—in recent years, it had always just been easier for Gramps to make the drive to see everyone here.

Gently, Alice pushed a wet strand of hair off Henry's forehead and he breathed in again in response. She wished Henry could've experienced the long evenings they'd spent on the pier after a rainstorm, when all the tourists had piled into the movie theaters and shopping malls to avoid the rain, Gramps closing the bike shop early as a result. He'd pull out a can of soda for both of them—she could still hear the snap and the fizz as he released the top with his thick fingers. She'd skip up next to him as he'd grab his tackle box and two poles from the corner of the shop. Sipping the sugary sweetness of the soda, the icy drink refreshing in contrast to the muggy heat that steamed from the asphalt road, they'd make their way to the pier.

After they'd fished, Gramps would bring her back to the shop, where she'd climb up on the counter, folding her legs underneath her, and they'd nibble on cookies that he would always make just for her—eating Gramps's cookies was one of her favorite memories. She could remember the smell of baking mixed with the tires of all the bikes and the salt of the sea. It was its own unique scent that could never be replicated.

She was unsure if it was the late hour or the fact that she struggled to let go of things, but she had a shockingly strong pain in her chest when she thought about never setting foot in the bike shop again. She tried to rationalize it, telling herself that Gramps wasn't there now, and she wasn't a little girl anymore, but no matter what she said to try to convince herself, the idea crept in that she might not be doing the right thing by selling.

She tiptoed out of Henry's room and called Sasha. She wanted to talk to her anyway to see if she could get out of her what was going on. By the way she'd acted during their ice cream date today, it certainly seemed as though Sasha was having some inner turmoil about something as well.

"I'm really having second thoughts about selling Gramps's property," she said honestly after Sasha picked up. "Even if I have no idea what to do, I'm struggling to part with it." The good thing about Sasha was that, while she always saw things through rose-colored glasses, she listened as well, and took in Alice's point of view. "I'm afraid I'll miss it."

"So what do you want to do?"

"I don't know anything about marketing or projections or inventory…"

"You're thinking about the ice cream shop!" she nearly squealed through the phone. When Alice didn't say anything, still trying to decide if she'd lost her mind or not, Sasha continued, "You have a natural knack for marketing! I remember the ideas you used to give me when I was in school. Was ice cream what you want to do? Or something else?"

Alice twisted a loose string on the throw pillow of her sofa. "Everybody likes ice cream." Was she convincing herself?

"True… I'm a bit rusty on the marketing side, but what if I helped you? We could do it together; we always have great ideas when we use both our brains! Remember the A you got me in my content marketing class?"

"I didn't get you that A. You got it. It was you who thought of that YouTube video on relaxation! Remember all those wonderful comments people left, feeling energized and excited? That video ended up getting almost five hundred thousand views!"

"Yes, but it was you who created the content. I just made the video."

"You're being modest, and kind," Alice said with a smile. "Anyway, I couldn't ask you to help me in North Carolina while you're trying to interview for jobs here." Sasha had been working at her husband Landon's real estate agency until the divorce and now she was in search of something new. She'd been pounding the pavement for months, and she was waiting for a call from the Martin Agency after a very successful round of interviews.

The line buzzed in silence for a moment, and then Sasha said, "What if I left the job search for a while and worked with you?"

Alice lay back on the sofa, causing Einstein to shift in his crate. The idea was making her prickle with excitement. "I couldn't afford you."

"You said your gramps lived above the shop, right? If we both lived upstairs and we split whatever profits were left after investing in the business, you could afford me. We could get by until we made enough that you could pay me a salary."

"That would be an awfully big favor…"

"It might be just what I need," Sasha said, excitement but also a near desperation in her voice. "We could wake up every morning and walk out onto the beach, dig our toes in the sand, and throw balls to Einstein, help Henry make sandcastles. But best of all, we could leave this place behind and make a fresh start—just the girls."

The idea did appeal to Alice. "No guys," she clarified. "No one to cloud our judgment and get in our way."

"Relationships are too difficult," Sasha agreed.

Alice knew why she wanted to get away, but she was baffled as to why Sasha was so eager to leave, especially with the possibility of employment at the biggest advertising agency in town. "Want to tell me why you're so happy to get out of here?" she asked. "You've been looking a little worried lately. Is something bothering you?"

There was a cough at the end of the line and silence before Sasha came back. "Nothing. There's nothing wrong. I just want to get away for a while."

"I know you…"

"Then you should know that I'm fine! I just want to enjoy the summer with my favorite people: you and Henry."

She let it go, although she still didn't believe her. "Running a business might be harder than it sounds at times," Alice worried aloud.

"Of course it will. But it might just be worth it."

"And you'd leave everything to do this with me?"

"Yep. I can't be here anymore, Alice."

"Why? Is there some reason you're not telling me?" she asked, trying one more time to give her friend the opportunity to share what was on her mind. She waited in the hush that followed, wondering if Sasha was struggling with how to say whatever it was she was thinking.

Finally, she said, "I have my reasons. I'll tell you everything later. Right now, let's focus on you and what you're going to do. If you want to keep the bike shop, just know that I'll be right there with you—all you have to do is ask."

The next morning, while Henry and Einstein ran around the backyard of her childhood home, chasing the new frisbees that her father had gotten them as a surprise, Alice sat across from him looking into those familiar green eyes with gold flecks—just like Gramps's.

"You know, your gramps had a good handle on people; he got a gut reaction the moment he met them. He always knew that you were like him, from the time you were just a little thing."

Alice grinned, trailing her fingers along the kitchen table where she'd spent countless mornings before school, her nose in a book to avoid the fact that she was alone most of the time. In those teenage years, it had made her feel different—growing up with just her dad, the house completely silent around them—but now she wondered if the solitary environment had been preparing her, making her strong, so that she could tap into that strength now that she had Henry and she had to raise him by herself.

"I could tell you had a similar personality to his, too," her father said from across the table. "There was a light in your eyes whenever you were going to see him, and I knew it was because your spirit had found its match with him. There are very few people in life who make you feel that way, you know?"

Alice nodded. Her dad was right: the very minute Gramps met someone, it was as though he'd known them for years. He'd throw his head back and laugh at something they said or put his hand on their shoulder if they revealed a worry. It only took a few minutes and Gramps would have them sharing things about their families or their jobs. He was a great listener. She knew that she was like that with her own friends, but would she be as great at it as he was with strangers? Would it come naturally for her?

"That's why he left the shop to you. He knew you'd know what to do with it."

Alice remembered the letter from Gramps, his words etched into her consciousness: *I'm giving you the shop, Alice, rather than your dad, because he's already lived his life, and I don't know if he'd be ready to take on something like that right when he should be settling down. You and Henry should have it—I know your dad would agree—so that you can decide the best use for it.*

But regardless of Gramps's wishes, Alice had felt like she couldn't make a decision about the property without first discussing it with her dad, so she'd called him right away to talk it out.

Her father slid a cup of coffee toward her. He'd learned to make coffee some time after Alice's mother had died. She remembered crying one day because she didn't have sugar and her mother had always put sugar in her coffee. Her father had gone out that very minute and bought her some. Then he came home and made her a cup, and it was the best coffee Alice had tasted. She told him that it was just as good as Mom's, and she saw the way pride filled his face. Until that moment, she hadn't come out of her own grief long enough to realize that, yes, he was grieving, but he was also terrified about how to finish raising her. After that, they had coffee every morning, and she talked instead of reading, even before she left for school. So now, when she wanted to talk, he made coffee.

"I think it sounds like a wonderful idea," he said, as he took a seat and lifted his own cup for a sip.

The sun came through the window at a slant, illuminating the grains in the surface of the table. She traced the circular pattern with her finger. "But I've never done anything like that before. What if I fail?"

He set his mug down with a clunk and leaned on his elbows, a grin on his face. She always made him smile. "You might fail," he said simply. "But you might surprise yourself." He straightened up, his chest filling with air as he collected his thoughts, clearly deciding what he wanted to say. He always did that.

"The one thing I think about all the time when I look back on my life," he said, "is that I wish I'd have taken more chances, not worried so much. I wish I hadn't played it so safe. Your mom wanted to go to Jamaica on vacation, and I kept telling her that I was concerned about spending that kind of money when something in the house could break or go wrong. With all the bills we had from her cancer, that little trip to Jamaica would've been a drop in the bucket, and I always wish I'd have taken her. I have a whole lot of what-ifs in life, and they eat me alive." He picked his mug up and looked down at his coffee, clearly collecting himself, tears brimming briefly. Then he met her eyes. "If you want to try it, then do. What's the worst that could happen? You could still sell it. It's prime real estate."

The excitement began to swell in her chest like a swarm of butterflies. "You're right," she said. "You're always right."

"Yes. I am," he said seriously, before giving her a wink.

Chapter Four

It had only taken a phone call, and, with the terms of the real estate contract nearing renewal anyway, the bike shop was off the market. From that moment on, things moved along quite quickly and Alice found herself having packed up and left her empty apartment, which she'd subletted to two students studying for their master's degrees. And now, here she was in that glorious childhood retreat, where the sound of the ocean was always there to greet her and the summer breeze seemed to go on forever.

The whole way there, Alice's thoughts were on all things ice cream. While the coastal wind whipped through her car, her hair blowing out the window—Henry and Einstein asleep in the backseat, the heat having its lulling effect on them—she'd been going over different words and their associations for possible names, running through angles for photograph opportunities to use in her advertising, and deciding what would need to be updated if she wanted to make the shop enticing to visitors. Alice already had a mental to-do list a mile long but she tried not to let her uncertainty about whether or not she could pull it off overwhelm her.

Truthfully, she'd never tested her marketing abilities; she didn't have a clue how the public would receive her ideas. She'd done some online research and jotted down a few thoughts, but ultimately, it was time to go full speed and put them into play without spending too much time worrying about it. The heavy summer season was about to begin, and they'd have to move quickly if they wanted to capitalize on that. It was imperative, actually, because, given the amount Alice wanted to spend for renovations, she needed to get her investment back as soon as possible so they'd have enough money to live on.

She'd spent the whole drive thinking about it all, but it was mainly because if she didn't use her mental energy for planning, her mind would drift back to the image in her side-view mirror of her father, waving goodbye, as they pulled out of Richmond for the last time. He'd met them for coffee before they left town this morning. She'd hugged him quickly so as not to get all blubbery, but he'd squeezed her just a little tighter, and she knew it was because he was going to miss her too. She'd never lived this far away from him, and she didn't like the idea of leaving him alone back home. He'd assured her that he would be just fine, but she already missed him terribly.

Alice had always liked the fact that Henry lived close to his grandfather. She would've done anything to live near Gramps. While her dad had made quite an effort to ensure she got to see Gramps as much as possible, she still wished she'd had Gramps around during the hard times when both she and her dad had needed someone there to listen.

Henry spent three days a week after preschool with Alice's dad, they stayed over on weekends, and her dad picked him up for his ball games. But he wasn't just there for Henry; he was there for her too. He'd been her shoulder to cry on when Matt left, and he'd talked her through it until her sobbing had subsided enough that she could think clearly. He'd held her hand and listened, offered his advice, and he'd been patient with her.

So instead of thinking about all that, making her chest ache, she put her focus on the business she was beginning.

The rental trailer her father had helped her hook up to her little Honda was now outside Gramps's bike shop. It was full to the brim with boxes, mattresses, her kitchen table and chairs… She had no idea if it would all fit in the tiny space above the shop. She didn't even want to think about what was in the other trailer that Sasha had just driven into the small parking lot, full of *her* things.

Sasha still hadn't told Alice what was going on with her, but it was now clearer than ever that something was wrong. Her friend had been overly emotional in the last week, as they'd prepared to move, jumping at the chance to be with Henry, even mentioning that perhaps she should get a dog. While Sasha was always thrilled to see Henry, Alice had never seen her quite this enthusiastic to drop what she was doing and be with him. Then, as they were pulling out of Richmond, she could see Sasha visibly crying. When they'd stopped for a bathroom break, Alice tried to get something out of her, but she just told her that she was fine and everything would be okay. Alice wondered if perhaps the divorce proceedings were overwhelming her, and she just didn't want to say anything. Maybe Sasha thought it would trigger Alice's emotions about Matt leaving. Certainly, a divorce could take its toll on a person.

Henry and Einstein jumped out of the car, having been squeezed into the backseat for four hours, curled up together and sleeping most of the way—probably to avoid the fact that they had no room to move. Henry grabbed Einstein's leash as the puppy tried to scamper off into the sand, pulling Henry along behind him.

Alice turned toward the view of the sea between the shop and the massive pier, and then to the little building itself, the display window

. .he gave of himself, how he had even repaired beach cruisers for two elderly women—Olive and Maple, his friends who lived in town. They brought him breakfast: egg sandwiches on buttermilk biscuits the size of Alice's fist, and little fritters with okra inside. They biked well into their eighties, their pastel beach cruisers sporting little baskets on the front where they'd hold their brown bags of food, folded over once and in a perfect line so as not to crush the contents.

Occasionally, in the afternoons, they'd stop by and ask Gramps to check their tires. He'd fill them up with air, free of charge. Olive and Maple were sweeter than the lemonade sorbet they were known for, and that was saying something. Alice wondered if Gramps was with them now, handing out Mason jars of iced tea while they all sat in their heavenly rockers up there in the land that, at the church Gramps took her to on Sundays, was promised to all who believe.

"I want to get into that water already," Sasha said, stepping up next to her. Her nose was still a little red, but behind her sunglasses it was difficult to tell if she was emotional again. It wasn't the right time to press her, though. Her friend's dark hair was pulled up into a ponytail, her aviators reflecting the pier. "It's gorgeous today, so warm already. Maybe we can unpack a few boxes—just enough—and spend the rest of the day on the beach. I'm beat from loading the trailer this morning."

Alice didn't want to think about how tired she was. If she let the exhaustion set in, she'd be asleep the moment she slowed down, and they still had unpacking to do. Six in the morning had come early for her today; she'd spent a good five hours finishing up the packing of the trailer the night before, staying up way too late, so she was beat before she'd even made the drive to the Outer Banks.

"I want to go swimming too!" Henry said, walking over with Einstein, who'd found a piece of driftwood and had it in his mouth, his tail wagging furiously. His chest was poked out to show his pride in finding such a trophy. The wind pushed Henry's blond hair off his forehead, showing off his blue eyes and making them look like mirror images of the sea. "Can we get my boogie board out of the trailer?"

"Of course," Alice said, her heart full of nostalgia. "Let's see if we can get just the essentials out for now, so food, chairs, and boogie boards!" she said with a smile. "We all need a break after that drive, I'm sure."

Alice carried in Einstein's crate first, and Sasha offered to take him upstairs. Then, once he was safe and secure, they brought in what they needed for the day, unloading the boxes into the shop before letting the puppy back out. It was muggy inside; the air conditioner had been turned off to save on the electric bill while it was vacant. The display window at the front didn't open, but Gramps had installed two regular windows at the back, which he raised on nice days, and a screen door to let the ocean air in.

"You need a little salt in your lungs," he'd say whenever he opened them.

Out of nowhere, a memory surfaced of that summer-day crush of hers at the window, his smiling face and penetrating eyes as he beckoned her outside. She'd met him with Gramps on the pier, and they'd spent the whole day together. Even after she'd gone inside, he'd convinced her to come back out on the beach with her and they'd talked until the stars had filled the sky, when Gramps had finally made her come in.

Alice thought back to her youth, when life was so much easier. That boy she'd met at Gramps's was so amazing that she'd compared every man she'd met to him since. She'd only spent one wonderful day with him, but he had made an impression that stayed with her into adulthood. It was so long ago, the details were fuzzy and she couldn't even remember his name, but what she could remember clearly were the fireworks that went off every time he looked at her. With one smile, he could make her feel like she was the most important person in his world. She never saw him again, but she'd chased that feeling for the rest of her life. It was the first and last time she'd felt such a strong connection with someone, but she'd been so young she hadn't realized at the time how rare that was.

The image of the boy wasn't clear anymore after all these years, but the way he made her feel remained strong in her memory. She blinked, clearing it, wondering why it had come to her now. Maybe the whole thing with Matt was lingering at the back of her mind, playing with her thoughts. Even though she didn't want to admit it, there was a tiny bit of shame lingering, making her feel like there was something wrong with her that had caused Matt to stray, even though she tried to tell herself otherwise. The reminiscence of that summer day long ago made her feel stronger now.

Alice unlocked the windows and pushed them up, the sea air soaring in. She hadn't been upstairs since her father had started packing Gramps's things. She hadn't had the strength until now. He'd told her there were still a few items left that wouldn't fit in the storage unit he'd rented to hold it all until he could go through everything, but she figured she could just push them aside for now and find a place for them later.

She could already feel the lump in her throat at seeing the emptiness of the shop again, let alone Gramps's apartment upstairs. She remembered how he would pin a sheet to the slanted rafter beams, each end of the fabric draping down onto the arms of the sofa underneath it, making a tent. He would fill the space with pillows and a blanket, just for her. She loved sleeping there. With the windows open and the sound of the ocean, it felt like she was really camping.

She'd let Sasha take the dog and his crate upstairs for her. But at some point, she'd have to go up so it might as well be now. The boards of the narrow wooden steps creaked underneath her feet, as she remembered them doing when Gramps walked up them. The treads were worn, the finish lightened in the center of each one. With every step, she could feel her heart hammering, unsure if she could face the onslaught of memories. She got to the apartment at the top and paused in the empty living and kitchen area to give herself a minute. The sofa was gone now, the space open and airy—just a few boxes, a trunk, and a lamp with its cord wrapped around its base on the whitewashed floor.

"It's so clean and roomy," Sasha said, now standing next to her. "This is going to be amazing when we get our hands on it."

The apartment consisted of one large room with four smaller rooms off of it; there was a modest kitchen at one end with white cabinets, gray countertops, and a view of the cottages and the sea just above the sink. The rafters were exposed, but Gramps had painted them white along with everything else: the walls, the floor—all of it white. He'd explained it to her once that he'd chosen a light color to make the place look bigger. Now that she could see it through adult eyes, he was right. Without his things in the room to age it, the place looked as new as her apartment back in the city. She walked over to the large double windows at the other end and opened them to let the heat out and the breeze in.

"Your gorgeous navy and gray patterned rug would be perfect right here," Sasha said, her voice animated as she pointed to the large space that Alice was already thinking would make a good sitting area. "Some white, gauzy curtains on those windows…"

Henry and Einstein clambered up the steps and joined them, Einstein getting right to business, pacing past his crate and sniffing the place.

"I just got white slip covers for my old chair and the sofa that were in my apartment," Alice added, the anticipation of starting over beginning to bubble up. "With the navy and yellow pillows I got, they'll fit right in."

"Oh my gosh, yes!" Sasha danced around the open space, taking Henry's hands and spinning him, making him giggle. "I have those glass floor lamps too! I'm imagining a painted starfish here on this wall…" She gave Henry one more spin and then let go, pointing to a small space beside the windows.

Alice was getting a vision for the place already. "Maybe we could go shopping later for knick knacks."

"And cocktails." Sasha widened her eyes suggestively, making Alice laugh. *That* was the Sasha she knew and loved.

"You know, Henry, there's a restaurant that makes cocktails for kids too," Alice said, "Fruity drinks with whipped cream and a maraschino cherry on top. Gramps used to take me there. I hope it's still open."

"I'm hungry now," Henry said, grabbing his tummy. "Do we have any food?"

"I didn't pack a whole lot." Alice walked over to the fridge and opened it. Thankfully, it had still been plugged in and was ice cold when they'd placed their food from traveling inside. She peered in at the half-empty bottle of water and a single-serve fruit and cheese tray she'd picked up on the way. Henry had eaten all the crackers. "I'll tell you what, why don't we run out and get a few groceries?"

Henry's face dropped, but he nodded politely. She knew that after that drive, asking him to get groceries was a little much, with the beach just outside. Einstein, who probably felt just the same as Henry, also needed to get out and run.

Sasha seemed to have the same thought because she offered, "I could run out."

Henry turned to her happily. "Oh! Can you buy me the little squishy fruity things that are in the shapes of animals? I like those for dessert. What are they called, Mom?" He'd squatted down and was threading his fingers through Einstein's fur, the back of his hair sticking up from sleeping in the car.

Alice's mind was so full, she wasn't placing the brand name. "I can see the box—it's blue with yellow writing... Why don't I just go? Would it be okay if you took Henry and Einstein to the beach while I run to the store? You could make me a list of anything specific that you want, and I'll just get it all. I know the area and there's a grocery store just down the bypass. I'd be less than an hour if I get us everything for a week."

"That sounds like a plan," Sasha said, grinning at Henry. "Let's get your swimsuit and your boogie board."

Chapter Five

The ocean breeze had all but erased Matt from Alice's consciousness; the brief memory of that boy at the window had been as close as she'd come to thinking about him. She could feel the tension fading away with every salty breath she took, exactly like Gramps had taught her to do. Even though she'd just arrived and there was a ton of work to get done, she was already glad she'd decided to make this move. Thankful to Sasha for talking her through it, she'd spent some time browsing in the local shops before getting the groceries, hoping to surprise her friend with a little token of thanks. She'd tried to be fast, running through them, eyeing trinkets and frames, cups and key chains, looking for something to give her, but when she peered down at her watch, Alice was flabbergasted at how much time she'd taken.

She'd settled on a blue and beige-colored coffee mug with OBX, the nickname for the Outer Banks, printed on it. The cashier had wrapped it in tissue paper and placed it in a white plastic bag with the shop's emblem—but she'd do one more quick swoop through a few more shops to see if there was anything else she could get to go with it. She had also bought Henry a kite—the expensive kind made of fabric and real woven string on a wooden spool. She felt like celebrating tonight, and she planned to buy a bottle of champagne to open after setting three chairs in the sand once the sun had started its descent. But she really needed to hurry. Henry had said he was hungry ages ago, and all they had at the house besides what she'd put in the fridge was a bag of chips and half a candy bar that they'd bought on the way down.

She'd walked from shop to shop, stopping in just a few more, and she'd gotten so far away from her car, which was parked outside the grocery store, that she found herself jogging in her flip-flops to make up time, the gift bags swinging at her sides. When she finally got to the grocery store, she was hot, out of breath, and tired, but she lumped her gift bags into a shopping cart and headed in, making a mental list of things they would need.

Then, she started down the aisles.

By the time Alice had gotten to the fruit and vegetable section, she'd slowed just slightly, the icy cold of the aisle giving her goosebumps. The hum of music over the speakers and the fluorescent lights helped her to focus. She stopped in front of the apples, reaching for one when a shiver from the cold air surprised her, causing her to fumble the fruit, bumping the stack next to it. Suddenly, an avalanche of apples came tumbling toward her.

"Oh!" Alice called, trying to catch them as they dodged her grasp, her tired limbs reacting too slowly.

Just as panic set in, the apples assaulting her while she shimmied back and forth in front of the display, two strong, tanned forearms swooped into her view, catching the rest and setting them right again. She tried to steady the ones she'd gathered, gently placing them back in their spots, one last defiant apple sneaking past her. It was caught in midair and returned to its place.

That was when Alice finally looked up to thank the owner of those arms—but also out of curiosity, because if the arms looked like that, what must the face…

"You were almost buried by apples," he said. His eyes were a sparkly green, creasing at the edges with a smile that took over his face. There was a kind look to his features, but it also seemed like he could command attention at an instant. His smile widened, if that were possible, when he looked down at her, making her knees feel like jelly. "You okay?" he asked, and she realized her look of horror at the falling apples was probably still contorting her face.

Alice nodded, willing words to come out of her mouth. But her sudden muted state and her expression weren't because of her battle with the fruit. They were because, for some cosmically unknown reason, he made her want to be at her best. She'd barely combed her hair this morning before the trip, the wind had erased any effort she'd put in at all, and she had a coffee stain on her shirt from the gas station cup with the ill-fitting lid. Her clothes were wrinkled, her flip-flops were the old ones she used to water the plants outside her apartment, and she hadn't even put on any jewelry. But why did she care what a gorgeous man in the supermarket thought? She was over that. Independent woman—that's what she was. She straightened her shoulders.

An apple teetered precariously at the edge of the pile. He leaned across her, his face next to hers, and caught it, sending a clean scent of cotton and spice her way. "Steady, boy," he teased as he scolded it. He looked at her in a way she'd never had another man look at her upon meeting her. It was as if he could see right through to her soul, but she knew that was just ridiculous. Not even the boy from her youth could do that. Could there actually be someone out there who would meet the expectations she'd set that day? No matter how hard she tried to tell herself otherwise, she could feel his compassion through his eyes. Once he righted himself, he said, "I'm Jack." He held out a hand, those arms coming back into view. "Jack Murphy."

As if his touch were electric, when she shook his hand, it jolted her mouth into working order and she found her words. "Hi, Jack," she said, putting on her most confident smile. "Thank you for saving me from the apple attack. Alice." She held out her hand in greeting and he shook it while warding off any further apple rolls with his other hand.

A charged, buzzing silence from their little encounter fell between them, and it took her a minute to realize why she was there. "Well, thank you so much again," she said, cautiously plucking three apples from the stack and setting them in her cart. "I'm in a slight hurry—I'm surprised my friend hasn't texted me wondering where I am…" She reached down to pull her phone from her handbag just to make sure she hadn't missed any texts, but then stopped, scanning the cart. The long trip, the apples, the hot guy beside her—was she going crazy? The cart was full of her shopping bags but her handbag wasn't with them. Her eyes flashed to the apple display, but it wouldn't be there…

"What's wrong?" Jack asked, and she met those eyes again, the concern in them robbing her of all her thoughts once more. Did he have to do that? She needed to focus.

"I can't find my handbag," Alice managed, feeling slightly panicked. "I've been all over the place shopping. I must have left it in one of the other stores." But as she processed this, she grasped the full consequences of not having her bag. "I have no phone, but also no car keys, no wallet…" she worried aloud.

"Do you think you can remember all the places you've been?" Jack asked, his voice so calm that her pulse slowed just hearing it, and she could imagine what he'd be like in the quiet darkness of the night. That was when she'd loved to talk to Matt: when the whole day was behind her, her clean body cocooned in her crisp bed sheets, as she lay next to him. Matt had hated it when she'd kept him awake, rolling around restlessly and telling her he had to get up in the morning. But she'd just wanted to know about his day…

"Well, don't worry if you can't," Jack said, breaking through her thoughts. "I don't mind driving you around. I happen to have the day off, and I have nothing planned at the moment."

"Yes," Alice said. Then, realizing by the way the skin between his eyes creased slightly that he didn't understand her response, she added, "Yes, I can remember all the shops. But I'd feel terrible if you were to spend your time off driving a stranger around."

"I couldn't just leave you here. I'd feel awful." That smile emerged again, and it was so friendly that it felt as if she'd known him for years. "Let's find your bag and then you can come back for the groceries."

As they replaced the few things she'd put into her cart on the shelves, she asked, "If you have nothing planned, what were you doing here? Or is the local grocery your hangout?"

Jack laughed, scooping up her shopping bags in one hand and returning her cart to the line of them at the front of the store. "I was going to try a new recipe."

He cooks? Handsome and handy in the kitchen; this guy was too good to be true. He must have flaws, although Alice was struggling to find any at a quick glance. "What were you going to cook?" she found herself asking.

Something had to be wrong with him. But as he moved his lips to speak, she still couldn't imagine anything but sweetness. She willed herself to make eye contact.

"It's a seafood stew. I found the recipe online. I was going to try to cut it in half since it looks like it could feed an army, and there are just two of us at home."

There it was: he was married.

Her cheeks burned with the thoughts she'd been processing about a married man. He was going home to the woman he loved while Alice was busy feeling all fluttery for someone's husband! Mortification setting in, she tried to get a look at his left ring finger, praying there was a mix-up, but his hand was in his pocket, fumbling with his keys. He pulled them out and pointed them toward a black Mercedes, the taillights blinking as he unlocked the doors. His hand swung by his side and she still couldn't get a look. Then, she scolded herself for even putting herself in this position. The last thing she needed was the distraction of a guy, anyway, let alone a married one. No. More. Distractions.

And then there was the fact that this perfect man was all in her head; he was wishful thinking. He wasn't real. He was a regular person with flaws. And probably that wife… Even if he wasn't married, she didn't need a stranger around Henry either. He had enough change in his life with Matt leaving and he would be starting a new school at the end of the summer, moving to a brand-new place where they didn't know anyone, and all the chaos that went along with opening a business.

All of a sudden, and totally unexpectedly, the weight of her choices came crashing down. What was she doing? Had moving here been an irrational decision to mask her need to escape the toxic environment Matt had left her and Henry in? Was this the right move for Henry? He'd left an apartment complex full of friends where the kids had spent Saturdays at the playground. They'd all been on his soccer team for the last two years. They were going to kindergarten together when school started. He'd left his Grandpa Frank. She'd thought it through and decided that the change would be good for him—that it would remove him from all the memories of the fun he'd had with Matt—but now she wasn't sure.

She'd brought him hours away from everything he knew, everything *she* knew. There wasn't a single person with kids on Beach Road that she'd seen; most of the properties were rentals. Gramps wasn't here anymore. No one was, except Sasha. Would Henry be able to make a life here? Jack leaned in and offered a consolatory smile.

"Do you mind if I use your phone to text my friend Sasha, so she knows what's happened?" Alice asked as they reached his car.

Jack pulled out his phone and entered the passcode, then handed it to her. Alice sent off a text, quickly explaining everything and telling her that she'd be home as soon as possible.

Sasha responded: *Take your time. We're fine here.*

With a little relief, Alice handed the phone back to Jack. Thank God for Sasha.

Jack put the bags in the backseat and shut the door. "Are you okay?"

"Yes," Alice said, not very convincingly. Then, out of nowhere, she felt tears fill her eyes. Maybe she was tired from the trip and all the excitement. How embarrassing.

"You're *not* okay." Jack took a step toward her, distress sliding across his face, only making her more emotional. What was wrong with her? When she tried to stop the tears, more came.

"I'm sorry," Alice managed.

"Don't be. We'll find it."

His comment startled her out of her uncertainties. She hadn't even been thinking about her handbag. "It isn't that," she heard herself say. She shouldn't be unloading all her feelings onto this stranger. She'd never done this before, so why start now? While the move had been a major decision, had the stress of it catapulted her into some sort of insanity?

"What is it?"

Alice shook her head, swallowing and blinking obsessively to get herself together, feeling absolutely humiliated. When she regained focus, those eyes were right in front of her. He took her hand, leading her into the shade under a nearby tree. They sat together on a bench there, her breathing shallow as she tried to get herself in check.

Alice leaned forward, hanging her head and trying to breathe more deeply, the coffee spot on her shirt blurring in front of her as her head started to spin. Was she having a panic attack? "I don't know why I'm crying," she finally said. She might as well come clean; she'd made a complete mess of things already. He probably thought she was a crazy person, which was fine. Maybe he'd stop looking at her, adorable and hunky, and she could forget this whole meeting. "I think I'm just a little overwhelmed."

"Why?" Jack's voice urged her to explain, that one word so soft it made her want to have his comforting arms around her. She was definitely losing it.

"I just moved here," she said, to offer an answer to his question, but she didn't provide any more than that because right now all she wanted was to get herself together.

"Oh?"

The breeze rustled the leaves of the trees, providing the only reprieve from the heat. A runaway strand of hair wound its way across her cheek as she squeezed her eyes to keep the tears in. Maybe she hadn't let herself grieve enough for the loss of her relationship or her grandfather. Perhaps she'd made the move too soon.

"I don't know if I made the right decision moving here," Alice admitted.

When Jack didn't speak, she looked up and met his gaze. She noticed how relaxed he seemed, how nothing—not even a random woman losing her handbag and then bizarrely breaking into tears and telling him her personal thoughts—ruffled him. His shoulders were comfortable, his face peaceful. She felt like it was just the two of them on the entire planet at that moment.

"All we can do in life is try," Jack said. "If it's the wrong decision, what's the worst that could happen?"

Alice didn't know. What *was* the worst that could happen? She thought about Henry. He'd eventually make friends here, become comfortable. But what if the business failed and she had to pull him away from yet another group of kids that he'd grown fond of?

"Want me to tell you?" Jack's head was turned to the side, his face so honest. "If you make the wrong decision, you just have to try a little harder to turn it into the right one. It'll be awesome if you decide it'll be awesome."

She let it sink in, her heartbeat slowing slightly, her shoulders beginning to relax. And, the more she thought about it, the more she realized he might be right. In that moment, this complete stranger had made her feel good about herself, about her choices, and before this instance, the only person who'd ever been able to do that was Gramps. Right in front of her, for the first time, was someone who had made her question her fears and see a different side to her choices. She'd never had another man talk her through things so easily before.

The two of them sat together on the bench until her tears were gone. And in the silence, she was so happy to have him there. What surprised her most was the thought that the outcome of those fears would've been very different without his words.

Jack broke through the silence with a slap on his thighs before he stood up. "We need to find your bag," he said, smiling down at her.

Alice stood up beside him and, together, they walked to the car.

"Where to?" he asked, opening her door for her.

As she tried to remember the last place she'd been, she wasn't as troubled by the missing bag, because with Jack, she felt like everything would be okay.

Chapter Six

"Wow, that was so nice of a complete stranger to do that," Sasha said as she hugged her new mug. She set it down to help unpack the groceries, retrieving the gummy snacks that Henry had asked for and placing them on the kitchen counter before rooting around in the grocery sacks again. "You bought wine, right?" she said, her voice muffled inside the bag. "Oh!" Sasha yanked out the champagne Alice had gotten and set it on the counter, beaming at her friend. She held up her mug. "This ought to be just the right size!" Then she set it next to the bottle with a wink at Alice.

Alice laughed, glad to see her friend in a lighter mood. She'd told her the whole story about how Jack had driven her around to find her handbag, and how she'd ended up locating it in the last shop she'd been in. Once she'd found it, she could remember perfectly how it had happened: she'd put all her bags down to unfold a beach towel so she could see the whole picture printed on it. It was a giant cocktail with little fruits embroidered on either end. She'd folded it back up and set it on the shelf, and when she'd picked up her bags, she must have missed her handbag by accident. Luckily, it was still where she'd left it, completely untouched.

"Wish we could thank him," Sasha said, as Alice peeked out the window at Henry, who was walking Einstein in the sand just outside.

"It would be nice to get to know a few people. And that would be an easy opportunity."

"I know." Alice did like Jack. He'd been so kind to her. He might be a good friend to have in the area as they got up and running. "I'd cook him dinner, but we really aren't ready for visitors quite yet." She looked around at the empty space, some of Gramps's things still in the corner, their bags spread along one wall. "Maybe if we run into him again, we could ask him to have drinks or something."

"That's a great idea!" Sasha picked up her phone and opened her texts. "But we don't have to wait. Is this his number you texted on earlier?"

Willing the cloud of excitement from her head as she looked at the string of numbers on Sasha's phone, she said with a smile, "Yes."

Alice trotted down the narrow staircase of the bike shop. She'd been getting her swim attire on: the new cover-up she'd gotten for the summer that matched the spaghetti straps of her swimsuit. On her way to answer the knock she'd heard, she noticed the back screen door was open, the breeze rattling it on its hinges. Sasha and Henry were already out on the beach, Henry splashing happily in the waves.

Sasha had offered to take him out again, doting on him and being overly sentimental, and while it was a very kind gesture, it was also a reminder that Alice needed to have some alone time to talk to Sasha. They'd decided to take it slowly to let Henry get settled, so they didn't have a whole lot planned for the redesign of the shop just yet, and it would be a good moment to find out what was bothering her.

Alice smiled, able to hear her son giggling from inside. Mentally reminding herself to fix the wobbly latch, she pulled it shut and focused on her original task. Through the display window she could see a woman who, to her surprise, was squatting down next to Einstein, rubbing his cheeks, a makeshift leash made of rope attached to his collar.

"I thought this might be your dog," she said through the front screen, as Alice opened the door to greet her.

The woman smiled. She was holding a large camera and her flip-flops scratched with her movements as they ground the sand against the weathered wood of the porch. There was no escaping sand on Beach Road; it was everywhere, trailing along the sides of the street, meandering through the wild gaillardias that grew along the edges of the walks, blowing up onto the porches, and drifting into parking areas.

"I'm Melly St. James." Her soft accent sounded as southern as the warm butter on Alice's mother's biscuits. "Everyone calls me Melly."

"Alice Emerson."

"I live in the cottage across the street."

The woman raised a delicate hand toward a small bungalow. It was quaint and beachy, just like she was. Alice delighted in her friendly demeanor. There was something slightly wise lurking under her lovely smile; Melly had the kind of face that made her seem like she had years of experiences bigger than any Alice had known. She was wearing a flowing skirt, her hair pulled back loosely, wisps falling around her face and onto her bare shoulders, her silky tank top matching her skirt.

"I saw him when you all arrived. He was wandering around in my backyard, so I figured I'd bring him over." She twisted her camera around so Alice could view the small screen. "I caught a quick snap of him first. I'd be happy to print it for you." She clicked a few buttons and held the camera out toward Alice.

"Wow, are you a professional photographer?" The photo looked like something out of a glossy magazine—Einstein was sitting among the tall beach grasses as if he'd been perfectly trained to do so, his chin up, his deep brown eyes directly on the camera, the sun coming in at an angle behind him.

Melly chuckled humbly. "No. It's just something I do as a hobby." She handed her end of the rope leash to Alice. "It took me forever to get this on him."

"I'm so sorry, he must have gotten out the back door." Alice patted her thighs, and Einstein came to her, his tail wagging furiously. "Thank you so much for bringing him back. We'd have been beside ourselves if we'd lost him." Alice gestured inside. "Would you like to come in?"

"I wouldn't want to impose," Melly said, but her obvious curiosity as she looked past Alice into the shop told Alice otherwise. "I'm sure you've got a lot to do, having just come into town. I only moved here myself in the last month. I'm still unpacking too so I totally get the chaos." She laughed quietly.

Alice let Einstein inside, slipped off the rope from his collar, and shut the door behind her to give her a moment to talk, stepping onto the porch. She was happy to meet another person new to the area. "Where are you from?"

"Not too far—South Carolina. How about you?"

"Virginia." The sun was still strong, the heat warming her skin despite the sea breeze. "I really don't mind if you'd like to come in. Please do. It's not that chaotic. I think I might even have... fruit gummies and whole milk to offer you."

Melly smiled. "Was that your son I saw when you all pulled in? The one walking your dog?"

"Yes." Alice ushered Melly inside and through the open area where she and Sasha had set up a small table and chairs, so they could sit downstairs and drink their morning coffee with the screen door and windows open to let in the breeze.

Melly's gaze traveled up the empty walls, along the cloudy front window where Gramps used to put his newest bikes, down the gritty, dirty floor, and then back to Alice. "What happened to the bike shop that used to be here?" She looked over at Alice. "I'd thought there was a man who lived on the top floor."

Alice was afraid to say too much for fear she'd burst into tears over losing Gramps. She'd been emotionally shaky since she'd gotten here and she didn't trust herself to go into detail. "My best friend Sasha and I own the property now, and we're opening an ice cream shop in its place. It's just us and my son Henry."

Melly frowned for a second, taking this in. Then she smiled at Alice, who was glad that Melly hadn't pressed her.

Einstein flopped down on the floor with his bone.

Alice grabbed the rag she'd gotten out and wiped the old wooden counters. Perhaps it was a nervous gesture, or having someone in the shop when it was exposed like this made her a little nervous. She didn't want any judgments to be made about Gramps's shop because, when he'd had it, it had been lovely. "He's outside at the moment with Sasha. I've got a few chairs in the back on the patio if you'd like to join me. I'll grab us some iced tea."

Melly nodded and continued to look around, her eyes moving up to the ceiling and then back down, her interest clear. "I love old buildings," she said. "This was one of the original fishing shacks on the beach, right? It's been around for so long, I'll bet it qualifies for the historical properties distinction. Mind if I take a few photos? I'd be more than happy to share them with you."

"Not at all."

While Alice prepared two iced teas, Melly walked around, snapping photos of the window overlooking the ocean, the old front door, the counter where Alice had sat as a girl while waiting for Gramps to pack his fishing equipment. When Melly slowed in her photo taking, Alice opened the back door, and a wide beam of sunshine cut across the floor, showing the age of the boards. She noticed Melly taking one more photo of that.

The squawk of seagulls and the static sound of the relentlessly crashing waves poured into the room. It was remarkably difficult to talk about Gramps's bike shop and share the space with a stranger without getting a lump in her throat. She'd thought she would've been fine having such a simple question about the original owner of the shop come her way, but the emotions that she'd experienced when she'd come back before came flooding in again without warning. She turned her focus to her memory of Jack and his calming voice, letting his words slide through her consciousness. *All we can do in life is try.* She just needed to try—day by day, if that was what it took. And then eventually the idea of Gramps's empty bike shop wouldn't seem as though her world had ended, like it did right now when she let herself look around.

"Follow me," Alice said, leading the way outside.

They walked out onto the patio and Melly took a seat, crossing her long legs, her flip-flop dangling from her foot. She set her camera down on the small table between the chairs as Alice handed her one of Gramps's Mason jars full of tea, the cold of the ice cubes causing the glass to cloud in the humidity.

"So," Melly said, "an ice cream shop?" With a grin, she added, "I used to work at a frozen yogurt shop in high school. I was known for making the biggest cones without the ice cream falling off. I even have a certificate." She giggled.

"Oh, that's funny! I decided it might be a good business move to open an ice cream shop here," Alice said, willing courage into her voice. "Who doesn't love ice cream, right? My son adores it."

Alice noticed contemplation in Melly's smile and the kindness in her eyes. She already felt better just having met her. It would be so nice to have a good neighbor.

Alice popped back in to grab Einstein. When she returned, Melly had taken her tea and scooted her chair to the edge of the patio, her eyes on Sasha and Henry—they were riding the waves on boogie boards. Alice safely leashed Einstein outside and he plopped down next to his bowl of water, shaded by the building. Henry caught a wave, the board under his belly sending him sailing forward as he bumped along through the choppy surf. He slid up onto the beach, his hair darkened to a golden color by the seawater. He caught Alice's eye and waved.

"I'll be down in a little bit!" Alice called, warmed by the sight. Henry was a great kid. So great that she often wondered what she'd done to be so lucky. It was as if, from the moment he was born, he just knew that they were a team. He looked to her for guidance, he listened when she talked to him, and he had a good heart. Her friends back home would tell her frazzled stories about how their kids would stomp up the stairs or talk back to them and Alice would smile and nod politely, but in the back of her mind, she'd think about how grateful she was that she couldn't relate. Henry was her little rock, her whole world.

"He looks just like you," Melly said with a smile. She took a deep breath and turned to Alice. "So, this ice cream shop… Does it have a name yet? Where will I be eating my delicious banana splits?"

"I've thought of a name, but I've only just mentioned it to Sasha. We're taking our time with this. I know we don't have forever, but we want to get it right. She's been researching the market and analyzing the best inventory while I've been focusing on interior design and aesthetics. I was thinking we'd call it 'Seaside Sprinkles'." Just saying the name out loud gave her a punch of happiness.

"Oh, I love that!" Melly said, her excitement genuine and clear. The ice clinked in her glass as she held it up toward the sun. "This tea is really good," she said.

"I'll tell Sasha; she made it. Or maybe you can." Sasha surfaced at the top of the dune, and headed over to the patio. She was wrapped in a towel, her dark hair in wet strands down her back.

"Hello," Sasha said as she approached.

"This is Melly St. James. She lives across the street."

Sasha beamed at her. "It's so good to meet a neighbor! I'm Sasha Miller."

"Hi!" Henry came up behind Sasha, dragging his boogie board on the string that was strapped to his wrist, his skin covered in beads of water, sand sticking to his feet and ankles. He moved around Sasha to give Alice a hug.

Einstein sat up, his tail wagging furiously at the sight of his boy.

"You're all wet!" Alice giggled, as he wrapped his dripping arms around her.

"Did you see me? I rode a big wave!" His attention was still on Alice as he squatted down and rubbed Einstein's cheeks. Einstein started licking the salt off his arms, the puppy barely able to keep still with the excitement of having Henry in the vicinity.

"I saw some of it! You'll have to show me all your skills in a little while. This is Melly."

"Hello," Melly said, leaning forward to greet him. "I saw you out there too—you were great, a real pro!" There was something so soothing about how she greeted him, as if she'd worked with children before.

It seemed to come naturally for her. "What do you think is the most difficult part of boogie boarding?" she asked him.

"I think it's knowing when to get down on your board. Too early and the wave goes whoosh," Henry said, flailing his arms in the air. Einstein stood up to reach him, and Henry bent back over to pet his head. "Too late and there's no water left, and let me tell you, you'll feel all that sand on your belly. Ouch." He nodded knowledgeably, his eyes round, making them all laugh.

"Why don't we come down to the water and watch you now?" Alice said, standing up to get Einstein, her iced tea in the other hand. "I think we can unpack the umbrella and the folding beach chairs pretty easily, can't we, Sasha?"

"I think so," Sasha said, shielding her eyes so she could participate in the conversation without being blinded by the sun. "They're at the back of my trailer. The sea wind is cooler closer to the ocean and, with the shade of the umbrella, the temperatures might just be bearable."

They were in for a hot summer, the radio had said on the journey.

Perfect for ice cream.

Einstein alternated between digging in the sand and sprawling under the shade of the beach umbrella that they'd dug out of the trailer and brought down to the shore. It hadn't been long before the champagne had come out. They'd opened it once they'd finished their iced tea, and it was clear that the alcohol had loosened Melly and Sasha up. Melly had kicked off her flip-flops, her feet buried in the sand, her head tipped back against the chair like she was trying to get some color on her face, that wispy hair dangling over the sand behind her, and Sasha had that familiar glazed look to her eyes and the funny smile she only got when she'd been drinking.

Alice could feel a slight buzz of her own, but she'd cut back, knowing she needed to keep an eye on Henry in the water. It was nice to see Sasha and Melly relaxing, though. Melly fit in like they'd known her for ages, but Alice could've guessed that right when she'd met her.

"I'm actually here because I've run away," Melly confessed. She said it like it was nothing, her head still tipped back, her eyes closed, but both Sasha and Alice stared at her, waiting for her to make eye contact. Run away? To what kind of running away was Melly referring? Alice observed her with different eyes, wondering if she was some sort of fugitive, or had she joined the witness protection program? Melly finally lifted her head to take another sip of her champagne and then clearly realized they were both gaping at her.

"Oh!" she said, looking back and forth between them. "My husband doesn't know where I am."

Sasha's eyes grew wider, that smile of hers dropping to a frown of confusion, shocking Melly into further explanation.

"I mean, my *ex*-husband. We're divorced. Nearly." As she said the word "divorced," her face looked weathered suddenly, worn and tired.

"Well, join the club, sistah," Sasha said lightheartedly. "That's why the two of us are here. My husband left too. And Alice's scumbag boyfriend ran off with his personal trainer." Sasha paused dramatically and eyed them both.

Einstein shook his body, sending sand onto Alice's leg, and then rolled over onto his back and tried to bite his tail.

"I feel like we need to start a women's support group or something. Look at us!" Sasha waved her hands in the air, the champagne sloshing precariously in her glass. (She'd opted not to use the coffee mug after all.) "We've all been hurt and we are smokin' hot women!"

Melly leaned forward, avoiding a laugh that would propel her sip of champagne onto the sand. She swallowed it down.

"And not just hot—we're strong, independent women. Am I right?" She winked at Alice, making her smile.

"I'd like to find someone I could grow old with, though," Melly offered, a far-away look in her eyes for just an instant before she snapped to, taking another sip of her champagne. "But we'll find someone if it's meant to be. There might even be someone right here—you never know!"

Sasha raised her eyebrows in Alice's direction before saying, "Alice might have found someone already! She met a guy at the grocery store. He grabbed her apples." She snorted with hysterics and Alice rolled her eyes.

"Do tell!" Melly said, stifling a grin.

Alice took in a deep breath, trying not to break out into an embarrassingly large smile at the thought of him. "His name is Jack Murphy, and he didn't grab my anything. I barely know him."

Melly's glass tipped precariously to the side, the liquid nearly spilling onto the sand, her eyes as round as saucers. "*Doctor* Jack Murphy? *The* Dr. Murphy?"

Alice met Melly's eyes, curiosity filling her. Doctor? "I guess. Do you know him?"

"I'm a nurse at the local hospital and all the nurses know who he is. He's this famous, uber-wealthy, single doctor that they all swoon over. He's in town, staying with his father."

An unexpected surge of excitement shot through Alice's chest. He wasn't married like she'd originally thought…

"Apparently, he used to live here," Melly continued, "but left his father all alone on the island to chase his millions in Chicago. He only came home, we hear, because he owed another doctor at the hospital a favor."

"Really," Alice said, her chest feeling like a deflated balloon, her hopes dashed. Well, that would make more sense than the picture of him that she'd created in her mind. Real life had slapped her in the face before she'd let herself get caught up in her feelings. She shouldn't feel disappointed; instead, she should consider herself lucky to have found out this soon.

Sasha was casting her protective stare at her friend, but she didn't need to. Alice wasn't going to allow anyone to hurt her like Matt had ever again, so she didn't need to worry. "So," she said, changing the subject. "Enough about Jack. I'm dying to know: how did you end up here?" she asked Melly.

Melly took in a deep breath as if to clear the air of all her thoughts. "I've never lived at the beach before, but I saw this job for a nurse at the hospital here and I jumped at the chance. I drove all the way here to interview and it went well! The director did say that he had to tell everyone the position could be only temporary, but he assured me that the warning was just a formality to cover himself on paper. The hospital is growing and needs the staff and I didn't have anything to worry about. While I'd normally wait and see, something in me told me to jump with both feet. I did a search for cottages on this street, and it was very difficult to find one, so when mine came on the market, I bought it sight unseen. It didn't matter what it looked like—I'd make it work. The cottage took all my savings, but I don't even care because I'd always told myself I was saving that money for a rainy day. This is my rainy day." Melly smiled, and looked out at the ocean, clearly proud of herself for making the move.

The three of them sat, looking out at the crashing waves, their similar circumstances unifying them—or at least that was how Alice felt about it. She'd scrolled through social media a thousand times after her breakup, peering down at all those photos of happy families; their new houses, or their vacations to exotic places, kids with new toys, anniversary celebrations—all of it made her feel like she'd missed out on something. And even though the three of them, sprawled in their beach chairs after having a little too much champagne, weren't comparable to those gorgeous photos she'd seen online, it made her feel like there really were people like her, that she wasn't alone, and that she could do this.

Chapter Seven

Henry rode the waves in the whole evening. Alice wondered if he would stay out all night if she let him. The sea enchanted him—she could see it in his eyes—and it gave her confidence that she was making the right choice by moving here. She'd never made such a major decision so quickly before, but like her new friend, this, too, was her rainy day.

Alice wriggled her toes, the sand dancing on her feet. She peered down at the grains, realizing they weren't sand but the little mites that the sandpipers chased as they pattered down toward the breaking waves. She shook her feet and set them on top of the earth, the surface like fire from the day's sun. She didn't mind. The drinks and the lapping waves had given her a sense of numbing calm that made her feel like everything would be okay as long as she just sat back and let it happen naturally.

She'd hardly thought about Matt all day, and from the look of it, neither had Henry, which was exactly how she wanted it. They were swept up in the magic of the Outer Banks, pulled from their old reality, and facing a bright summer ahead.

Melly grasped the arm of the chair with one hand, her nearly empty glass in the other. "I suppose I need to go home and get some things done. I have an early shift in the morning."

Alice stood up beside her, the spray from the ocean floating through the air, cooling her skin where the alcohol and sun had heated it. She'd enjoyed making a new friend. Today had made Alice feel like she belonged in the Outer Banks.

Sasha stood up too, grabbing the bottle between her fingers.

"Yes, and Henry needs some dinner," Alice said, as the three women looked out at him. Einstein sat up, his ears perking in interest. She reached down and stroked his head, her gaze out in front of her.

A wave pummeled Henry's little body, the boogie board flying from the surf like a rocket. He popped above the bubbling crash of the wave, shook off the water, and sent a thumbs-up their way, a smile enveloping his entire face.

"Are you hungry?" Alice called down to him.

Henry shook his head, his board—neon green and black with an orange flash of a logo on the other side—under his arm. He hadn't been this excited about something since baseball, and it was nice to see. She couldn't help but feel the thrill that this interest was something different than his father's baseball. It was uniquely Henry's. He had a whole strip of islands to explore, full of new opportunities. Perhaps he'd find himself here.

Alice walked down to him. "Well, come in anyway. It's probably good that you take a break. The waves will be there whenever you want them."

They all gathered the chairs and put down the umbrella. Alice shook the towel downwind to free all the sand that Einstein had put on it and folded it up, wadding it under her arm, while Sasha held Einstein's leash in one hand and the chairs in the other. Seeing the umbrella lying alone in the sand, Melly grabbed it, and they walked back up to the house.

Once all the beach gear had been safely stored against the house on the patio, Melly said her goodbyes and Alice and Sasha went inside with Henry and Einstein.

"I like Melly," Sasha said, peering at their new friend through the window as she crossed the street to her cottage.

"Yes, she's so much like us, isn't she?"

Sasha nodded, and the solidarity in her eyes told Alice that Sasha felt just like she did about Melly. It was as if they were all meant to meet. Alice hadn't asked Melly why she'd run from her ex-husband, but Alice could understand without an explanation because, in a way, she was running too; Alice was escaping a life of mediocrity, a life of trying to make things work that just didn't.

Once they were upstairs, Alice pulled a blue and white check tablecloth from one of the boxes and fluffed it out before putting it on the table. Einstein tried to grab it, jumping in the air, but she shooed him away playfully. He settled on the floor, his oversized paws causing a thud on the hardwoods. Not long after, he allowed the exhaustion to take over from spending the day on the beach and he laid his head down, sprawled across the floor, closing his eyes.

Alice fixed Henry a sandwich in the small kitchenette and set it in front of him as he climbed up onto the chair. His hair was fuzzing up on top, the humidity taking hold of the drying strands. She also noticed that his cheeks were pink from the sun, reminding her that here, where the rays were so strong, she'd have to reapply his sunscreen more often.

"Did you have fun today?" Alice asked, sliding a glass of milk with one of his favorite bendy straws next to his plate. He got on his knees and leaned over his plate to take a sip from it. Einstein heaved himself to his feet and moved under the table, where he curled up sleepily with a chew toy Alice had gotten the day she'd bought him, his tail thumping the old wooden floor.

"It was so much fun!" Henry picked up his sandwich and took a bite from the middle, leaving crumbs on each cheek. "Can I go back out after I eat?"

"Maybe wait a little while so you don't get a cramp."

Alice had no idea how she was going to get anything unpacked with Henry outside all day. Sasha would gladly watch him, but she didn't want to put that burden on her friend—Sasha had her own unpacking to do—and nor did she want to make Sasha decorate the whole upstairs apartment while she was outside. But that was what being a single mom was all about: figuring it out. At the end of the day, she had to do it all.

From the time she was a young girl, Alice had wanted to be a mom. As a child, she never asked for just one baby doll for Christmas; instead, she'd ask for three or four, pretending to adopt them all and have her own little family. She cared for each one, changing its diapers, feeding the ones that actually cried like real babies, and putting them all to bed individually. Perhaps she was practicing early for her role as a single mother. The difference was, Henry didn't have a house full of siblings. And while taking care of him was difficult all by herself, she would gladly have a house brimming with kids.

Having also grown up as an only child, she knew what Henry's childhood was like, and she wanted more for him. Perhaps it was her deepest yearning to have a sister of her own—someone she could share things with, someone who wouldn't judge her because after all, they were family, and family does anything for one another. But she was lucky in other ways. She had great friends like Sasha.

Alice pulled the white porcelain water jug from the box and set it in the center of the table. "I'd like to get some yellow daisies for this."

"That would be so pretty," Sasha said, her phone in the palm of her hand as she sat down in the chair beside Henry.

For the most part, Sasha had seemed to enjoy the afternoon and she'd been more herself than she had recently, although she wasn't quite as lively as she normally was. To a passerby she would look completely normal, but Alice knew better; she could see something lurking below her skin, weighing her friend down. Henry offered her a potato chip.

"Thank you," she told him as she popped it into her mouth.

Alice leaned on the windowsill to take in the view of the ocean through the small window. "We could open this wall up a bit when we renovate to get in some light." She turned around. The walls were white clapboard, and with the blue of the tablecloth she'd placed on the table, it had a nautical feel already. She was really just making conversation with her remark about opening the wall, though. The majority of her money would go toward the restoration downstairs for the ice cream shop rather than anything upstairs, but she could just imagine the potential of this place. With a few alterations, it could be amazing, and the views were stunning.

Sasha was madly typing on her phone. "Guess what," she said, her eyes never leaving the little screen in her hand. "We've got a dinner date with Jack Murphy. I just set it up." She finally made eye contact and waved her phone in the air.

The champagne had clearly had its way with Sasha's discretion. She would usually at least ask Alice before throwing her out on a date. At least it was a group date. "What did you say to him?" Alice asked, her heart speeding up at the memory of those arms. She tried unsuccessfully to free her mind from the image as Melly's little anecdote surfaced.

"I just told him that we wanted to thank him for helping you."

"Who's Jack Murphy?" Henry asked, and Alice prickled with unease.

"No one important," she told him. "Just someone I met in town. He helped me find my handbag." But, despite her own caution, as she remembered the adorable look on Jack's face when he caught the last few apples, she had to straighten out the smile that kept wanting to surface.

Chapter Eight

They'd spent the whole next day unpacking while Henry busied himself with building a model train he'd found in one of Gramps's trunks. As young as he was, he had meticulous attention to detail and he was able to focus for quite some time on it. Alice had been so grateful for those trains because they had allowed her and Sasha to spend the entire day getting things done. It was as if Gramps had offered to watch Henry for her. She looked over at the train, now completely assembled, and smiled at the thought.

By the time Alice had gotten ready for dinner, she'd completely convinced herself that she wasn't even going to think about Jack after this evening. What Melly had told her about him kept running through her head. As she'd gotten her sundress on—the white flowy one that she'd brought along for special occasions—she'd wondered against her will about the type of girls Jack liked, immediately scolding herself. It was an indulgent line of thinking, but there was something about him that made her yearn to know more. Just pondering these things, she wanted to kick herself. So, as she clasped her last silver hoop earring, she reminded herself that she and Henry were just fine on their own, where neither of them could get their heart broken again.

Henry had on a pale blue surf shirt that she'd picked up for him at the local shop when she'd run out for more milk after Melly had left yesterday. All his clothes were wrinkled from being packed, and she wanted him to look nice. She didn't know why—it was none of Jack Murphy's business whether or not she dressed her child in wrinkled clothing—but for whatever reason, she wanted to make a good impression. The color of the shirt against his sun-kissed skin and white-blond hair brought out his sapphire eyes.

"You look handsome," Alice told her son as they walked into the beachside restaurant.

Henry puffed out his chest with a smile. "Thank you."

Alice put her hand on his back to lead him inside. The restaurant was open to the air, the beach waves competing with the island music playing. Bright lanterns hanging from the top of the bar swayed in the breeze that had wound its way in from the shore. The whole place had floors made of thick planks of wood salvaged from old boats and cottages, and the walls were covered in surfing stickers, competition posters, and snapshots of locals.

She zeroed in on Jack as he stood up and waved, beckoning them over to a table for four, menus already in place in front of each chair.

As she neared him, he locked eyes with her and produced a smile that could warm the heart of the coldest person on earth, robbing her of all rational thought. He held her gaze long enough to cause a fluttery sensation to snake through her, heat settling in her cheeks, she was sure. Then he greeted Sasha.

"Jack Murphy," he said, holding out a hand. "You must be Sasha." His hair was combed, but the wind had clearly had its way with it on the walk into the restaurant, making the gold strands curl just a bit.

He had a hint of stubble this evening, and with those green eyes of his, she had a hard time keeping herself from staring at him.

"And what is your name, sir?" he asked as he looked down at Henry.

"I'm Henry."

"Hi, Henry," Jack said, patting him on the shoulder. "It's nice to meet you."

"Henry's my son," Alice heard herself say.

She always did that when she met people, especially men. It was her safety net, her way of getting it out there right then that any friendships that may start would be with both her and Henry. Sometimes, she could see the fear right away in a man's eyes when she said it, and she was inwardly hoping it would be that easy with Jack, but instead, she found a quiet affection lurking in his face as if he could see all the difficult times she'd had at once. She swallowed and tore her eyes from him, focusing on Sasha, who was gawking at her, before snapping her mouth shut and biting back a grin.

"Is that so?" he said, looking down at Henry. "When Sasha texted me, she'd said to make reservations for three adults and a child, so I've come prepared." Jack winked at Henry and pulled a conch shell from a bag on the floor. "Have you ever heard the ocean in one of these?" he asked, handing it to Henry and pulling out a chair for Alice. She sat down, willing Sasha with her glare to stop what she was thinking. But Sasha knew her all too well, and she could read her mind—she could always do that. And right now, Sasha could see right through her mannerly nods and polite thank-yous as Jack pushed in her chair. Sasha could tell that she liked how Jack looked at her, that despite her fears, she felt an explosion of happiness just having him there.

"What do I do?" Henry asked.

"Have a seat first."

Henry climbed up on the chair next to Alice. Jack reached over and positioned the shell against his ear. "Close your eyes. Listen very carefully."

Henry sat, motionless, the enormous pink shell pressed to his ear. Then his eyes snapped open, astonishment on his face. "I heard it!" He listened again, wrapping his little hand around the shell, allowing Jack to let go.

"Cool, right?"

"Yes!"

Jack went around and offered Sasha a chair, Alice hiding behind her menu to avoid any further mind reading. She grabbed the small pot of crayons the waitress placed on the table and pulled them forward for Henry, who'd been given a paper kids' menu. It had a maze covering the entire page and Henry, brandishing a green crayon, immediately went to work on it, the shell now on the table beside him.

Music was flowing freely through the space, the cool breeze finding them just in time as Alice started to feel warm. There was something dreamlike about the Outer Banks. She'd always thought so as a child whenever she'd visited, but even now, she knew the magic was real. Her whole life, she'd been chasing happiness, and now that she was with Henry and Sasha here, she might have just found it. She looked over at her friend, and the sense of calm that had clearly enveloped her today made Alice wonder if Sasha thought so too.

"I think we should all have a fruity drink full of rum to celebrate new friendships," Sasha said, raising a discreet and suggestive eyebrow at Alice. She wondered if Sasha was suggesting it to try to forget whatever it was that had been bothering her. She certainly was putting forth a lot of effort this evening, and it was clear that being happy was her number one goal. When Alice didn't respond, Sasha turned back to Jack. "You're a local, right? What do you recommend?"

"I'm not actually a local," he said, picking up the drink menu and scanning the list. "I did live here, but I haven't been back in a very long time."

"Oh," Sasha said, glancing over to Alice.

When he looked down at his menu, Alice shrugged inconspicuously to let her friend know that she didn't think it seemed to bother him that Sasha had known he'd lived there. Maybe he'd thought she'd just guessed. The way Melly had spoken about him, it had seemed like people knew who he was, so maybe he was used to people knowing things about him.

"So did you just move here then?" Sasha asked, obviously covering herself, but also, she seemed a bit too interested, and it hit Alice as to what her friend was probably doing.

Poor guy. When Sasha set her mind to something, there was no stopping her, and it was clear by her glances at Alice and her questioning that she might be trying to play matchmaker. She'd done that before and it had gone horribly wrong. Once she'd set up a profile for Alice on some awful dating site and promised to do all the scouting work. The next thing Alice knew, she was out with a guy who wouldn't stop talking about his cars, except to inquire whether they were going back to her place or his. "He'd seemed so nice," Sasha had said. Don't they all?

"I'm only in town for a short time. I'm down here finding a house for my dad and I'm working locally at the hospital—I'm a doctor—I'm doing a little research with a colleague."

So Melly's information was correct.

"I live in Chicago."

Yeah, we know…

"It's cold in Chicago," Sasha said.

"It's cold here. You haven't experienced winter with coastal wind yet."

"Touché."

The waitress came to get their drink orders and Sasha leaned over to Alice. "I like him, I can already tell," she whispered quickly. "And he's a *doctor!*"

Clearly, his charm had made Sasha forget what Melly had said about him. "Great. Maybe you two could go out sometime. Before he *leaves*."

"Would that be okay?" Jack cut in.

Both women stared at him blankly.

"Coconut smashes? That's what I'd suggest for a rum drink. It's got crème de coconut and two rums in it. Henry, they have chocolate milk if it's okay with your mom."

"It's fine," Alice said, turning to Henry. "Is that what you want?"

"Mm hmm." He had hit a wall on the maze game printed on his menu three times, and she could see unusual tension in his shoulders. She took in his demeanor. Suddenly, he looked almost worried, frazzled. She'd never seen him like that before, and it surprised her.

"Need any help?" she asked carefully, picking up a blue crayon.

"No. I can do it." His voice was quiet and controlled, but it was clear that he wasn't keeping it together at all. With his lips pursed and his brows pulled together, he dragged the crayon down a long stretch of the maze, hitting another wall, causing him to take in a frustrated breath. Alice pointed to a spot that might lead out and he said as sternly as she'd ever heard a five-year-old, "I can do it." He slid the paper away from her. He'd been fine just a second ago, but now it was as if everything had changed.

Henry had never acted like that before, and while he was still being respectful, keeping his voice down and obviously trying not to snap at her, he was definitely upset. She wondered if maybe he was just tired from such a big day, but she knew deep down what was going on because she'd felt it before. It was the kind of feeling that crept in during the wee hours of the night, lingering in the darkness: the feeling of being left by someone, not being good enough, of knowing that a piece of his life had ended, never to be recovered. But on top of all that, Henry had had a lot going on in the last few days and all the change might finally have caught up to him. Was Jack's presence making it worse?

"Don't think of it as dead ends," Jack said calmly, breaking through her thoughts. He scooted his chair closer to Henry and looked down onto his paper. "You're just finding all the paths that *don't* lead out. Sometimes you have to discover those first before you find your way."

Alice stared at him as Henry took in what he'd said. With a gentle hand, those same fingers that had caught the apples for her reached out and touched each dead end, counting them. "You've found five so far! Five ways that don't lead out. That's some great research."

Jack couldn't have said anything better. That was her whole life: finding the dead ends first—her job, the men she'd dated, her life's choices—before she found the way out, the way to her happiness. A wave of worry washed over her as she wondered if the magic she'd felt here had been because of what her grandfather had built rather than what was ahead of her. What if this *wasn't* the way out and just another dead end? Gramps had always had everything together, and *he* was happy here. That was it. He never seemed to have any uncertainties at all. When he spent time with her, it was just the two of them, smiling, fishing, enjoying the salty air. Simple, like happiness should be.

"I did it!" Henry said, smiling and lifting his paper to show Jack.

"See? You didn't need any help, did you? You did it all by yourself."

The waitress came with their drinks and set them onto the table. Alice and Sasha's both had a plastic shark jutting from the cup with a maraschino cherry in its mouth. She twisted the straw and took a sip, the sweet rum concoction like nectar.

They ordered just as a band started setting up in the corner—bongos, an acoustic guitar, a steel drum, and a couple of maracas. The regular music faded and the band tested their instruments as Alice took in her view of Jack, a white sailboat on the horizon behind him.

"I'll bet it was great growing up here," she said, only realizing when he met her eyes that she'd said it out loud.

"It was." Jack smiled at her, lifting his beer bottle to his lips. It was some sort of local lager, light yellow and refreshing looking. He took a drink as the music started.

"What kinds of stuff did you do here?" Henry asked him.

He set his beer down and leaned on his forearms toward Henry. "I used to fish. A lot."

"I love to fish," Alice said. "My grandfather taught me how right here in this town."

"Sounds like you two have a lot in common," Sasha noted.

"I like to fish too!" Henry piped up, cutting off Sasha's line of conversation, thank goodness. "My grandpa taught *me* too!"

"Maybe we could all go fishing sometime before I leave," Jack said.

"Yeah! I want to fish off a pier like Mom did. I've never done that," Henry said, after telling Alice what he wanted to eat.

Jack turned toward her, thoughtfulness on his face. His hand was still, relaxed, and wrapped around his bottle of beer. "We definitely need to do that before I leave. I haven't fished in so long that I don't even have a fishing license. I could get one on the way home tonight at one of the shops along Beach Road."

"I need to get one as well," Alice said, pulling the maraschino cherry from her drink and popping it into her mouth. She set the stem down on her napkin. The salty air and the music were making her feel like she was on vacation. Would it be like this every day? Would the sea, the atmosphere, and the friendliness of the locals, make her feel like her whole life was spent on vacation? She hoped so. Alice and Sasha had a lot of work ahead of them before they'd be able to sit back and enjoy it, but she wasn't going to think about work right now.

"Well, there are tons of little shops still open. After dinner, I can take Henry home while you and Jack find one to get your licenses so you all will be ready to fish whenever you can organize the time."

Convenient.

Sasha was in overdrive. Her friend was liable to be planning their wedding by September. One thing she'd seen over the years, and something only Alice knew about her, was that whenever Sasha had something big bothering her, she didn't know how to deal with it because she was always so optimistic about everything. And it was apparent by her laser focus making sure everyone was having a nice time that she was struggling.

"I'm jealous," Jack said as he walked beside Alice on the beach. They'd decided to make the journey to the shop for their fishing licenses by foot via the shore, leaving both their pairs of shoes in his car. Henry and Sasha had gone to get ice cream—Sasha had claimed that it was research. "We should've gone with them for ice cream before setting out for the licenses."

Alice smiled at him, the sand soft and cool under her feet.

Jack looked down at her, his face flushed from the alcohol at dinner. "I like Henry. He's a good boy."

"Thank you." Alice turned her head toward the sea to let the breeze blow the hair out of her face. Her protective nature set in when Jack mentioned Henry, the picture of Henry's face when she'd told him about Matt coming to mind. She watched the waves rolling angrily onto the shore, nearing them, trying not to let herself get too anxious over it. It was just a comment. Jack wasn't close enough with Henry to hurt him, and she'd like to keep it that way.

"Is it just the two of you?"

Alice nodded, beating down the swell of Matt's indiscretions in her subconscious before he could cause any more unease for her. She knew it was her mind's way of reminding her heart that this walk tonight wasn't real. It was only the thin slip of time when two people hadn't gotten to know each other's inner workings enough to realize they could never live together.

"I have Sasha, though. She's my best friend in the whole world."

"It seems so. She's very good with Henry and she traveled all the way to the Outer Banks for you."

An ocean wave came in higher than the others, sending white foam spraying over her toes, lightening the moment. She tried to dodge it, but she wasn't fast enough. With a grin, Jack moved, not very subtly, further toward the next wave. His gently playful demeanor piqued her curiosity. Sometimes his actions were in complete juxtaposition to Melly's description of him. It made her want to follow to see what he did next, so she wadded her sundress up in her fist, another wave rushing in toward their ankles.

Jack stopped and turned, facing the dune. Jutting out from behind the sea oats was a sign for ice cream, and she immediately thought of Seaside Sprinkles. Just above the sand, she could see the line of yellow umbrellas and the people gathered under them. There wasn't an ice cream shop down by the pier where Gramps's place was, and she knew it would be the perfect location for one. It just felt right.

"I wonder if that's where they are," Jack said.

Alice shrugged, lifting her eyebrows in optimism, but there were tons of ice cream shops dotting the Outer Banks. That had been one of her and Sasha's discussions at the outset: how would they set themselves apart?

"Want to get one?" Jack asked. "My treat."

"Okay," Alice replied, looking for the familiar wooden public access steps to the street.

"Let's walk straight up the dune," he suggested.

"But we're barefoot. It's full of sand spurs."

Jack looked thoughtful, the fizzing surf behind him the only sound. "There aren't that many. You just have to keep a lookout for them."

Alice considered this, unsure. When she was six, she had had to go to the bathroom and she had run from the beach through the brush to get to the bicycle shop. She fell down, those prickly little balls embedding themselves in her knees and feet as she got back up to run. She'd cried all the way to the house, and Gramps had to pick them off her one by one. He'd rubbed her skin with a special lotion to make the sting go away and then he'd made her chocolate chip pancakes for dinner—her favorite. She'd never forgotten.

"I'll give you a piggy back ride."

"What?" Alice laughed. But she thought again about the pain from those sand spurs. Her dress *was* flowy; it would be easy to climb up on him… "I'm too heavy," she decided.

"A wisp of a woman like you saying you're too heavy is an insult. At least make me feel like my four days a week at the gym aren't for nothing." Jack squatted down, his back to her, his broad shoulders ready for her to wrap her arms around. "Up," he demanded playfully. She liked how easy it was to be around him. She thought about what it would feel like to embrace him. He turned to look over his shoulder. "I'll get you a double-scoop."

Alice put her arms around his neck and, with a little hop, she was on his back. Jack stood up, holding her thighs to keep her from sliding down, and as if she didn't weigh a thing, he strode across the beach, her sandy, pink-pedicured feet dangling on either side of him.

He maneuvered the two of them around the largest dune, finding a small path where the sand had worn down. Carefully, he took deliberate steps but then flinched, his body tensing just slightly.

"You stepped on one, didn't you?" Alice said, making her point.

"When I was a kid, I ran all over these dunes without a care in the world and never stepped on a sand spur. I come up one dune when I'm trying to make a good impression and trample one right away." He shifted her weight. "It's okay, though. I think it fell off my foot. I can hardly feel it—ow! Maybe not."

Alice giggled, despite herself. He turned around to try to look at her. "Sorry," she said. "I warned you, though."

When they got to the smooth sand that led to the deck of the ice cream shop, he set her down and inspected his foot, plucking out the culprit and flicking it back into the brush. Then he led her up the stairs to the counter.

Alice looked around, but there was no sign of Henry and Sasha. She hadn't thought they'd be lucky enough to stop at the same shop, but it was worth a look. She took in the color scheme, analyzing every choice the owners had made, reading the signs. This place was pretty busy, but it didn't have the friendly feel she and Sasha were going for with Seaside Sprinkles. Would her ideas sink or float in this town? Her confidence faltered every now and again because she'd never done anything like this before. She didn't have the big degree that Sasha had, but she tried not to let it get her down.

"What's your favorite?" Jack asked, peering up at the list scrawled across a painted board above them.

"I like mint chocolate chip."

"That sounds good. I might have the same. Or rocky road…"

"No rocky road for me, thanks." Alice lifted her chin and played with her new hoop earring, remembering that last tub of rocky road she'd had after Matt had left. He'd admitted it all over a spaghetti dinner she'd made just for him because he loved her homemade meatballs, telling her that he couldn't help it, he was in love. Their plates had sat cold on the table after she'd made him leave.

"Mint chocolate chip it is then."

Alice grabbed an empty table, which was a rarity on a gorgeous night like tonight—she remembered that from visiting Gramps. Jack waited his turn in line and then headed toward her with two small waffle cones full of mint chocolate chip, wrapped in napkins.

Ice cream and summer just went together like nothing else did. Her nights with Gramps almost always ended with some sort of ice-cold treat. It was indulgent—she knew it—but it was a tradition she wanted to continue for Henry. She could just imagine Seaside Sprinkles full of people sharing their stories of sunshiny days on vacation, where they'd come from, and how different it was here. She thought about Henry sitting on the small stools she'd planned to cover in bright fabric to match the vibrant surfboards or beach décor that would hang from the ceiling, and the little matching lampshades on every table—all in soft greens, blues, and pinks, against her white furniture and driftwood walls; Einstein plopping down next to the café tables.

"I wonder where Sasha took Henry," she said, looking one more time for them.

"There are so many places they could go." Jack sat down across from her and handed over her cone.

Alice took a bite of the ice cream, still thinking about Seaside Sprinkles.

"So what brought you back here to do research? You said you were living in Chicago." She wanted to get to the bottom of what Melly had told her about him. He certainly didn't seem like he was so awful, but perhaps it was just wishful thinking.

"It wasn't work, actually. My dad has called the Outer Banks home his whole life, but he's renting a place right now. He needs a new place. His is so old that it's literally falling apart, and his lease is almost up."

"Mmm," she said, listening while taking another bite of her ice cream. "So have you found anything for him?" Alice licked her ice cream down until it was flat with the cone and then began to nibble around the edge.

"There's a strip of beach that I've had my eye on since I got here. I just need to call the agent and put in an offer. I want to build him a little house that he can spend the rest of his days in. He can fish and drink his Bulldogs, he calls them—Mexican beer combined with margarita mix. I tell him the alcohol's bad for him, but who am I to pass judgment when I'd have the same thing every evening if I could?" He chuckled.

"That sounds wonderful," Alice said, turning toward the coast, her bare feet grazing the surface of the decking as she swung her legs back and forth.

"The house or the drink?"

Alice grinned. "Both."

"I'll show it to you tomorrow."

"I can't wait." She couldn't—it was true. She still wanted to get to the bottom of his story. At least that was what she told herself, instead of admitting that she couldn't wait to see him again.

Chapter Nine

Alice woke to the sound of the ocean through the windows upstairs. They were all still on air mattresses, having not set up the furniture yet. Today she'd planned to move everything else in. They had to get a move on, despite her wish to pretend she had nothing to do all week.

Last night, she'd asked Jack to let her walk home from the fishing shop after they'd gotten their licenses. He hadn't liked the idea of her alone, in the dark, and he'd adamantly advised against it, but she assured him that Beach Road was crawling with cyclists and tourists taking evening strolls, and she'd be just fine; plus, she was a grown woman and she'd walked home from places many times on her own before. She could see the indecision in his eyes, but the more she looked into them, the more she could feel her resolve crumbling and she had to get out of there. As it was, she'd already somehow agreed to see the beach location for his father's new home with him when she'd told herself not get swept up by him. He'd charmed her again, and, as they'd walked to the fishing shop, she'd let her mind work over her heart, bringing her back to reality.

So when it came time to leave, she'd insisted. She'd needed to clear her head. Her emotions were flying around, scaring her. Jack was too good, too perfect, and she knew that if she gave it enough time, something would break and she wouldn't allow it to be her heart.

The fresh air had done her good. She tried to get her mind off him by thinking of all the plans she had for Seaside Sprinkles. She wanted to run the décor and a logo that she'd thought of past Sasha today, so when they took a break from unpacking, she was going to tell her friend all about her ideas. She was excited, energized.

With the small paper fishing license under the white pitcher on the kitchen table to keep it from blowing away, she set off downstairs to join Henry and Einstein. "Want to fly your new kite today?" she asked him, as she leashed up Einstein for his morning walk in the sand.

"Yes! Then, after that, can we get in the water?"

She threw a quick glance over at Sasha, who was sitting, cross-legged, in the kitchen chair, drinking her morning coffee in her new mug, a far-away look in her eyes. She'd made a cup for Alice and had it sitting on the counter. Sasha had always been her rock; nothing fazed her. So to see her like this for so many days was unnerving.

"We'll take turns watching him," Sasha offered, clearly swimming back into the present.

Alice liked that idea. Then they could still unpack and maybe Henry would get so tired from all the sun and surf that he'd fall asleep early and she'd finally get a chance to talk to Sasha about what was going on with her.

"Sounds good to me! Sash, want to take a walk with us?"

Einstein flopped into the sitting position, leaning on his hip, and turned his head to the side; he, too, seemed to be expectant of an answer. His ears perked up just before he started to pant lightly, his dark brown eyes on Sasha.

Grabbing Alice's mug and handing it to her, Sasha took her own and slipped on her flip-flops. "A walk actually sounds amazing." As she said it, her eyes became glassy. Quickly, she slid those aviators of hers on and put her mug to her lips. Henry, oblivious, grabbed Einstein's leash and opened the door. Alice followed but not before giving her friend a look to let her know that they would be talking about this sooner rather than later. They couldn't wait any longer.

The sun had yet to burn through the morning haze and the surf was quiet and subdued, the water lapping onto the shore as Einstein bounded ahead of them after a sandpiper that was scurrying its way down the smooth, wet part of the sand from where the waves had just retreated. Henry giggled as he ran along the shore to keep up with his puppy, and Alice was so happy to see him feeling a little better this morning. But she knew first hand how those feelings came in waves and she'd be ready the next time he was unsure.

Sasha sipped her coffee quietly as they plodded through the sand, and Alice turned to her once Henry was out of earshot. "You're either overly excitable or totally zoned out and on the verge of tears. Tell me. What's going on?"

Sasha cleared her throat, still hiding behind her sunglasses, her lip starting to wobble.

Alice stopped and turned toward her friend, her voice as soft as the wind. "What is it? You've been different for weeks."

"I thought I could escape it, coming here. I thought if I could just refocus…" Sasha tipped her head up to the sky as if she were trying to keep the tears from spilling over.

"Is it the divorce?"

She shook her head.

Einstein and Henry ran down to the surf, both of them splashing in it. The waves danced around them, sending spray into the air. Each droplet looked like a diamond, shimmering in the sunlight on its way to the sand. Henry was laughing, happy, and his squeals of joy were in stark contrast to the atmosphere between her and her best friend.

"You can tell me anything, you know that."

"I know I can. It's just so hard to get the words to come out because they break my heart." She drew in a jagged breath. "Landon doesn't even know."

It wasn't like Sasha to hold in something this distressing without even sharing it with her husband. Even in their tumultuous times, Sasha would've confided in him with a problem so huge. She hadn't even told Alice, which was surprising. These facts alone told Alice that whatever it was, it was bigger than Sasha had ever dealt with before. She waited for her friend to talk in her own time.

Finally, after a long pause, searching the ocean, her attention turned to Alice and she said, "Before Landon asked for a divorce, I found out I was pregnant. Landon and I were having a baby." Her words came out in almost a whisper and Alice had to lean forward to hear her.

"Oh my gosh." She allowed her gaze to fall on Sasha's toned tummy, her hot pink tank top fitting firmly against her torso. Alice's mind went a hundred miles an hour: she thought about how Sasha barely ate and Alice had always been starving when she was pregnant; she'd had a steady stream of coffee in the last few weeks, and Alice remembered how she had been told to keep the caffeine down when she'd been pregnant with Henry; *and* Sasha had lifted the heavy kitchen table without a flinch… Before Sasha could say anything else, Alice already knew.

"I lost it." A tear slid out from under her aviators and she let it fall. "I'd primed myself to be an amazing mother. I was ready. I wanted that baby more than anything—Landon or no Landon. I bought a little outfit, a set of booties." She tossed the rest of her coffee from her mug, the tide erasing it from the sand. "I was so prepared for all the joy of it that I neglected to get myself ready for anything that could go wrong. And when it did, it hit me so hard I'm still struggling to recover. I don't know why I never told Landon. I guess I was waiting for the right time, but there just wasn't a right time because something would set him off and we'd get to arguing, and then the baby was gone. The day before I had the procedure to remove the fetus, after I had been told there was no heartbeat, that was when Landon told me he wanted a divorce. I've never been that low in my life."

"Why have you held all of this in, Sash?"

"To make it go away." Sasha put her hand to her heart and Alice wondered if it was a subconscious action to try to keep it together, because Alice's own heart was breaking for her friend.

"Those kinds of feelings don't go away, Sasha. You have to deal with them. It's okay to be sad. You *have* to be sad. Once you let yourself grieve, you can move on."

She nodded, but it was clear she was deep in her own thoughts. "I had names picked out."

Alice smiled gently, remembering the moment she'd thought of Henry's name. She had been alone in her apartment, leaning on her elbows over a box of takeout Chinese, her belly barely allowing her to do so, when the name Henry John Emerson came into her mind, and she just knew it would be a boy. She'd said the name over and over out loud in her quiet apartment, a huge grin on her face.

"What names did you choose?"

Sasha looked out at Henry, and Alice followed her line of sight. He and Einstein were soaking wet. With this new information, Alice felt a little guilty. She'd had a perfectly healthy little boy. She hadn't ever had to experience what Sasha had gone through. She remembered what it felt like when Henry kicked in her belly, letting her know he was there, that soon her life wouldn't be just hers anymore. She remembered what that excitement was like and couldn't imagine it being ripped away from her.

"A girl would've been Amy Elise and a boy would've been Chuck, short for Charles. Charles Christopher."

"Those are nice names."

Sasha agreed silently, emotion clearly getting the better of her. Alice could actually see her mustering the energy to speak again. "I look at Henry and I think how amazing that his little soul made it all the way. He got himself here to be with you. My little one had to go back home for a while, but he or she will try to find me again, I pray."

"I'll pray too," Alice said, the weight of her friend's statement making her feel like she, too, had lost out on knowing this little soul.

Alice clicked off the screen and slipped her phone into her pocket, hiding her smile.

She climbed the ladder, pinning the paper with her Seaside Sprinkles logo to the wall as Sasha came into the room. Alice had asked a local artist to help her with it and when she saw the final design, she'd been positively tickled. She'd ordered a window application for the front door and she'd gotten it printed on napkins and cups for the ice cream. The logo was pink and drawn out like a circular stamp, with the 'S' in both words long and swirling, dropping off into a wave of little multicolored sprinkles. She and Sasha had used the one white wall at the back of the shop downstairs as their planning board, pinning all their ideas to it. It was covered in papers, plans, and lists.

"I love it," Sasha said, taking a step back to look at it from afar, her hands on her hips, and her head to the side.

Alice was glad to see her smile. It was as if their talk this morning had lifted the burden off her heart just a little and allowed her to move on with the day. That loss was still in her eyes, though, and Alice knew it would never go away completely, but now that Sasha had shared with Alice what it was, she seemed to be able to handle it a bit better as they planned for the ice cream shop. Jumping into the planning was a great diversion for them both.

They'd ordered equipment today; gotten two quotes to replace the small rental counter with a larger one made from pastel tiles and painted shiplap, with a tall, rounded glass top for viewing the flavors; and they'd spoken with a local flooring place to have a few boards replaced on the hardwoods. The shop already had recessed lighting, which was actually very nice, but they wanted to add more shiplap in white on the ceiling to give it a nautical look. They'd priced it at the local hardware shop, and with the purchase of a saw, they thought they could do it themselves. As they made all their lists of changes, they realized that they'd really have to make Alice's dollar stretch to pull this off, and some of the things on their dream-shop list might not happen just yet.

They'd planned to put up some porch swings with oversized cushions in pastels on the front porch, lots of potted flowers, and a couple of paddle fans, but now they were down to a row of plastic chairs. Nevertheless, things were starting to come together in Alice's mind. She was getting a feel, a vibe, a springboard for more ideas.

"I'm so glad I have you with me to do this," Alice admitted to Sasha. Her insecurities were welling up again. There was something about having Sasha's expertise when making decisions that made Alice feel like she was doing the right thing. "I don't ever feel secure about the marketing decisions until you say okay."

Sasha squinted at her friend and shook her head. "You don't believe in yourself. Why is that? You're awesome at this, but you won't allow yourself to trust it."

"I don't have the training."

Sasha rolled her eyes. "Yes, I took classes, so I have a baseline of strategies, but it's really down to instinct." She turned to the wall of ideas. "Do you realize that I didn't do a thing to that logo—*you* created that all by yourself with the artist; it was *your* vision. I didn't change it at all. I haven't had to change a thing that you've created because you have God-given talent. Who's to say your strategies aren't better than the ones I studied in my books?"

Alice wanted to believe Sasha, and she knew she had some good instincts, but would she be consistent? And did she have the background knowledge required? She'd bounced her ideas off Sasha, who'd discussed every angle with her. "There's a reason no one will hire a marketing person at your level without a degree. And I don't have one. That's all I'm saying."

"What would you have done if I hadn't come? Would you have tried to do this alone?"

Just the thought sent a cold shiver through her because she knew the answer. "I'd have probably sold the place," she said, nearly breathless at the thought.

Things were speeding along like a runaway train, her ideas shooting off like a rocket, and she was holding on for dear life. She'd never felt so energized, so alive in her career. She couldn't imagine, even this early on, walking back through the doors of the dentist's office and sitting behind that desk again. But she'd watched *American Idol* enough to know there were people with dreams who wouldn't realize those dreams. Those people believed in themselves—they were driven, they planned, they did everything they should do—but their talent fell short. Would she fall short as well?

Sasha huffed indignantly as her eyes landed on the ideas wall. "That whole board is yours; it's all from your mind," she said. "I've let you lead because this is your destiny. I'm just along for the ride."

"The ceiling shiplap was your idea," Alice said, scratching for something to prove her point.

"And shiplap has been proven to sell ice cream?" Sasha raised an eyebrow. "You've created the Seaside Sprinkles brand: the idea of togetherness, of family and friends experiencing this place instead of just stopping in. Look at the colors you have: all friendly and cozy instead of the usual neon that people are so accustomed to. Your typography is lower-case, unassuming, subtle—which makes it feel like home. It's totally different from anything else here in the Outer Banks. And it *will* sell ice cream, Alice. But it will sell more than that. It will sell a gathering place where families will return year after year to drop in and say hello, to try the new flavors you're thinking of trying—those are great, by the way—and to meet up with others who are stopping in for the same reasons. It's all from you, not me."

Alice looked over at the board, scanning all the sheets of paper, the drawings, the lists, the phone numbers for different work that would be required.

Sasha handed her their last idea, for a painted ice cream display with faces cut out for photo opportunities. They'd planned to put it outside so people would have something to keep them busy when the lines got long. *If* the lines got long.

"I'll let you off the hook," she said. "Now, tell me! Why were you smiling at your phone when I came in the room?"

Alice felt the heat crawl up her neck as the subject changed. "Jack texted, and he wants to meet me for a drink in about an hour," she said.

Henry walked in with the coloring book she'd gotten him for the move. He waited for an explanation, having evidently heard what she'd said, while he opened it to a clean page and chose a crayon.

"Then," Alice told him, "he wants to come back to get you for fishing."

His yellow crayon was still in his small fingers as he grinned up at her, eyes wide. "Can we fish off the pier?"

"Of course."

"Henry, may I color too?" Sasha said, waving her friend upstairs so she could get ready. Her gesture was an offer to watch Henry earlier than expected; Alice knew her so well that they spoke with only their actions, and she could read it without any prompting. She smiled gratefully at Sasha.

Alice went upstairs, feeling so thankful that Sasha had offered to watch Henry for her, especially now that Alice knew what her friend was going through emotionally. Alice finally relented, wondering if Henry was actually good for Sasha—he could keep her mind off the loss she'd suffered. She wished she could do something to support her friend, but she wasn't sure what to do.

Still pondering, she pulled a pair of shorts and her favorite tank top from the suitcase and laid the garments on one of Gramps's old trunks. She remembered how he'd set her up on it to tie her shoes, her little feet dangling above the floor as she sat atop the large, glossy wood planks that striped the lid.

Its contents had never occurred to her. Curiosity mounting now, she moved her clothes and flipped the heavy brass latch, the hinges groaning as she pushed it open to peek inside. With a knowing smile, she pulled out an issue of *Saltwater Fishing*, his favorite magazine.

He'd earmarked the page on shifting sands. As she set it aside, a small circular case caught her eye. She opened it to find it was a wind-up travel clock, an old analog in gold leaf. She turned it over in her hand, admiring it. At the bottom, peeking out from more magazines, she could see an ink pen with his initials, a few photos of an old Ford truck he'd restored and sold at auction, and a couple of postage stamps from different countries. She didn't have time to look at it all now, but the next time she had a free moment, she couldn't wait to go through it. Gently, she folded the little travel clock and snapped it shut before placing it gingerly back into the trunk.

But just as she was about to close the lid, the tarnished gold of something small got her attention. It wasn't a coin; it was something else. She felt around through the contents until her fingers found the bottom of the trunk and she tried to pull the object from under the magazines. When she got hold of it, she brought it up into her view. On closer inspection, it was a round locket, the front engraved with roses. Alice pressed her thumbnail between the sides and pried it open. On the left was a baby picture that looked like her and on the right, another baby. She squinted at the image, wondering if it was her cousin Susie. They were about the same age.

What a sweet reminder of family, she thought, and closed her fist around it as she shut the trunk. It was just like Gramps to have kept something like that. It had most likely been Alice's grandma's, and when she passed, Gramps had probably held onto it to keep it within the family. Her aunt Claire was always putting up old photos online. Alice would have to let her know that she'd found another one of Susie. Setting it on the dresser, she put her clothes back on the trunk and went to get ready, promising herself she'd go through Gramps's things as soon as she could. Maybe there were more treasures in there.

Chapter Ten

Alice ran her hand along the sea oats as she crossed the boardwalk of one of the beach bars in town. Multicolored arrows directed her along the path around back, where the entire side of it was open to the sea. She read each one of the signs: "This way to happiness"; "You're almost there"; "We're all waiting for you." Then she reached the back where the largest of the signs read, "We're so glad you're here." When she took her eyes from the sign, Jack was smiling down at her, a fruity drink in his hand.

"Hello," he said, handing it to her, those biceps peeking out from under the sleeves of his T-shirt. The light green of the fabric brought out his eyes, but she kept her attention on the emblem of his shirt to keep her composure as she took the drink from him. It was a faded picture of a sailboat with the name of a rum that she didn't recognize. It must be local; the lettering said: "Outer Banks, NC" in curly script underneath the name.

"Thank you," she said, filling her lungs with the sea air before finally looking at him. She smiled, unable to resist the feeling of how great it was to see him. "What is this?" She looked down at her drink. It was a creamy yellow with pineapple slices and shaved coconut on top.

"It's called 'The Smilemaker'. Looks like it works."

Only then did she realize she was still smiling. A tingle of warmth spread over her cheeks, and she hoped he actually thought her reaction had been to the drink, although the fondness in his eyes told her otherwise.

Jack pulled a barstool out for her and she took a seat, placing her drink on top of a white square napkin on the bar.

"I know we've only just met, and this is a somewhat personal request, but I was wondering if you'd go with me to see my father today. I told him I'd pop in on him and I was wondering if we could go before we went fishing. He's all alone and I think he'd really enjoy the company."

"Of course." She'd just been asked to meet the man that Jack had supposedly abandoned to move to Chicago. Her curiosity was getting the better of her, and she couldn't wait to meet him.

"We don't have to stay long."

"It's fine. I don't mind at all." And she didn't. She was intrigued to see the man who had raised the person sitting in front of her, the person so different from Melly's description of him: the mannerly apple-catcher who was also great with kids and had the most gorgeous eyes she'd ever seen. Which version of Jack was real? Suddenly, she was second-guessing her decision to go because she might just find out definitively that it was Melly's, and she wanted to hold on to the idea that it wasn't for a little longer.

"Great." Jack sat down beside her in front of a bottle of beer. With his strong hands resting on the table, he twisted toward her. "So, are you settling in okay?"

"Yes. I've even met a new neighbor. She's lovely. We've spent a ton of time together already and it feels like I've known her forever. You might know her, actually. She's a nurse. Her name is Melly St. James."

"I do, actually," Jack said, his eyebrows rising in interest. Then she noticed something in his expression, as if there was more to tell. He lifted the bottle of beer to his lips, his gaze shifting to the ocean briefly before returning to his bottle. He held it out as if reading the label and set it down.

"What is it?" she asked, interested in what information he had about her new friend.

He turned the bottle around slowly before meeting her eye again and then frowned, shaking his head. "Nothing at all. Glad you've already met your neighbor!" His face lifted. "I haven't met mine in Chicago and I've lived in that building for three years."

"Three years and you don't know your neighbors?" Wait. She wasn't letting him change the subject. That was a definite expression—a weird expression—she'd noticed when she'd mentioned Melly. "What do you know about Melly?"

"She's one of the new nurses hired at the hospital."

"Yes." She pursed her lips. She wasn't being crazy. There was something very off about his response when she'd mentioned her, but she worried she was making a mountain out of a molehill. However, if it were nothing, then why wouldn't he just say whatever it was? "You're holding something back about her," she said anyway, her interest at maximum levels. "Why won't you tell me what it is?"

He leaned forward, surrender flashing in his eyes, and licked his lips as if buying time. "I'm not at liberty to say."

"Why?"

"How are you able to mind read like that, anyway? I didn't even say anything about Melly St. James and you somehow start grilling me on the hospital drama."

"Drama?"

He shook his head and then smiled. "Remind me never to try to keep a secret from you. You're killin' me here."

She grinned. At the end of the day, it was hospital drama like he said, and for whatever reason he wasn't allowed to tell. She was putting pressure on him to spill the beans, and from the look on his face, he was torn between making her happy and keeping the secret. So she decided to let him off the hook. "Fine. I'll let it go." She held his gaze.

"Grab your drink," he said, his attention moving to the dartboard at the corner of the room. "Let's have some fun."

Glad to have something pulling on her attention besides those eyes of his, she followed him over.

Jack took his beer bottle by the neck, between his two fingers, and led the way. Setting the drink down on a keg-barrel-turned-table, he plucked the darts from the board and handed her the ones with red tails, their fingers brushing each other's as she took them. "Give it a few practice shots."

Alice took an enormous drink from her glass, hoping the alcohol would relax her enough to take an accurate shot. Holding the dart between her thumb and forefinger, she zeroed in on the center of the board. When she felt like she had the shot lined up, she let the dart go, surprised by the slight heaviness of it. The tail wobbled as it sailed in an arc, barely catching the bottom of the board.

"My dart game needs some work," she said.

He grinned at her, maneuvering the dart between his fingers in such a relaxed and casual way that she wondered how often he played this game. "I have an idea," he said, his green eyes aglitter. "I get this shot—bull's eye—and you go on a boat ride with me tomorrow. I miss and we both go about our business as usual."

"You don't have to work?" she questioned.

"I do, but it's research and I'm heading it up, so I'm on my own time. I'll figure that part out."

She looked at the dart in his fingers, considering.

"Do we have a deal?"

Alice assessed his confidence. He was charming her, and she wasn't entirely sure she had time to go on a boat ride with him. She had things to do.

"Well?"

"You get me here to have a drink and suddenly I'm meeting your dad, visiting a potential property with you, fishing with my son, and now I'm about to plan a boat ride. You're good!"

Jack laughed.

"Fine. But you have to make it from here." She took a few giant steps backward, lining herself up with the end of the bar and putting him back a considerable distance. She'd leave it up to fate to decide.

Jack tightened his lips as if thinking it over, his eyes moving from the bar to the dartboard. Was that uncertainty she saw?

"Confident?" Alice teased.

Jack laughed again, affection swallowing her up.

The dart still twirling easily through his fingers, Jack paced over to the spot she'd chosen and unexpectedly, the bull's eye seemed awfully far away, too far away, her determination crumbling. Despite all the things she told herself, she wanted him to make that shot, but she'd made it nearly impossible. The more she thought about it, the more she realized that by making it a near unreachable target, it was her brain telling her heart to quit dreaming.

There was a smirk on the bartender's face, but before she could process the meaning of it, Jack let the dart go and her concentration moved to the sailing object, her heartbeat speeding up despite the scolding from her inner voice.

It seemed to take forever, and then there was a light thump as the point made contact with the board. She stared at it, blinking to be sure she was really seeing what she thought she was seeing. Or was it wishful thinking?

"Bull's eye," she heard from the bartender behind her, as he laughed quietly and turned toward a customer.

Jack took the darts from her hand and, one after another, hit the center of the board, not missing a single shot.

"So is this how you get all the girls to go out with you?"

The corner of his mouth turned up in an adorable way. "Only the ones opening ice cream shops. I'm hoping to get free dessert."

Alice tried to keep a serious face. "I think you need more of a challenge if a boat ride is at stake."

"Nope. You agreed. I even let you choose the distance. But I'll tell you what: you can pick the challenge the next time."

"Next time?"

Jack nodded, his gaze roaming her face. "Wanna meet my dad now?"

"Okay," she said, happy to just be with him. He was proving to be nothing at all like Melly had described, and, while that fact thrilled her, it also scared her to death.

"When I was a boy, my dad wasn't around a whole lot. He was a sales-man—what he sold changed by the year. But the one thing he was good at was talking to people, and with that gift, he made a living for his family. He always researched every single one of the products he sold, so he could tell the customers exactly what they were buying, which made them feel like they could trust him. He spent his whole adult life providing for us, and now it's my turn to give something back to him," Jack said as he pulled up outside the small bungalow, nearly hidden in the woods among the pine trees. He hopped out and opened Alice's door for her.

An old man with a white beard and broad shoulders, wearing denim overalls, walked over to greet them. He'd been chopping wood, a split piece teetering haphazardly on an old tree stump. The pine straw crunched beneath Alice's feet while she followed Jack over to the man to meet him half way. She could see the immediate boost in the man's features when he saw his son; his pride was clear.

"Hey, Dad," he called before they reached him. "This is Alice."

The man clapped his hands together and wiped them on the front of his overalls before offing one to Alice in greeting. "Butch Murphy." She could tell by the gentle way he took her hand that he was kind, and with that smile, it was no wonder he'd been a good salesman. He had the sort of face anyone would trust, just like his son.

"You don't have some big news to share with me or anything, do you?" he asked, his gaze darting between the two of them.

Jack laughed. "No, Dad. We just came to say hello."

"Mmm," he nodded, looking unconvinced.

"You know chopping wood won't help your back, right?"

"My back is just fine." Butch stroked his beard defiantly but a slight uncertainty flickered on his face. "I'll go crazy if I stay inside. You know that."

"Yes. I do. But you could take a walk, go out for a nice cup of coffee. Anything but chop wood. You don't even need firewood. It's summer."

"It'll rot if I don't chop it and get it off the ground."

"You have central heating for the winter anyway."

"Yes, but there's no better way to spend a winter evening than by the fire. That's when I can relax."

"Two seasons from now?" Jack chuckled, clearly just giving his father a hard time. Their banter was enjoyable to watch, and it was obvious they were very close.

"You have got to be the worst date ever," Butch said. "You've brought a girl to see me and you never bring girls home." He leaned in toward Alice. "Even in high school, he brought very few girls over." Eyeing Jack, he said, "And here you are talking about central heating. A regular Casanova, you are."

"Then what do you propose we do?"

Butch rolled his eyes dramatically as if the answer were clear. "Follow me." Butch turned and headed into the woods.

Alice questioned Jack with a look, but he seemed to be just as unclear as to where they were headed.

"Why are we going down the old path?" Jack put his hand on Alice's back to help her keep her footing as she stepped over a downed tree limb.

"Remember all that fishing line I had you buy me?" Butch asked, his eyes staying on the trail, his back to them as he led the way. "I'm going to show you why."

"Did you find a pond back here or something?" Jack thrust a vine out of the route, clearing the way. After Alice stepped past it, he let it go and it snapped back over the path again.

"Nope. I learned how to relax."

They pushed past the last of the brush and Alice gasped. "Oh my gosh," she said. "Did you do this yourself?" She tipped her head up to see them all. The woods had been cleared, raked clean, and the trees' limbs had been pruned, letting the sun in through the canopy. There were benches made of logs, highly sanded and glossy, but what had really floored her was what was hanging from the branches by the nearly invisible fishing line: there were little, perfectly carved wooden birds—hundreds of them. Not only did Jack get his friendliness from his father, he'd inherited Butch's precision as well. "It looks like they're flying," she said, her words coming out breathlessly.

"Dad, this is incredible."

Jack walked around slowly, his head tilting back, viewing each one individually, and giving every bird his full attention. Alice liked how he did that: he took his time with everything, just like he had with her when she'd had that moment the day they'd met. He was deliberate, focused.

"I had to do something to fight the boredom," Butch replied.

"I had no idea," Jack said, running his hand along one of the benches. "It's quite a departure from cutting firewood." He turned to his father. "When did you start doing this?"

"Shortly after I retired." Butch sat down, noticeably worn out from standing. "Remember when I whittled that truck for you?"

"Oh, yeah. I'd forgotten about that. I used to take it outside and make ramps for it. I haven't seen it in ages."

"Well, I have it." His head dropped and he seemed to be gazing at the forest floor when he looked up suddenly. "Forgive me for getting personal, Miss Alice, but I don't mind if you hear this." He cleared his throat, his attention on his son. He took in a deep breath and let it out. "I found that truck and I realized that I made it for you, Jack, but I never got to see you play with it. Not once did I see you play with it. I was too busy running around trying to make us money. This all started when I was sitting by myself one day thinking about that. I thought, 'I'd like to make young Jack another toy. Too bad he isn't young anymore to enjoy it.' But I made one anyway, one for every time I thought about how I'd missed that."

Alice felt the prick of tears in her eyes and, at the same time, she felt like an outsider, eavesdropping on a very personal moment between Jack and his father. She took a step back and viewed more of the beautiful birds Butch had made to give herself a minute.

"I don't fault you for working," Jack said. "You had to do what you had to do to support us."

"I enjoyed the travel, the nonstop movement of it. I liked meeting people and the rush of great sales as a result of my work. But now that I'm an old man, that's all gone, and, by the grace of God, and your mother's hard work, you've become a man I'm proud of—but I hold deep guilt that your success was nothing to do with me. I wasn't around to help build you into the man you are. I wish I had been."

While this was a very delicate conversation, Alice was glad to hear it. She found it incredibly moving and a testament to who both these men were. Gramps used to tell her that there's a certain grace in how we deal with things that tells others about the kind of person we are. That grace was present here.

"Sorry. I've gotten sentimental in my old age," Butch said, now standing beside her and placing his hand on her shoulder. "Maybe we can find something wonderful to do with these birds one day."

Alice looked over at Jack, a quiet smile reaching his eyes. She thought again about how Melly and the other nurses had it all wrong, but she was too afraid to let herself believe it.

Butch walked over and clapped Jack on the back. "Come on up to the house. Let's have some coffee."

Chapter Eleven

"I can't wait to show you this property," Jack said, as he turned a curve leading them back toward the coast. "Dad doesn't know I'm buying it for him. It's a surprise. I'm going to completely renovate the building." He beamed at Alice. "Well, once I put in an offer."

Her knowledge of the summer market gave her pause at his statement. The time for selling was nearing its high and it would be a seller's market for the next few months. "If you've decided to buy it, why haven't you put a contract on it yet? I'd be worried it would sell to someone else and I wouldn't get it."

He raised his eyebrows, seemingly sure of himself. "I'm not too worried. I'd just outbid the offer. I'm prepared to do whatever it takes to get it. And I did tell the agent that I'd be in touch. I'd planned to call her after shopping the other day, but a certain someone lost her handbag." He winked at her.

"If I don't get a move on, though, Dad's going to hurt himself trying to keep that house of his from falling apart. It's only a rental, but you can't tell him that. It was a good house for many years, but it got to be too much upkeep for him, so I sold it, and we're just renting until I can get him somewhere else to live."

Over coffee, Butch had mentioned how the roof was leaking and Jack had warned him not to get up on the ladder to try to fix it, although Butch had clearly done it a few times to hang all of his wooden birds.

"I used to visit this area all the time as a kid. We lived about a block away from the beach during my younger years, and I would walk to the shore every single day, even after school once the summer was over. I have so many memories here."

Alice took in Jack's profile, the creases around his eyes visible through the side of his sunglasses as he looked at the road while gripping the wheel at the bottom with one hand. The windows were down, blowing Alice's hair. She propped her elbow up on the car door to hold the runaway strands out of her face, relishing the familiar straw feeling of her hair as it was coated with the salty air.

She couldn't wait to see what Jack had planned for his father. It was such an enormous and thoughtful gift that she wanted to hear every single detail. Completely relaxed, she allowed herself to imagine more days with Jack, sitting by an open window as the sun streamed in, while he showed her floor samples or paint colors. They could have working lunches: she planning the latest order for ice cream at Seaside Sprinkles, while he chattered away on his phone to the architect with a hundred ideas for what would make Butch the perfect home.

The ocean was outside her window now, that familiar stretch of beach just over the dune. They were nearing Gramps's old shop, and she got a punch of excitement, thinking that perhaps the property was close to hers. Certainly, a remodel could take all summer and that would mean she'd have all those glorious months to see Jack.

And how wonderful it would be if she were lucky enough to see the look on Butch's face when Jack revealed his new home. She imagined a long front porch with a few of his birds hanging from its ceiling, rocking chairs underneath, all of them sitting together.

But she also reminded herself that this was only fleeting. Jack was going back to Chicago. Why had he moved away in the first place and left his father here all alone when it was so clear that Butch felt like he'd lost time with his son? Jack knew how he felt—she'd seen Butch tell him with her own eyes—but he hadn't said a thing about staying. Did he care at all how his father felt? When he'd finished whatever this favor was for his doctor friend, he was leaving, and that fact was screaming at her loud and clear. But she pushed it out of her mind, wondering if she was overthinking things and perhaps she should just live in the moment and think about all the wonderful things they could do this summer.

Jack slowed down outside the shop, and she wondered how he knew where she lived. Was he planning to pick up Henry first so they could go straight to fishing after? Were they going to fish from the same pier she'd fished from with Gramps? He leaned over her to look out her side of the window as she searched his face for answers.

"I wonder who that is," Jack said.

She stared in the direction of his gaze, and he was looking directly at Sasha's car. Alice's was parked on the side of the house, so he hadn't seen it yet.

"This is the property." Jack pulled in next to Sasha's vehicle and turned off the engine. "But it looks like someone's occupying it. It couldn't have sold that quickly; the closing procedures alone would take at least ninety days."

Her skin prickled with unease. Alice couldn't speak, all those hopeful thoughts about the summer becoming a muddle in her mind as confusion set in.

Jack misread her bewilderment and offered her that gorgeous smile of his. "I'm sure it will be fine. Maybe the agent's here to check on the property. I'll find out what's going on." He shut off the engine and, as he opened the door to get out, she caught his arm.

But before she could say anything, Henry burst from the door and ran over to them with bare feet, stopping right in front of Jack. Henry's hair was wet, beads of water still lingering around his shoulders. He must have been waiting for them on the beach.

"Hi!" he said, noticeably delighted to see Jack. "Are you here to go fishing? I've been waiting!"

Jack's eyes were on her son, obviously processing the situation. But then, he cleared whatever had filled his mind and grinned at Henry. "Hey, buddy! You're ready to go fishing? I've got everything in the truck. Go grab yourself a shirt and some shoes and we'll head up to the pier."

Henry ran back inside as Sasha peeked out the door, waving at them.

Jack waved back, and with his face still turned toward Sasha, he said, "This building is yours?" His eyes were unstill, his words coming out hushed. He ran his hand through his hair.

"Yes," she said, after Sasha had gone back inside. "This is going to be my ice cream shop." Alice felt terrible suddenly, thinking of how Butch wouldn't get to have that beautiful cottage she'd conjured up in her mind.

"But it couldn't have sold that quickly," Jack said matter-of-factly, his gaze darting over to her before he looked back at the property, his hands in his pockets. While he was keeping a straight face for the sake of conversation, his disappointment was evident.

"I was going to sell it, but then I decided to open the ice cream shop, so I took it off the market."

His brows furrowed with this news, his mouth set in a contempla-tive frown. A car drove by, its tires grinding the sand on the street as the sun beat down, both of them standing in silence.

"Ready!" Henry said, running out the door and greeting them.

"All right." Jack put on that million-dollar smile and reached into the back of the truck, pulling out three fishing rods and his tackle box. "We're close enough to the pier that we can walk right over. How lucky is that?" he said, all the words coming out on an exhale, as if he were still trying to get his disappointment in check. He handed the smallest rod to Henry.

When they got to the pier, Alice found it surprisingly empty. Usually it was swarming with visitors who were there to see the floor-to-ceiling fish tanks and to buy souvenirs from the gift shops before they walked the length of the colossal landing, stopping to peer through the complimentary binoculars and sit in the rocking chairs that lined the center. There was normally a huge sale going on at the gift shop—everything 50 percent off—but today, it was closed.

Jack bought the tickets for their entry, and Alice reminded herself that she'd have to pay him back. She wanted to do something nice for him anyway—it was such a shame that he wouldn't be building Butch his home on that stretch of beach now. Jack was quiet, and, even though she hadn't known him very long, she could tell his mind was still whirring—it showed right on his face.

Henry ran ahead, stopping at the edge to view a flock of seagulls that had dipped down into the surf.

"I'm sorry about your dad's house," Alice said quietly. "There's got to be something else available."

Jack blinked over and over, looking down at the pier as if he were looking for something before meeting her eyes. "You own that building?" he asked, as if he hadn't heard the answer before. He was visibly baffled. He looked out to the ocean, that mind of his still going. Then he shook his head, his brows coming together in concern before he forced a smile. "It will all work out," Jack said. "Let's talk about it later." He walked up beside Henry. "Ready to catch some fish?"

Chapter Twelve

Jack hadn't spoken any more about the property, focusing mostly on Henry and helping him catch fish. They'd thrown back everything they'd caught so far, which was eleven fish, the last one nearly breaking the line it had been so big.

"So you fish with your grandfather?" Jack asked, leaning over him to keep his line from getting tangled under the pier. The sky was an electric blue, making them both squint as they talked to each other.

"Uh huh," Henry said, without taking his eyes off the line as he waited intently for a bite. "Grandpa Frank and I fish in a pond, though. I've never fished from a pier before."

Jack smiled. "When I was your age, my dad was always gone, and I'd walk to this pier sometimes because there was someone who would fish with me here. The man who owned that old bike shop where you all live would fish here too. I got my line tangled once, and he helped me. After that, I started to watch what he was doing and he began to tell me as he did it. Before long, we were friends."

Alice, who had sat down on the nearby bench to soak in the sun and watch the two of them, straightened up.

"I used to love to fish with him," Jack said.

Henry finally took his eyes off the line. "That's my great-grandpa."

Alice watched the way Jack's back tensed as he heard this, the tilt of his head as the information sank in, and the slow revelation of what she, too, was realizing at that moment. He turned around, his expression questioning, as he looked at her.

She stood up and took a step in front of Jack, the wind pressing against her. "I used to fish with him too."

Jack.

Both of them stared as if they'd only just now actually seen one another, and she wondered if Jack was remembering what she was: that one day when Gramps had introduced her to a boy on the pier and they'd sat together, pushing their feet through the railings, the salty spray grazing their toes every so often as they shared stories about school, those green eyes of his making her feel like she was a princess. Gramps had bought them both an ice cream cone, and if she closed her eyes, Alice could still remember her sticky fingers and the heat in her cheeks at the boy's crooked smile when he looked at her. They'd been about fifteen.

"Strawberry ice cream," he said, a smile playing on his lips.

She nodded.

"I thought you were the most beautiful girl on the beach that summer," he whispered.

The flutter in her stomach was starting to be a normal sensation these days. "How come you didn't come back? I visited after that."

"That was the summer before I moved inland to the home that Dad has now. It was too far to walk, and I didn't get a car until after college when I moved to Chicago." He baited his hook and tossed his line out a little way from Henry, who was still waiting for a bite. "Your grandfather was a good man," he said to her over his shoulder.

"Yes, he was."

As Jack's comment settled in her mind, she remembered Gramps saying that one day, when she met a man, he hoped it would be someone like Jack. She'd laughed it off, too consumed by young flirtations to take his words to heart.

"You got one!" Jack said, steadying his fishing pole with one hand while he reached around Henry to hold his rod as it bent down toward the sea, Henry's little hands madly reeling. "It's a big one!" Jack gripped the rod, holding it steady, the end of it looking as though it might break in half. Henry's hands were barely able to maneuver the reel.

Alice got up and took Jack's rod so he could help her son. Together, they worked to get the fish into the air. Jack's arms were around Henry, the two of them pulling and winding the reel together, and to anyone else they looked like a little family, like some sort of cosmic fast forward from that day when Alice was fifteen. She shook her head to clear the idea of it, just as Jack and Henry brought up an enormous fish.

"It's a red drum!" Jack said, grinning. He held it by its mouth and unhooked it. "Want to hold it for a photo before we throw it back?"

Henry put his hands out and Jack set the giant thing in his arms. Then he pulled out his phone and took a photo. "Okay, throw it back!"

Henry tossed the fish and it disappeared in the surf.

Then, with her mind still on Jack and Gramps, the line Alice was holding yanked and pulled her forward. Before she could respond, Jack's arms were circling her like they had Henry, reeling, his fingers on top of hers, the spicy smell of his neck at her face, making her dizzy.

"It's a good day for fishing," he said into her ear, causing the hair to stand up on the right side of her body. "Look! Your mom just caught a speckled trout!" He let go of her to take the fish off the line. "Want to take a picture with it?" he asked.

"That's okay," she said, not particularly wanting to hold a slimy, wet fish. She'd done it without flinching as a girl, but then she hadn't had on her best DKNY tank top that she'd found on sale and would never encounter at that price again.

"Come on," he said, beaming as he held it out by its mouth, its tail flailing around, flapping back and forth. Jack was obviously ignoring her don't-you-dare look.

He wiggled it nearer to her. She darted backwards, trying not to squeal and make a scene. Gramps would have rolled his eyes at her right now, that grin he got when she was being silly on his face.

"You sure?" Jack poked the thing in her direction again, making her jump and nearly bump into an elderly woman as she made her way to the binoculars. Alice apologized, but the woman didn't seem overly placated.

"I know!" Henry piped up. "You hold it, Jack, and you can stand with Mom, and I can take the picture."

Still holding the fish in one hand, Jack pulled his phone from his back pocket again, hit the passcode with his thumb, and tossed it to Henry. "Great idea!" he said, putting his arm around Alice, startling her.

Then, just as Henry called out, "Say cheese!" Jack put the fish up to her cheek as if it were giving her a kiss, making her yelp.

Henry doubled over in laughter as he viewed the photo on the phone.

"Not funny," she said in mock seriousness.

"Sorry." He screwed his lips up, trying not to smile. Then, after he tossed the fish into the water, he leaned over toward her and said, "In the next photo, I'll kiss your cheek instead."

"Next photo?"

He certainly seemed to think they were going to be together again. First he'd said she could have the next bet and now he was planning to kiss her...

"Henry," he called. "Take one more."

She turned to ask what he was doing just as his lips landed on hers and for an instant, she forgot how to breathe. Before she could get air into her lungs, he'd pulled back and the moment was over. As playful as he'd been, when he looked down at her, he seemed speechless in that moment, as surprised as she'd been.

Jack quickly turned his attention to Henry. "How about I take one of you and your mom now," he said, clearing his throat.

"Okay," Henry said. But then, addressing his mom, he added, "Don't kiss *me* on the lips. Ugh." Still giggling, Henry walked over to his mother and wrapped his arms around her waist. Her head was humming, none of her thoughts coming through clearly in the haze of panic that had overtaken her at the idea of leaving this man.

She put on a smile and Jack took the picture.

Chapter Thirteen

"I came as soon as I saw your text," Melly said with a kindhearted expression. She was wearing her scrubs, but she'd slid on a pair of flip-flops to walk over for coffee this morning. She'd said that she'd just come off the night shift, but she wasn't going to sleep for another few hours, and she'd be happy to have coffee as long as they had decaf.

Alice had already consumed plenty of fully caffeinated coffee, because she'd been up all night thinking about fishing yesterday. She hadn't talked about any of it with Sasha for fear that if she said it out loud it would make the situation real, and she didn't want Sasha to feed her with all the what-ifs and maybes that Alice knew her friend would. If Sasha knew Jack was the boy from her past, Alice would never hear the end of it. Sasha would spend the rest of her life trying to convince her that they were perfect for each other, when, in reality, could anyone really be perfect? She'd lost sleep over that question last night.

And then, to make matters worse, Alice had roped herself into a boat ride over that little game of darts, further filling her brain last night. Jack had promised to pick her up this evening after Henry had gone to bed, and she knew that the idea of being with him on a boat alone would rule her mind all day while she tried to work. That was why she'd asked Melly to come over: the more people to grab her attention, the better. She'd also called Melly because an ice cream wholesale distribution company had delivered samples of their ingredients to try, and she needed an unbiased opinion on her churning skills. She had Henry and Einstein, but they were both easy to please.

Alice and Sasha had spent the morning cleaning and setting up their first machine. They'd settled on a salted caramel flavor with an almond milk base. The first time they'd tried it, they'd put in a little too much air, but after a few attempts, they had it down pat. Once they'd had their coffee and chatted for a bit, Sasha scooped them all a bowl and Henry sifted the sugared caramel chips onto the top.

Melly, who'd looked quite tired when she'd come over, had perked up a little after the coffee. She'd said her shift had been super busy. The hospital was trying out a few staff configurations to see what worked best, and she'd been two people short. She took the first bite of ice cream. Her eyes wide, she said, "Oh my gosh, this is delicious!"

"You think?" Alice couldn't help but get excited, although they were a long way away from being ready and, while they were going to take the time to do it right, they didn't have forever. They needed to start making money. It was a step in the right direction, though.

Henry, who had nearly finished his bowl already, was rolling a tennis ball from the back of the shop to the front while Einstein chased it, sliding into Henry on his paws as he brought it back.

"You look worried," Melly said, reading Alice's thoughts.

"I'm just thinking of all the things we have to do to get ready, and I'm nervous that we're biting off more than we can chew. It's not just about having ice cream. It's about having *the perfect* ice cream, about having what everyone is waiting for, that complete family experience. That's a lot of pressure." She allowed her gaze to roam the wall of ideas. "What will make Seaside Sprinkles the best place on the beach?"

"Maybe we can catch some of the traffic from the pier once we open," Sasha offered. "That can't hurt."

Alice nodded, still pondering what could make the shop amazing. It needed something. It needed what Gramps's bike shop had: that feeling that everyone was family. How had he done it?

"Have you *heard* about the pier?" Melly asked, dragging her spoon along the inside of her bowl and scraping the last of her ice cream.

The ball rolled past them on the floor, Einstein scrambling to get it.

"It's in need of repairs and it isn't turning over a profit like they'd hoped. Shops are pulling out. I've heard they're closing it."

"What?" Alice said, her spoon rattling against the table as her hand thumped down in surprise. All the memories of her and Gramps slid into her mind. Then she thought about the wonderful time she'd just had there with Jack, but also about how empty it had been. "They can't close it."

"Well, I think they are."

"That would be sad," Henry added, taking the ball from Einstein and throwing it again.

Einstein didn't chase it. Instead, he walked over and scratched at the back door.

"Yes," Alice said, "that *would* be sad." Without warning, a new wave of worry washed over her. With a closed pier and nothing else in the area, would the ice cream shop survive? The traffic to her part of the beach would greatly diminish without the pier to bring vacationers down there.

"I'll be back," she said, standing up. "Einstein needs to go out." She was glad to get outside; she wanted to listen to the ocean. She needed answers. If only she could talk to Gramps. She needed *him*. Alice grabbed Einstein's leash, the jingling sound causing him to spring to attention. He bounded over to her and she clipped the leash to his collar. "Back in a sec," she said. Then she walked all the way out to the water's edge.

Gramps. Tell me what to do. I'm scared I've made the wrong decision.

Einstein pulled on his leash, forcing her to take a step toward the water just as a large wave crashed in front of them, the spray shooting up her bare legs and soaking the bottom of her shorts. Another wave slammed down right after it, fizzing and roaring its way toward her.

She stared, waiting for an answer that didn't come.

Please, Gramps, she pleaded silently.

She took stock of the shore, noticing how few people were on the beach. Was that because it was morning and they hadn't gotten out yet, or was the area thinning out? Were people moving further south near the new restaurants and diversions?

Einstein tugged on the leash and she followed blindly, trying to do damage control in her mind, the surf bubbling around her ankles. Not only did the pier bring in tourists but also, unattended, it would be a dilapidated eyesore and no one would make a drive to have ice cream on a beach with an awful view. Would she even be able to sell the shop for what she would've sold it for, if the pier fell into disrepair?

The whole day Alice had worried about the pier, about the fate of the ice cream shop, about the fact that they were living on their savings—all of it rolling around in her mind, restless. They'd made two more flavors today, and they'd confirmed the color scheme for the logo on their paper cups. But the entire time, uncertainty about it all lingered. Alice thought about getting her old job back at the dentist's office. She could probably return with just a phone call. She might need to find another apartment since she'd sublet hers for the remainder of the year until the lease was up, but their things were still mostly in boxes, so, if she had to, moving back would be easy...

She'd fretted so much about everything that she hadn't even been able to allow herself to get excited about the boat ride with Jack. But she'd gotten ready and now it was time to put all that out of her mind for a few hours. She went up to tuck Henry in just before she left. He was already under his covers, the small lamp on in the tiny hallway they'd created with two white folding screens that Gramps had made from old doors.

She sat down on his bed and ran her fingers through his hair.

"You look pretty," Henry said, his voice groggy from exhaustion.

Alice smiled. "Thank you." She'd chosen a powder blue sundress with little matching flats and a pair of her dangly earrings.

"Mama."

He only called her "Mama" when he was serious or worried.

"Yes?"

"I wanna go home. I miss our house."

She took in a breath to steady herself. This wasn't what she wanted to hear after all her thoughts today. "This doesn't feel much like home yet," she said. "We haven't made it our home. You haven't had a chance to make friends, but you will when school starts..."

"I miss Tommy Malone."

Tommy Malone was Henry's best friend at preschool. Henry had been to his birthday party at the roller rink and Tommy's mother had invited them back to her house that day. They had a big, sprawling home on two green acres of land and an oak tree out back with a tire swing. Henry loved it there.

"There isn't anyone like Tommy Malone here. There aren't any kids at all."

"They're here. We just have to find them."

"I miss my old room."

Henry rolled over on his side, away from her, and the two of them sat in silence until his breathing was so deep that Alice knew he'd fallen asleep. She understood how he felt. If she let herself, she missed living near her dad. She missed being able to run across town to see him any time something was bothering her. She missed their cups of coffee… She wondered if he was alone every night, what he was doing. Did her childhood home feel empty without her and Henry popping in? She could pick up the phone and call him, but it wasn't the same. He couldn't reach over and place his hand on hers to comfort her worries; he couldn't look into her eyes and smile like he always did. He was getting older, and so was Henry. Henry had already missed out on so much time with Gramps because of the distance. Would he miss out on time with his Grandpa Frank too? With a deep breath, she got up quietly and left the room, heading out to see Jack, her heart heavy.

She needed a diversion from reality right now.

It was early enough in the summer season that the days didn't stretch too far into the night yet, but even though it was nearing seven in the evening, the sun was still lingering. That was the thing about summers here: the days demanded their presence.

Alice padded down the dock in her baby blue flats to the spot where Jack had told her to meet him. She knew the public boat landing well from the days when Gramps had a boat. He'd always said that the very best days for a captain were the day he bought the vessel and the day he sold it—the darn things needed more care than an infant and were just as temperamental. But when he'd had it, those had been the best times in her memory: when the motor would kick up, the water spraying out like a fan on either side of them, the wind plowing through them, causing her to hang on to the railing even though she was sitting, pushing her little body around the bench's cushion.

Then, when he found the spot where he thought the fish were biting, he'd slow them down to a stop and they'd cast their lines, nothing there with them but the sun, the pelicans, and the cooler full of soda cans and the bologna sandwiches he'd made that morning.

When Alice got to the end of the dock this time, however, the boat waiting for her wasn't quite the little fishing schooner she'd been used to. Instead, there was a small yacht, its lights gleaming on the water's surface, the sleek white exterior cutting through the hues of blue from the sky and the sea. She forced her focus toward Jack, who was waving from the lower deck. He headed over to meet her.

"Is this yours?" she asked, as he greeted her with a big smile.

"No, it's just a lease while I'm here. In Chicago it's a little too cold for me to think about owning a boat. But maybe if I retire somewhere warm, I'll splurge on one."

Just the idea of: one, a person being able to lease something like this beauty; and two, considering buying one a "splurge," was difficult to understand. "What kind of doctor are you?" she heard herself say, before tearing her eyes away from the boat and trying to cool her burning cheeks with sheer will. Had she really just asked that?

He was smiling, happy. "I specialize in pediatric neurosurgery."

"Oh," she said, surprised. He was an actual brain surgeon. For children.

"I'm assisting in the pediatric wing here while I finish my research." He led her onto the boat. "I'm studying neurological disorders in children and what happens physically to the brain during things like epileptic seizures."

She remembered what Melly had told her about him only returning to the Outer Banks to do a favor for one of the doctors. Was this the favor? Did the hospital need more help in its pediatric wing?

"So what made you decide to study that field, in particular?" she asked indulgently. It seemed so specific that she struggled to understand how the idea of it had even occurred to him.

"I like a challenge," he said with a smile. "I didn't really set out to do one thing or another, but as I moved through school, what excited me most wasn't the actual task I was learning but the act of learning itself. I liked the adventure just as much, if not more than, the destination, I suppose." Handing her a glass of sparkling wine, he added, "But enough of the work talk. I do plenty of that during the day, and I'm sure it would bore you to death. Let's enjoy the evening."

"Well, it does explain why you were so precise with the darts," she said with a grin.

He held out that masculine hand of his, showing her every still finger. "Steady as they get."

"You *know* you tricked me with that bet," she said, as he offered her a seat aboard the yacht. She sat down and took a sip of the wine, the crispness of it against the warmth of night taking all her other thoughts away.

"Nah," he said, sitting down beside her.

For a split second, she wondered if they were just going to sit there at the dock, but then she noticed there was a captain at the wheel. He nodded with a smile when she met his eyes.

"If you hadn't agreed to play the darts game, I'd have just asked you outright to take a ride with me."

"You're very sure of yourself." She took another drink of her wine, delicately holding the stem. His commanding smile was making her nervous, but she was proud of herself for keeping the glass steady.

He pursed his lips, seeming to contemplate her observation. "Mm. I'd say I'm sure about my *decisions*."

"And what decisions have you made?"

The boat engine growled, the vessel vibrating just slightly as it started to pull away from the dock.

"The decision to see you again."

She cupped her wine with both hands, as if that would calm her heart. Her fingers might be still, but inside, she was all abuzz. The boat's noise gave her a moment so she wouldn't have to respond, but Jack's eyes were on her, his body turned toward her, his arm stretched out on the back of the bench so that if she scooted near him, he could put it around her.

Her mind raced with his admission that he'd decided to see her again; he'd made a conscious decision to spend more time with her. Why? Was she his next adventure? He'd said himself that it was more about that than the end result. Perhaps he only liked the chase. Would he be stifled after the newness of their whatever-this-was had worn off? The engine was loud against the clatter of all this in her head, her temples starting to feel the pressure of it.

Then everything stopped. The noise gave way to the quiet hiss of the sea as the boat sliced through it, the stars peeking out of the dimming sky, the horizon darkening and the shore glowing pink as the sun finally let go. As Alice sifted through her confusion, she tried not to think about how fate had thrown them together again, how the only person at the grocery store that day to catch those apples had been the boy she'd met all those years ago with Gramps, and how she had just stood at the ocean and asked Gramps what he wanted her to do. She tipped her head back to view the stars, wondering if he could see her somehow, wishing he could help her get a handle on the muddle of thoughts she was having.

Gramps had always told her that the future—good and bad—was directly correlated to her fate, what was destined for her, and she just had to relax into it. She'd never believed him, and she still didn't. But this moment did make her wonder if all his talk about destiny had *some* merit. What if she stopped worrying so much and just let what was ahead of her happen?

"What are you thinking about?" Jack asked. He'd set his wine down and scooted closer to her, interest written on his face.

"Gramps."

Jack looked up too, his chest filling with air and then releasing slowly as he thought about whatever it was on his own mind. Perhaps he was thinking the same thing. Then he met her eyes and smiled, his lips pressing together in the sincerest way. "He really was such a fine man."

"Yes. He was an amazing grandfather."

"I was always alone, and he stepped up when Dad wasn't there. He didn't have to do that, but he did. He bought me lunches and fishing bait. He taught me the right times to fish, and he even stood outside with me in the rain when I'd walked all the way there and didn't want to go back home where boredom would set in. He called my mother and introduced himself, telling her that she was welcome to get a bike from him any time she wanted and he wouldn't charge her. She and I actually took a few rides together on his bikes. I'd never been inside the shop until then. After that, I went all the time."

"That sounds like Gramps."

"Today, kids and their parents would be leery of that kind of hospitality, but it didn't seem odd at all. I always came and went from that pier of my own free will, and he never asked a thing from me. It was like meeting one of my buddies up there. I hardly even noticed his age."

"I know what you mean."

"He was quiet, but when he asked something, it was clear that he really wanted to know. He asked about school, about my friends. I wonder if he was curious as to why I wasn't at the pier with kids my age."

"Why *didn't* you meet any friends there?"

"I liked hanging out with him," he said with a chuckle. "I was always interested in adult topics as a kid. I read non-fiction, I watched the news, I followed foreign events. While my friends were chasing girls at the mall after their parents had dropped them off, I was reading about chemistry. My friends found it funny, and it didn't bother them, but when I wasn't playing football or at the beach, fishing with your grandfather was a way for me to have someone to talk to about the things that interested me. Like having a dad when mine couldn't be there. I'm so glad I met him."

"How did we only cross paths the one time?"

His eyebrows raised in contemplation. "I don't know. I didn't knock on his door whenever I thought he had visitors, because I didn't want to be rude. But now I wonder if some of those times it was you who'd been inside. What would it be like now if we'd have met more than just that one day at the pier?"

As she looked into his eyes, the idea of it made her wonder if perhaps he could've saved her from all the heartbreak she'd suffered over the years. But as Gramps had said, that wasn't her fate. If they'd spent time together too young, Henry might not have come into her life, so it wasn't meant to be… Until now?

"We'll never know," she said.

Jack twisted on the bench and, just like she'd hoped earlier, his arm was further behind her. The boat slowed, dropping anchor in the middle of the darkness, the sky and sea both velvet black, the stars like diamonds. The captain disappeared from view, leaving the two of them alone. Without even a thought, Alice put her head on Jack's shoulder, not realizing her action until his arm was around her, her pulse quickening. Then, before she could calm herself down, she felt the warmth of his breath near her cheek, his lips mere inches from hers, every exhalation of his doing the work for her until she was completely still and relaxed.

There was something so different about this moment than all of the others she'd had before. Despite how much she'd tried to warn herself about him, she'd never been so sure of her feelings, her heart winning out. She'd also never been so aware that there could be no returning to mere strangers, and yet, despite what she'd been through in the past, she knew that it was right. She turned her head infinitesimally, just enough, and Jack read her body language perfectly, his soft lips landing on hers, his hand at her face, his arm drawing her near. His scent, the feel of a day's growth of stubble on his cheek, the perfection in his breath as their mouths moved perfectly together—she'd never had anything like it.

Jack was the first to pull back, his lips still near to hers. "I want to see you every single day," he whispered. Then he kissed her again.

Chapter Fourteen

"Mom!" Henry yanked on Alice's covers, the sun streaming in through the window. "I can't find Einstein."

She swam out of her sleep enough to realize that she was the last to get up, having slept like a baby. She took in a deep breath and stretched.

"I can't find Einstein," Henry said again.

The statement finally registered, and she blinked her eyes into focus. "What time is it?"

Henry leaned across her to view the digital clock they'd set up by the front window. "Eight thirteen."

Alice sat up and ran her hands through her hair. "That's late. Where's Sasha?"

"She took a walk. I took Einstein out, but I brought him back in. And now I can't find him."

"Ohh," she said. "Did you pull the screen door really tight? It doesn't latch."

Henry ran downstairs to check.

She swung her legs over the edge of the bed, the hardwoods already warm under her feet from the heat outside. They'd have to get some rugs for the winter, she was nearly sure. The boards creaked under her as she pulled on a pair of shorts and changed into her T-shirt. When she got downstairs, the door was unlatched and Henry was outside calling Einstein. Knowing she'd have to go out looking for him, she ran back upstairs, threw her hair into a ponytail and quickly brushed her teeth.

"Any luck?" she asked when she got down to the beach. The sky was a glorious shade of blue without a single cloud.

Henry shook his head, worry crumpling his little face.

"It's okay. He has his tags on and we'll find him."

She went barefoot down the beach with Henry, calling the puppy's name, shielding her eyes from the sun with her hand and wishing she'd grabbed her sunglasses. The beach equipment companies were already setting up all the chairs and umbrellas in the sand for the local hotels, and the shore was dotted with people taking their morning walks. But no Einstein.

"You know what?" She stopped and looked back toward the bike shop. "Last time he got out, he went over to Melly's. Why don't we check with her to see if he's there?"

"Okay."

Henry stepped in line beside her and they made their way back up to the bike shop so they could cross over the street to Melly's. But before they could get there, they both stopped. When they approached the shop, Sasha was leaning on the back door; something was wrong with her.

"Sash, you all right?" Alice asked, walking more quickly to reach her.

Sasha was slumped with her arm on the door, leaning on it as if she needed support to stand.

"Sasha?"

Just then, Sasha slid down to the ground. "I don't feel well," she said weakly.

"Oh my gosh, you're sweating terribly." Alice scooped her up under her arms and helped her inside, steadying her as she sat her down in a chair. "How long have you been like this?"

"I've felt bad for about a week, but I figured it was just nerves with everything going on."

"Don't move. I'm going to Melly's. She might be able to help until I can get you to a doctor." Alice grabbed Henry by the hand. "Let's get Melly and we'll look for Einstein too."

They ran across the road, the surface burning her feet, and up the stairs to Melly's door where Alice, feeling the panic of everything, banged her fist on it.

Melly answered. She was wearing scrubs again, this time mint green. "What's wrong?" she asked, coming out onto the porch and shutting the door behind her.

"Sasha looks like she's about to pass out, and I was wondering if you could take a look at her. She seems feverish and she can't stand." As Melly started down the stairs with purpose, Alice took her arm. "And we can't find Einstein. Have you seen him?"

"No," she said, concerned, as they all went down the stairs to the driveway and ran back across to Sasha.

When they entered the bike shop, Sasha had her head down on her arms. She didn't look up. Melly went over to her, pressing two fingers to her wrist. Alice waited, apprehension overwhelming her. "Her pulse is low. Let's get her to the hospital."

Henry followed them out to the front, tears spilling from his eyes. "Einstein!" he called. "Einstein!" His voice withered into a whimper, his cheeks pink.

"I'll bring my car over," Melly said. "I'll take her to the hospital. You go with Henry to find Einstein. I'll text you once we're settled."

"I shouldn't leave her." Alice offered a consoling look to Henry, feeling torn.

"She'd want you to find Einstein for Henry. I've got her."

"I came as soon as I heard," Jack said, walking toward Alice down the hospital hallway.

He was striking in his white coat and pressed trousers, a large and very expensive-looking watch peeking out from his shirtsleeve. He looked distinctively different: his hair was combed perfectly, not even a hint of a whisker on his face. He didn't look like the kind of guy who took kissing-fish pictures, but instead, the kind who lived in high-rise buildings and bought dinners that cost more than those highlights Alice had gotten after Matt had left. The sight of him like this jolted her into some sort of reality check, but he spoke again before she could allow her mind to move to how different their lives were.

"How's Sasha?" he asked.

"She'll be coming home later with a round of antibiotics." Alice didn't know how much Sasha would want her to divulge to Jack, so she left it at that, but the doctors had said that the miscarriage procedure had introduced bacteria that had caused the infection, and she should pay close attention to her body as she recovered. The medicine would help, but if there were any other signs of infection, she needed to come in immediately.

Jack sat down next to Alice, his posture now familiar, and only then did she finally allow herself to exhale. Having him there made her feel like everything would be okay. He put his hand on hers and squeezed. She closed her eyes for a second, feeling exhausted.

"We can't find our dog," she said suddenly, craving his reassuring response. He always made her feel better. She wasn't sure what he could say to this one, and she was glad she could discuss it without Henry.

Melly had taken Henry to get some snacks while they waited for Sasha's discharge. They'd been there all day long and poor Henry hadn't eaten a thing. He'd been too worried about Einstein. But Melly had talked him into a few packages of saltines and a juice box.

"Einstein's been gone since this morning. He got out the back door. It doesn't latch like it's supposed to." Alice swallowed to keep the tears from coming. She was so worried for him. He was just a little puppy. She'd checked her phone every five minutes to make sure someone hadn't called the number on his collar, but there had been no messages.

Jack must have been able to read her emotions because he'd started gently moving his fingers back and forth over hers as if to comfort her. "Why don't I come by after work and we can look for him?"

She nodded, the words not coming. She was so tired.

Henry had cried when they'd arrived home and opened the door to an empty crate and untouched water bowl. Alice had finally gotten him settled, and he'd fallen asleep in his bed. Sasha was resting as well, and Alice found herself sitting on the small front porch step, her toes in the sand, the lull of the ocean behind the house making her eyelids heavy.

She opened her hand to look at the locket she'd found in Gramps's chest. She'd carried it down to the porch, hoping it would give her some sort of magic wisdom or at the very least, take her mind off everything else. She turned it over in her palm. Maybe she'd just wanted to hold Gramps, and having something of his made her feel closer to him.

She'd been thinking a lot about the choice she'd made to come down here. They'd spent a ton of their savings and still had more to buy; Henry wasn't terribly happy here; Sasha was supposed to rest for the next few weeks, and they hadn't even properly unpacked; and the pier was closing, which would leave them in a low-traffic area.

"What do I do, Gramps?" she whispered into the silence, her eyes on the etched gold of the locket.

With no answers, she opened it to view the two baby pictures. Permitting herself a small digression from her thoughts, she took out her phone and snapped a photo of the open locket in her hand. Then she texted it to her aunt, Claire. *Aunt Claire, look what I found*, she typed, and hit send.

In a few seconds, the little bubbles emerged on her screen as her aunt checked the message.

The words floated up to her: *What is it?*

She took a closer picture and texted it, then typed, *It's a locket Gramps had. Of Susie and me.*

Her aunt texted back: *That's not Susie. Not sure who it is.*

How odd. The only other family member her age, or even within the right age range to have a photo so dated yet still in color, was Susie. If it wasn't her, who was it?

Her phone lit up: *Are you sure it isn't a photo of you?*

It definitely wasn't Alice; she could tell. *I don't think it's me*, she typed. *Oh well. Maybe someone will know. I'll hold on to it.*

Okay, honey. Hope you're doing well!

Yep! she lied, just a little. *Tell Uncle George I said hi.*

I will. Give Henry a kiss for me.

Okay. She slipped her phone into her pocket just as the sound of sand under tires tugged on her attention.

Jack pulled up out front and got out of his car. He'd changed into a T-shirt and shorts with a pair of leather flip-flops, and seeing him like that eased her tension just a bit. Perhaps it was because she'd met him under casual circumstances, but she felt that he looked more like himself when he wasn't in his work clothes, though she knew that probably wasn't true.

"Hey," he said, smiling at her. "How's the crew?"

"Ha. They're all sleeping."

He sat down next to her. "Any sign of Einstein?"

She shook her head. "I called the local shelter to see if anyone had turned him in, but they haven't seen him."

"You've had a tough day," he said.

"Yeah."

Since the very moment she'd met him, she'd shared her feelings and he'd listened. She'd never allowed anyone else in on her worries before, but she trusted him with her real emotions, holding nothing back. It was new and a little scary to let someone else in, but Jack made her want to take a chance; he made her feel comfortable about telling him her vulnerabilities. She didn't want to whine on and on, but she felt like she needed to say what she was thinking out loud or she might explode, and Jack was kind and such a good listener. He seemed to know just what to say to ease her mind, and he wasn't as close to the situation as Sasha, who would tell her it would be fine just to keep her from losing it, so it would be easier to believe him when he said it would be okay—he'd be objective.

She *needed* to hear a caring voice to help her see the bright side of things, and she felt like Jack was the only one who could give her that.

"I'm worried about a lot, actually," she said, before looking at him.

He was focused on her face, his head turned just slightly to the side.

"I'm still worried I haven't done the right thing coming here," she said. "I thought it was so right…"

Everything seemed to be against her, even though in her heart she felt like she should do this. Whenever she was at that wall of ideas, Alice could almost sense Gramps's presence. Nothing else did that for her, not even the ocean. Planning things for the shop, she felt like the entire universe was with her, the ideas coming one after another as if a force outside of herself propelled her. But other than that, nothing was the way it should be. Was she forcing things?

"The more I try, the more I feel like this might not work. I've thought about getting my old job back." She chewed on her lip, the idea of it settling uneasily.

He was quiet before finally saying, "I didn't want to bring it up right now, but since you mentioned it, I have a proposition that might make it all easier for you."

She stared at him. "Which is?"

"Sell the bike shop to me."

Alice didn't respond, but a tiny voice in her head was getting louder. It was the voice of reason that had warned her about leading with her emotions. She'd let herself believe that Jack could be there for her, support her. But instead, real life had just slapped her in the face and it took her a moment to regain mental control of the situation, her heart slamming around in her chest.

"I'm willing to give you well over the purchase price. Up to a million."

Heat spread over her like an angry tidal wave. She fumbled for that feeling—the universe feeling—wondering if perhaps this was what was meant for Gramps's bike shop, and she was being unreasonable, but all she could feel was resentment. There was nothing telling her it was the right choice and she knew why.

She'd allowed herself to fall for this man, and she'd let her guard down. But who was he really? That doctor with all the money who wanted the bike shop. And now, when she needed him, when she needed that calming voice that said it would be okay, instead, it felt like he'd used her vulnerability to his advantage, giving her a lucrative offer she would find hard to refuse.

And, as if it had been waiting in front of her face for her to discover, she remembered what he'd said about the thrill of the adventure. Was all of this just a way for him to satisfy his urge to get the next big thing, his newest conquest: her shop? All her fears washed over her once more. Just like the other men in her life, she'd thought he was different and now she was furious for putting herself in this position again. When it came to the big moment when things weren't all roses and she needed someone, he'd failed.

And now everything was becoming clear: he planned on leaving again, so maybe Melly was right and he had abandoned his poor father before. It would make sense, since Butch had practically poured his heart out to Jack and yet he would go right back to Chicago once he got Butch a house. He kept secrets about Melly that he wouldn't trust Alice enough to tell her. He wouldn't tell her *anything* about work, actually. And now, he was trying to take Gramps's shop right out from under her for his own personal gain. And she'd actually let herself have feelings for him…

At least this time she hadn't let it go as far as she had with Matt. But what was eating at her was that, little by little, she was losing hope in the idea of her life moving forward. What was money when she and Henry didn't have anyone to share it with? Her dreams of a big family and a loving husband had now slipped completely away in this one moment, because Jack—who had been her gauge for all her relationships since she was a girl—had taken her hope away, just like the others.

"I don't know what to say." She swallowed the lump in her throat.

If she sold the shop to Jack, Butch would have a beautiful home that he deserved. He'd be able to carve wood sculptures, possibly even sell them… The shop would be in a great location for something so specialized, she thought, because while vacationers might not go that far down the beach to get ice cream when the pier wasn't in business, customers searching for a one-of-a-kind souvenir might make the short drive, with only a few print ads required to spread the word.

But what about her? She'd have to try to explain her failures to her son. What kind of example was that: dragging him all the way down to North Carolina, pulling him away from his friends… For what? So she could tell him she'd changed her mind?

Jack was clearly waiting for her to say *something*.

She didn't like the position Jack was putting her in. He had money on his side, he had Butch to pull on her emotions—and he knew it. Didn't he care at all about the fact that she'd uprooted her whole life to do this? Was a piece of land more important than what they'd started? Clearly it was. Truly, it wasn't his fault she felt this way—he didn't owe her anything. But she knew what she wanted for herself and she wasn't going to settle again. She didn't want someone who put his needs above hers anymore; she wanted a person who would share every single decision with her.

She stood up, her head pounding with anger and frustration. "I *do* know what to say: no, thank you." That was all she could get out, for fear tears would spill down her cheeks. She opened the door. "I'm tired. And I don't want to talk about this anymore."

"Wait," he said, moving toward her.

She ignored him.

"Alice!"

She looked back at him, his eyes searching hers frantically, his face so distraught that she almost faltered. But she knew the truth of the situation and she had to be strong. She shut the door before allowing her emotions to well up. He'd let her down tonight in the biggest way. But that was just the dose of reality she needed to move forward. She decided right then that she wasn't going to talk to Jack Murphy again. He could find someone else to flaunt his money in front of.

Chapter Fifteen

Alice awoke the next morning with a new sense of purpose. She'd make this shop a success all by herself. She'd show her son what hard work could produce. She'd do whatever it took. She'd keep hustling until everyone in the Outer Banks knew the name Seaside Sprinkles.

She'd been at the paint store right when it opened and purchased five gallons of paint in "Perfect Pink," "Luscious Lime," and "Daybreak Blue," a bag of sponge rollers, five paint brushes, painters' tape, and some mixing buckets and pans. Then she bought a box of Sasha's favorite chocolate truffles and made sure her room was comfortable, unpacking an extra blanket to go under her—the super fuzzy, soft kind—and opening the window to let the breeze in.

After she checked on Sasha, with Henry's help, she started painting. She and Sasha had talked about ideas for how Alice might want to paint the shop, but they hadn't finalized anything and Sasha wasn't in any shape to think it through with her, so Alice decided for herself.

Alice had studied the light coming in through the windows, remembering how it hit at different angles throughout the day, and she'd chosen paint based on how it would look under the changing brightness. She'd pay attention to the logo they'd created and its position on the wall once the surfaces were painted. Bright pink stripes covered the old brown paneled walls of the bike shop as she dragged the roller up and down. With every swipe, she felt that zinging energy return.

"Is this good, Mom?" Henry asked, his face streaked with baby blue paint. She'd given him the job of painting the wall that would eventually be behind the new counter they'd ordered.

"It looks great!" she said with a grin, walking over to him. She wished she had an extra pair of hands, but knew that she could carry the full weight of the task if she had to, as long as it helped Sasha to get better. Her friend needed the rest. "But it looks like you missed a spot."

"Where?" The roller dripped blue paint onto his bare foot.

"Right there," she said, brushing pink onto his nose.

His mouth dropped open, and he lunged forward, the roller precariously close to her hair. Alice squealed and ducked out of the way, her brush spraying paint on the clear plastic covering she'd laid down to protect the wood floor. They both looked at the little pink dots against the dark wood underneath, where the paint had gotten through. It actually looked awesome and she imagined the whole floor full of pastel paint drops.

Alice grinned. "Oh, you're in trouble now." She tried to grab him with her free hand, but he dodged her, the plastic crinkling under his feet as he ran to the back of the store. She chased after him, diving and catching his ankle with her paintbrush.

Henry collapsed, giggling uncontrollably.

She was glad to see him smile. He hadn't since they'd lost Einstein.

Alice's phone had buzzed a few times this morning, flashing Jack's number. She'd ignored his calls. Her focus was going to be on Henry, Sasha, and getting Seaside Sprinkles ready for business. She'd been up most the night, and she'd thought of an idea: what if she could raise funds to keep the pier? She'd planned to look into what it would take today.

"What are you two crazies doing?" Sasha said, coming in from the stairway in the long T-shirt she liked to sleep in, which Alice remembered her mother bringing back for her from her trip to the Bahamas. It was bright blue with a wave on the front.

"Painting," Alice said with wink. "How are you feeling?"

"Better, but weak. I think the antibiotic is already helping, if that's possible."

"We still haven't found Einstein," Henry said, his distress obviously not far away, even with the diversion of painting.

They'd told Sasha about losing Einstein when they'd gotten home yesterday, but Alice had assured her not to worry, that they'd find him, because she knew Sasha needed to focus on getting healthy again. Henry went over to the window in the front door, paint in his blond hair, and looked out at the food and water bowls he'd left on the porch in case the puppy came back. They were untouched.

Sasha walked around the table and stood next to him, her steps labored. "I'm sorry," she said, giving his shoulders a squeeze.

Alice didn't want to think about that defenseless little puppy out in the world all by himself. She worried so much about him. Where had he gone? She prayed that if they couldn't find him, at least maybe another family had, and that they'd taken him in and would give him the love and care that he needed. Alice knew Henry was beside himself with worry for his puppy. Einstein had been his security after Matt left—his source of complete goodness, of loyalty—and now the puppy could be in danger and, even though Henry was young, Alice could see in his eyes that he knew that, and it was killing her. She wanted so badly to do something but she just didn't know what.

Sasha turned around, her chest rising with her breath as she surveyed the new paint. "I wish I could help you two get this room ready," she said, shaking her head.

"It'll be fine!" Alice said, feeling completely confident. She couldn't find Einstein, but this, she could do. "We're one man down, but we're still going! Henry and I will have the painting done in no time!"

There was a knock at the door and Alice's heart filled with excitement, thinking it could be someone who'd found the stray dog and was dropping him home. Henry opened it to see Melly outside on the porch. She was holding a bouquet of wildflowers: lavender, rosemary, baby's breath, and gaillardias, and a stack of photos.

"Hi," she said, walking in and greeting everyone. "These are for you." She handed the flowers to Sasha. "And I thought I'd bring by the photos I took of the shop. I'm so happy with how they turned out."

Melly held up one she'd taken of the sun streaming in on the old hardwoods and it was beautifully simple; the marks in the floor radiating with the sense of all the people who'd walked those boards, the bikes that had rolled across them, and even the history that had come before; the beam of light like an angelic ray of happiness. Another photo had been taken through the window, the frame dark with shadows, the center the most vibrant blue showing the sea and sky, with a strip of white sand between them. Melly placed them back down on the stack of the others and handed them to Alice.

"They're just gorgeous, Melly," Alice said, in awe of her friend's talent. "I can't wait to frame them and put them up in the shop!" She flipped through the photos, stopping on a perfectly posed portrait of Einstein, the pine trees behind him a vibrant green, his black fur like satin against the brightness of it. His dark eyes bored into her as if he were telling her that he missed her. Swallowing the lump in her throat, she quickly covered it up before Henry could view it, placing the photos on the shelf above the workspace they'd been using for the paint samples.

"These are gorgeous, too, Melly! Thank you." Sasha gave Melly a hug and then pulled a Mason jar from a cupboard and filled it with water at the small sink for the bouquet, the scent of the flowers wafting into the air and making the whole room smell like summer.

"How are you feeling?" Melly stepped over a large piece of plastic to join Sasha.

She arranged the flowers and set them on the counter. "I'm doing okay. Just need to get my strength back."

"I understand. Well, if you need me, I'm here."

"Do you paint?" Sasha teased, grinning at Henry.

"I can paint!" Melly said. "I'm unexpectedly off today." When she said this, Melly's voice wobbled just enough that Alice noticed, but she wouldn't make eye contact. With Sasha in her current state, Alice didn't need to get drawn into anything else, so she let it go.

"Need some help?" Melly asked.

Alice wiped her hands on her paint-splattered shirt. "If you're offering, I'd love to have a little help. That would be amazing." Maybe painting could ease whatever it was that Melly was upset about.

"Of course! Let me run back home and get changed into some old clothes."

"Oh my gosh, you're awesome!" Alice said. "I'd hug you, but I don't want to get paint all over you."

Sasha offered, "I'll be in charge of pizza orders, music, and wine!"

"Wine?" Melly said, raising an eyebrow. "Is that on your doctor's list of acceptable beverages?" Her voice was teasing, but Melly's concern was evident by the look in her eyes.

"Okay, wine for you all, and Vitamin Water for me."

"Excellent." Melly gave her an empathetic smile.

The three women sat in their chairs on the small patio out back while Henry played in the ocean. Alice and Melly, both still covered in paint speckles, had finished painting the entire room, carefully backing out of the rear door as they lightly spattered the floor in pink, blue, and green paint. Unable to walk back in until it dried, Sasha had ordered a pizza and Alice and Melly had taken turns diving into the waves with Henry, but now they'd settled in the sun with the food. Melly hadn't mentioned a thing about the reason for her sudden day off, and Alice was beginning to think she'd imagined her new friend's flicker of emotion earlier.

Unable to hold in her own feelings any longer—she'd managed all day—Alice told the girls about Jack's offer. She'd replayed their conversation over and over in her head all of last night, and no matter how she tried to spin it, the truth was that he'd been looking out for Butch; and while that was honorable, he'd still taken advantage of the situation without any regard to Alice.

"I don't think he meant to be awful," Melly said. "I've spent some time with him at the hospital and I don't know if those rumors I'd heard about him are true. He seems like a very kind man. Perhaps he was just trying to give you options."

"Well, his delivery needs some work," Alice said, pursing her lips and shaking her head. The whole situation made her uncomfortable. She felt guilty about Butch, worried that she was going to run herself into the ground with this place, and angry that Jack hadn't said what she'd wanted him to say, which was that he believed in her and she could do it. Maybe her expectations were too high, but shouldn't they be?

Melly smiled. "You'll find where you fit," she said. "With Jack or without him, ice cream or no ice cream, you'll figure it out. That's what I tell myself too." She took in a jagged breath and looked out over the ocean. That, right there, was the emotion Alice had seen earlier. She hadn't imagined it after all. She waited, honing in on Melly, wondering if she would share what was bothering her. But Melly kept quiet. When Melly didn't respond to Alice's glances, she looked out at her son.

Henry was on his boogie board, riding the surf that took him all the way up to the dry sand. He waved at them and they all waved back. Alice assessed Sasha, trying to decide if she was strong enough to support Melly if something was wrong. Alice could see in Melly's eyes that she wanted to say something, but she wasn't giving anything up, when, in truth, she should feel like she could tell them. They should all hold each other up in times of crisis. One thing Alice knew was that Sasha was emotionally resilient, and even if she was physically exhausted, she'd probably still be amazing if she needed to offer encouragement to Melly or help her through something. So Alice decided to ask.

"Melly, is something bothering you? You look like you've got the weight of the world on your shoulders right now."

Only then did Sasha seem to notice Melly's demeanor. She scooted her chair closer. "What is it?"

Tears sprung to Melly's eyes and when she tried to blink them away, they spilled down her cheeks. She wiped them with her hand. She seemed unsure about divulging whatever it was, but Alice urged her on with a look that let her know they were there for her. "I heard they're going to let me go at the hospital," Melly said quietly, as if it were still a shock to her.

"What?" Alice said, disbelief causing her voice to almost squeak as she said the word. "They just hired you!"

Melly nodded in agreement, dragging her fingers under her eyes as the tears spilled over. "I didn't want to bring it up. You two have too much you're dealing with right now. You don't need my issues making it worse." She shook her head, a bewildered look on her face. "I came highly recommended. I had reference letters from the top surgeons in my field. I don't understand it at all." She spoke as if she were talking it out with herself, her focus inward as she worked to arrive at some conclusion that wouldn't come.

"Who told you this? How do you know?"

"One of the nurses has a friend in HR. She let it slip last night while they were out for drinks. She said it came down to funding. There just isn't enough money to keep us all—that was why it had been a temporary position. I think the hiring manager assumed they'd get the funding. It's probably a surprise to him as well. The hospital partners thought if they could stretch their dollar, hire top-notch staff, bring in high-level research... They were trying to elicit donations from a few large private sources, but they backed out and the community just doesn't have enough revenue to support us."

That was the favor Jack was doing. He'd been asked to do research for them to get their name out there. And he knew something about Melly, but he wouldn't say. It was all making sense now.

"I can't go back home," Melly said, before putting her face in her hands. "And that's the only option I have. I'd have to sell the cottage and get my old job back... I can't face my ex-husband."

"Lots of people live in the same town as their exes. It wouldn't be so bad, would it?" Sasha offered.

Melly bit her lip in thought, her features overwhelmed with fear. Clearly, there was more to this than she'd shared, and Alice wondered what it could be.

"You can tell us," she said, in an effort to support her friend.

Melly swallowed, taking in a few breaths before meeting Alice's eyes and then Sasha's. "We tried to have children, and we just couldn't—nothing worked. It put a strain on our relationship. I went to the doctor and we found out it was me. I can't have them. So every day after that, things got worse. We tried to make a go of it, but I could see the disappointment in his eyes whenever he looked at me, and it made me feel broken. I couldn't take it anymore, so I left. I feel whole here. If I go back, that brokenness will overtake me."

Sasha was visibly stricken by Melly's confession, and Alice knew it was because of her own recent loss. Alice worried about Sasha, hoping she was well enough right now to handle this conversation, but she seemed to be finding the strength for Melly.

"There are other ways to have a family," Sasha said, patiently trying to help talk her through it. "Would you two have ever considered adoption?"

Melly's mouth turned down, her pain obvious. "I suggested that, but he wasn't interested. That was when I knew what we had wasn't really as strong as I thought. We just started to exist in the house—two people with different expectations in life. I wanted a family just like he did, but when he wouldn't contemplate adoption, I felt his disappointment and his blame; I had to get out."

Sasha's phone lit up on the little table beside their beach chairs, pulling them all from the moment. She swiped the screen. "It's a text from Jack." She held the phone up for Alice to see. "He said he's been trying to call you, but you won't answer. Maybe we could ask him about Melly's job."

"No." They needed to be there for Melly. And Alice did not want Jack in on this conversation—it was for the three of them to discuss. He might not sympathize with her since he was one of the senior doctors. "I don't want to talk to him. I have nothing to say."

"He knows I've opened the text. How should I respond?"

"Just tell him that, I guess."

"Don't mention me," Melly said. "I don't want to get anyone in trouble for letting the news slip before it should've come out."

Sasha tapped on her phone. Then she set it down on the arm of her chair. "I told him you aren't interested in his offer to buy the property and you'd like to focus on getting the shop ready." Then the little bubbles appeared on her screen and she picked it up again. "He's typing back," she narrated. "He says he has something of yours. He'd like to return it."

"What could he possibly have of mine? Tell him whatever it is, he can keep it."

"What if it's Einstein?" Sasha said, as she tapped some more on her phone. "I'm asking him." She waited for his response and then read it. "He said it isn't Einstein, and he'll meet you on the pier at seven when he gets off work."

"Tell him I'm busy. He can leave it on the front porch."

Sasha typed the message and then turned her phone off. "Enough of that," she said. "We need to get back to Melly." Sasha leaned toward their friend with a smile. "I say we do something with just us girls and Henry tonight to take your mind off everything for a while, something low key that I can be a part of."

Melly sniffled, a smile emerging. "You could come over to my place," she said. "We could have a movie night."

"That sounds amazing," Alice said with a smile.

She'd be glad to focus on having a little fun.

* *

Empty bowls holding remnants of popcorn were scattered on the coffee table amidst a half-full box of Junior Mints, a bottle of wine, and Henry's cup of milk. Alice, Sasha, and Melly were sprawled across the sofa. They'd watched a movie for Henry, but he'd fallen asleep halfway through, so they'd put him on Melly's bed and then they'd watched *Roman Holiday*, an old Audrey Hepburn movie, under a light blanket. The heat creeping in from outside and the wine had warmed them pretty well, but it was still fun to get cuddled up like Alice and Sasha had done as girls. Melly was the perfect addition to their friendship and it had been a great night.

Alice kept drawing parallels to the movie, wishing her life could be all happy endings and last-scene kisses. Jack had come out of nowhere and completely knocked her sideways—she couldn't get him off her mind.

"I'm so glad we met you. What brought you to the Outer Banks, specifically?" Sasha asked Melly. Alice turned her attention to them.

Melly sat up and started tidying the table, stacking the bowls. "The nursing job."

Sasha was leaning back against the pillows, her eyes heavy. "How did you hear about the opening at the hospital?"

"I just looked it up online," she said quickly, but that same expression she had when she'd discussed her ex-husband came rushing back onto her face.

Alice wondered if there was more to their story than Melly was telling them. Had he hurt her beyond what she'd divulged? As good a friend and neighbor as Melly had become, Alice would let Melly tell the rest of her story in her own time; if there was any more to tell. Sasha seemed to have caught on to her unease as well, and she didn't ask her anything else.

When the dishes were cleared and the room put back together, all the pillows in place, the blankets refolded, Alice scooped Henry off the bed and she and Sasha walked back across the road. The floors were most likely dry enough now to walk barefoot across them carefully, just long enough to get upstairs, where they could sleep and allow another eight hours of drying time. Alice couldn't help but look down both sides of the street for Einstein, hoping that she'd see him. She wanted to call his name, but she knew it would only wake up Henry, and then he'd be worried the rest of the night.

As they got closer to the shop, Alice noticed a figure sitting on her porch. She squinted to see if she could make out who it was, but she didn't recognize him until they'd made it into the lot. It was Butch.

He stood up as they approached.

"Hello, Alice," he said quietly, and then nodded to Sasha. "I was wondering if I could have a word with you."

She whispered, "Let me get Henry into bed. Would you like to come in?"

"Oh, thank you but no, dear. The fresh air will do me good. I'll wait out here." Then he took a seat on the step again.

"Who is that?" Sasha said on their way up the narrow staircase, once they'd gotten inside.

When they reached the top, Alice carefully laid Henry on his bed and covered him with his blankets. "It's Butch," she whispered. "Jack's father."

"Oh. Wonder what he wants."

"I don't know, but I'll find out and come back up to tell you."

"Okay. I'm here if you need me. I think I'm going to lie down but wake me up if you need help with anything." She yawned.

Alice went back downstairs, past the bouquet of wildflowers Melly had brought, and opened the door, joining Butch on the step.

He faced her. "Jack said that you don't want to see him, but he needed to give you this." He held out his fist and dropped the locket that she'd found in Gramps's trunk into her hand. "He says it's your grandmother's locket."

Alice looked up, surprised. "How did he get this? And how did he know it was my grandma's?" *She* didn't even know that; she'd only guessed.

"I'm not sure. You'll have to ask him." His eyes stayed on her, thoughts behind them. Then, as if he'd decided something, he said, "He's a wreck, Alice."

"What?" She rubbed the locket with her thumb.

"He didn't ask me to tell you this, but I can't help but intervene. I don't get to meet the women that he dates. And he doesn't stop his hectic life to date very often. He's usually too busy saving the world. But he is so worried about you that he can't even sit still. I have no idea what happened between you two, but you need to talk to him. I've never seen him like this, Alice."

That fear crept in: the panic that, by meeting him, she might get hurt again. Why hadn't he come himself tonight? Why had he sent Butch instead? If he really wanted things to work out, wouldn't he have been there? But she remembered she'd told Sasha to say she didn't want to talk. And there was his offer to buy the shop that she was struggling to reconcile in her mind. "I don't know…" she answered. It was too complicated already, too hard.

"You lost your dog, right?" Butch said, staring out toward the road, his lips pressed together and visible through his beard. Without waiting for an answer, he continued, "Jack has been out looking for it every couple of hours since you told him it was missing. He even checked the bypass." Finally meeting her eye, he said, "Meet him, Alice. You need to talk to him. Let him get whatever it is off his chest before the poor guy bursts."

Her resolve crumbling, she finally agreed. Butch stood up and gave her a hug. "I hope you two work it out," he said, sincerity in his face.

But she knew they wouldn't. She wouldn't allow it. It was too much, too soon after Matt, and she just didn't want to go down that road for a second time. This had been a close call, but she'd stopped things before they'd gotten messy. She'd fallen hard and fast, and she wouldn't let that happen again. The truth was that while she did want a big family and a loving husband, this wasn't one of those movies, and things didn't always work out like that. She'd rather have a small family with wonderful memories than a big one that was a disaster.

Chapter Sixteen

"Guess what I found," Alice's dad had said to her on the phone this morning. "An old ball cap of Henry's. It was behind the bookcase."

"How in the world did you find it there?" Alice asked, so glad to hear her father's voice. She hadn't wanted to think about how much she missed him, or she wouldn't have the energy to finish Seaside Sprinkles. She'd have wanted to run back to her childhood home instead, settle in with a box of donuts, and have coffee at the table all morning, talking to him.

"I cleaned out all the old books that I'd read and donated them to charity to make room for new ones." He cleared his throat and then added, "I've resorted to parting with books because I'm running out of things to keep me busy. The house is too quiet without you and Henry, and if I stand still, the silence bothers me."

Alice felt the lump forming in her throat, and she didn't speak for fear that she'd blubber into the phone. She remembered that same quiet after her mother had died; it was a unique kind of silence, an emptiness, the absence of something settling in the air. She didn't want to even consider that she and Henry had left her father with that silence again.

"I was thinking I could stop by…" he said happily, the way he did when he had a surprise for her. He used to leave little treats on her bed, and he'd always say, "I've got a little something for you…" His tone was the same now as it had been then.

"What?" she managed, the thrill of seeing him causing her to smile through the tears that had found their way to her eyes. She blinked them away. This new development changed her mood in a flash.

"I've been visiting a friend in the Tidewater area. Remember Ricky Gleason? He and his wife invited me to stay for a few days after I told them about your move. They thought I might like to have the company. I figured it's only two extra hours to the Outer Banks. I could come by and surprise Henry."

"He would love that!" She was almost giggling. "I would too. I miss you."

"I miss you too. I can't wait to see you."

It was as if a weight she didn't even know she'd had was lifted off her chest, her shoulders feeling lighter, her worries drifting away. Just knowing she'd get to see her dad made it feel like nothing else mattered.

"Would it be okay if I took him back home for a few days? It would be nice to have him around the house."

Alice was delighted. While she hated to be away from Henry, she liked the idea of him being able to see his friends again and spending some time with his Grandpa Frank, and it would give her a few extra hours to really put some work into Seaside Sprinkles.

"Of course!" she'd said.

Later that morning, her father had picked up Henry. He'd only stayed a short time, Henry hurrying him along, nearly bursting at the idea of going back home. Henry had been chatting a mile a minute about the places he wanted his grandpa to take him and the friends he wanted to see. Her father had promised that he'd spend more time catching up on their return, but right then he wanted to get Henry back as soon as possible so he didn't waste a minute with his grandson.

So Alice found herself in an empty shop for the first time since they'd gotten there. While Sasha napped upstairs, recovering from the infection that was still making her tired at times, Alice had called the county office and spoken to the supervisor in charge of historical properties about the pier. Mr. Blankenship had told her that it required quite a bit of renovation—most of it needed to be replaced—but the problem was that the small retailers on the pier weren't bringing in the revenue needed, and two of them had even decided to pull out completely once their contracts were up. Mr. Blankenship had said that even if the funds were raised to rebuild it, the pier needed something big to move in, something like a restaurant or major retail chain, and, in that area, he just didn't expect it to happen.

With her hands on her forehead, Alice stared at the table, her mind reeling. Jack had put her in the very worst position. She was chasing a dream that might not come to fruition, even with all her efforts, and she might fail. But even if she could deal with failure, she might not be able to manage emotionally, given the fact that she could've avoided it all by taking the money, which might have been the most sensible option for herself and her son. She looked up at the wall of ideas and wondered if this place would be better as a home for Butch than a business, her head starting to throb.

The clock clicked over to four forty-five. She needed to leave to meet Jack. He'd texted and she'd agreed to see him, to keep her promise to Butch. She got up straight from her work, grabbed the house keys and dropped them into her handbag. This meeting was going to be a very quick one. She planned to tell him that she was thankful for all he'd done for her, but she really needed to be on her own right now. She wasn't even going to go into her reasoning or the fact that she was still upset that he'd made her that offer on the shop. This was closure—nothing more.

Alice kept repeating that in her head as she walked down the beach toward him. He'd told her he'd find her halfway. When he neared her, she could see he was carrying a rolled-up beach mat. Unease settled in her shoulders when she saw it. She didn't have the strength to spend any more than a few minutes with him. She didn't want to give him time to put on that charm of his and make her reconsider her decision to end this.

"Hi," Jack said, with the mat still under his arm. He was cautious in his approach.

He looked tired and that smile she loved to see wasn't there. He was searching her face as if he were trying to find answers to his questions. He turned toward the ocean, breathing it in, not saying anything as a seagull flew over them. Then he unrolled the mat on the sand, motioning for her to sit down. After seeing his face, she didn't have the heart to deny his offer, so she lowered herself onto the mat.

That endless ocean stretched out in front of her, still giving her no answers.

"I didn't mean to offend you with my offer," Jack said, as he sat down beside her, getting right to it. "I'd never intentionally do anything to hurt you. I'm so sorry." He went to take her hand, but she moved and he drew back. If he touched her she might lose her resolve. Even if they could get past this, it just wasn't the right time with him leaving and her wrapped up in opening the shop, and, at the end of the day, she didn't know if he could be what she wanted him to be.

Alice didn't say anything, all the emotions running together in her head.

"Did you get the locket?"

"Yes. Butch brought it by." Glad for the diversion from the topic at hand, she added, "He said you told him it was my grandma's. How did you know that it was hers?"

Jack leaned back on his hands, his legs stretched out in front of him and crossed at the ankle, a small line still present between his eyes, that seriousness on his face. "Your grandfather showed it to me once."

"What?" she asked, disbelieving, twisting toward him. Why had Gramps shown Jack something that she'd never seen?

"He had it on his counter in that little dish with the roses on it."

"My grandma's dish—yeah, I know it. It was in there?"

"Yep. He showed me the photos of his grandkids." Jack smiled. "You and Grace."

"Who?" What in the world was he talking about? She didn't know anyone in her family named Grace. Who was that? "You mean Susie?"

Jack squinted, trying to remember. "No," he said, shaking his head as if he were reassuring himself, "It was Grace. He said, 'This is Alice and that's Grace. They're my grandkids.'"

None of this made any sense, and she thought he must have it all wrong. "My cousin Susie and I are his only grandchildren."

Jack frowned, obviously confused. "That's weird. He talked to me about someone named Grace. About her as a baby. How pretty she was."

She'd known Susie her entire life and she'd never been called Grace. Susie's name was Susan Elizabeth McMichael. And why had it just been the two of them in that locket? Why wasn't it Susie and this Grace person? Alice considered calling her dad right then, although he was probably busy with Henry, and she didn't want to disturb him. And she'd rather ask him in person. But she needed answers. She'd never heard anything about anyone called Grace in all her life. It definitely wasn't anyone in her immediate family or she would've known about her. Right? And certainly, she'd know if she had another cousin. There had to be some mistake…

"Did he tell you anything else about her?"

"Not much. That was really it. It had been more of a comment than a conversation, but I could see the love in his eyes when he showed me the photos."

Gramps had kept this locket the whole time and there might have been an entire story—someone else's life story—behind it, and she'd never had even an inkling about it. Her mind went to that old trunk full of things back at the bike shop and suddenly, she wanted to sprint down the beach and sift through every last thing to find answers.

"Would you come back to the shop with me?" she asked, getting to her feet. It was apparent that Gramps had said things to Jack that he hadn't told her; she needed him there in case she found something in the trunk that she didn't understand.

"Of course," he said, standing up and folding the mat.

"Would you help me carry this downstairs?" she whispered to Jack, so as not to wake Sasha. The trunk was more awkward than heavy, and the two of them could easily get it down. She'd have him carefully help her set it on one of the sheets that she'd laid down to protect the new paint on the floor.

Jack got on one end and lifted, backing down the steps as she took hold of the other side. As quietly as possible, they shimmied it down the narrow staircase until they came to rest at the bottom, lowering it down on the sheet and scooting it gently into the middle of the room.

"What are we doing with this?" he asked, coming over to her side and standing so close to her that she could feel his warmth.

Her tummy did a flip-flop when she caught his scent, her memory going back to those arms around her, his lips on hers, and there was a part of her that wanted him to hold her again and tell her it would all be okay.

"It's full of Gramps's things. There might be something about Grace in here." The name "Grace" felt odd on her tongue; it was a stranger's name. She couldn't get the niggling feeling out of her mind that she was a little angry that Gramps had told Jack about Grace and not her. Why had he felt more comfortable talking about a possible family member with Jack? Or had he deliberately kept it from her? If so, why?

Alice opened the lid and pulled out the stack of magazines and papers, folders and documents, and set them on the floor. Jack took the top magazine off the pile and flipped through it, stopping at a fishing article. His curiosity seemed so genuine that it had distracted him briefly, which made Alice smile and shake her head, Jack's interests reminding her of Gramps. She much preferred Jack's casual side to the one she'd seen in the white coat. In a perfect world, he'd spend all of his days there in the Outer Banks, instead of in a cold, stark hospital.

"You're supposed to be helping," she teased, the now familiar ease of being with him settling between them again. She couldn't deny it. It wasn't something she could control, it just *was*, like air or light or… love.

"Right. Sorry." Jack took another small piece of paper from the trunk, looked it over, and then marked his place in the magazine, setting it aside as if he'd return to it one day. Alice stared at it for a moment, trying to squash the silent wish that he would. Why was he getting to her like this? She'd never had such a hard time being rational before. She always stuck to her decisions with 100 percent accuracy. But she found herself constantly changing direction when it came to him. She couldn't stand her ground. Jack reached over and took another few magazines, flipping through them and making a new stack.

They continued looking through everything, and Alice was just starting to think they weren't going to find anything when she noticed a folded piece of paper hidden under the last file folder. She opened it up and with every word she read, her skin felt prickly with apprehension.

"What did you find?" Jack asked, concerned.

"Something from Gramps…" She let her eyes run over Grace's name.

"Read it," Jack urged her.

She smoothed the paper on her leg and began, her hands shaking, the implications of what was about to come out of her mouth making her stomach hurt.

To my dearest family,

For Susie, I've set aside a trust fund, knowing how much she adores the west coast and would never leave it. And I already know what Alice should have, but I've always wanted to give something to Grace as well, because, over the years, I've missed out on showing her how I feel about her. And I love her. I love her just as much as I love Alice and Susie. She, too, is my granddaughter. After Annie's death, I have been painfully aware of the limited days that I have, and I can't help but think how I'd like to leave the shop and my remaining assets to both Grace and Alice—they can split my belongings down the middle. Please send them all my love.

Paul Emerson

"Who's Annie?" Jack asked.

"My grandma." Alice looked back down at the letter. "I only own half the bike shop? Gramps signed his name, Paul Emerson, which makes it official. That can't be right," she whispered. Alice turned the paper over in her hand. "Does this have any bearing on my inheritance?"

"It's sort of a written will, but you have a signed, dated will that most likely was written after this, so I wouldn't think it has any bearing at all." He leaned over to look at it.

"You're right," she said, more to reassure herself. "He wrote the will right before he passed away."

"Then I think you're fine. The bike shop is yours."

But the pinch in her chest didn't go away. She had a family member out there that she'd never known about. Why? Who was she? Had Gramps had an affair? Did she have other aunts or uncles out there with children? Or was Grace some hidden secret of her Aunt Claire's or even her father? Had her father strayed from her mother? Never. That would be impossible. Any answer to those questions would be unthinkable. Her hands felt cold and clammy all of a sudden and she wiped them on her shorts. "Did Gramps tell you anything more about Grace?"

"Like I said, not much. I do remember now that he said he hadn't seen her in a long time. Sorry, I didn't commit his exact words to memory because at the time it hadn't meant anything to me. But he'd only mentioned her that one time anyway, so I don't think I'd have a lot to tell you even if I had remembered it perfectly."

"I need to call my dad." It didn't matter that Jack was there with her. She stood up and pulled her phone from her pocket, then dialed her father's number, her back to Jack. Through the years, her dad had shared everything with her. He'd always been completely honest. Did he know about Grace? She only had one aunt, and that was Aunt Claire, who seemed to know nothing about the person in the photo. If it was Gramps's grandchild, then the baby would have to belong to either Claire or Alice's father, unless Gramps had fathered other children and Alice had an aunt or uncle with a child she knew nothing about. None of it seemed feasible at all.

The phone continued to pulse in her ear with no answer. She ended the call. When she turned around, Jack was facing the Seaside Sprinkles idea wall. "No luck?" he said, without taking his eyes off the board.

"He's probably with Henry." She walked over and stood next to him, all the pieces of paper with her handwriting and Sasha's almost taunting her, playing on her insecurities. She pinched the bridge of her nose to alleviate the ache that was forming. "I'm glad my dad's busy. Henry's been a mess since we lost Einstein, and I've pulled him away from everyone he knows except Sasha and me. I hope he's having the time of his life."

Jack smiled sadly at her. "I've been looking for Einstein."

"I know. Butch told me."

"He asked if I'd bring you over again. I think you really brightened his day when we stopped by last time." Jack met her gaze. "I'd like to."

The truth was, she enjoyed Butch's company. He was such a friendly person that he made her feel like she belonged here, like it was home. But spending time with Butch would just make her feel worse about her choice to keep the shop and would confuse her feelings about Jack even more. And she didn't know if she could cope with Jack leaving if she continued to spend time with him.

"I don't know," she said, honestly.

"He makes a cherry cobbler that's out of this world."

That made her smile. "Are you trying to bribe me with desserts?"

The corner of Jack's mouth turned up in an adorable way. "If that's what it takes." Then seriousness took over his features. "Come tomorrow," he said. "Then, maybe over pie, you'll tell me why things have changed between us."

Chapter Seventeen

When Alice arrived at Butch's the next day, she noticed three rocking chairs on his small front porch and three Mason jars full of iced lemonade. The screen door creaked as Butch greeted her.

"I was just setting up for us," he said, his delight at her presence clear. "The heat from the oven is liable to reduce my years on this earth, given the temperature outside. No one needs a heatstroke over cherry cobbler. Jack told me he offered you some, so I figured I'd better get to baking." Butch picked up one of the glasses and handed it to her as she reached the top step.

"You didn't have to," Alice said.

"What I *didn't* have to do was make the lunch that we're having before the cobbler, but I'm happy to."

The door squealed again as Jack walked through it. "Hi," he said, that all-too-recognizable affection in his eyes making her reconsider how long she wanted to stay. He grabbed his Mason jar and took a sip of lemonade as he claimed one of the chairs, seemingly unbothered.

Alice found his demeanor quite difficult to comprehend because she'd hemmed and hawed all morning about whether to actually show up, what to wear, how to treat Jack when she saw him... She'd been so angry at herself for the position she was in. She had made a decision not to see Jack anymore, yet he kept finding his way into her days. She had a ton of things to do to get Seaside Sprinkles ready if she wanted to open any time this year, and she really didn't like leaving Sasha, even though she swore she was feeling better. But despite all of that, she had refilled Einstein's bowls on the porch like she'd promised Henry she'd do, gotten ready, and found herself in the car, going down the bypass toward Butch's house. On the way there she reasoned she was going because Butch was kind and deserved to have a friend if he wanted one. And he'd asked Jack to invite her. But it didn't make her any less tense about how to act.

Jack patted the rocking chair seat beside him, inviting her to sit. She sat down, leaning forward and holding her drink with two hands, the icy surface cooling her just slightly. Butch did the same.

The three of them sipped their lemonade, and Alice noted how quiet it was without the ocean at the back door. The humidity sat on her skin like a wet blanket, and she could feel it crawling down the back of her neck. Absent was the ocean, but also the coastal breeze this far inland. Exhaustion finally took over in the silence. She hadn't slept well at all, thinking over everything and now about Grace as well. The truth was she had a relative out there to whom Gramps may have wanted to give the shop, and the unanswered question as to why he didn't in the end kept going around in her mind all night. She felt like she couldn't move forward without having some sort of answer.

She'd tried to call her dad again but he only got out a few words in greeting before Henry called him, and she realized that that wasn't the time to speak to him about it. She needed to see him, and she planned to have a talk with him once he came back to drop Henry home.

"It's stifling hot here in the woods, but you know, it's the most serene place to live," Butch said, tipping back in his rocker and taking a sip of his drink. "So much has built up around here… Not many places like this left." He shot a worried glance over at Jack.

"It is a nice spot," Jack said, standing up abruptly. "What's for lunch? Wanna go in and eat? I'm starving." He opened the screen door as a request for the two of them to rise and go inside too.

But they'd just sat down. Why was he so jumpy all of a sudden? Before she could find out, Butch had gotten up and tottered inside and Jack was fiddling with the thermostat, turning it colder to combat the heat.

"Whatcha got for us today, Dad?"

The tiny kitchen counter was full of dishes: bowls of potato salad and fresh vegetables, sliced chicken and wedges of cheese, homemade bread…

"You outdid yourself," Jack said, removing the cellophane from the top of one of the bowls.

"In my next apartment, I'd like to have a bit more counter space," Butch said, as he shifted a bowl to make room for their stack of plates. He looked over his shoulder to address Alice. "Jack's finding me a new place to rent," he explained.

Alice tried to read Jack, wondering if he'd abandoned his idea of building something wonderful for his dad. He wouldn't make eye contact with her, but she could see that Butch's line of conversation wasn't sitting well with him.

"I wouldn't mind staying here, but…" He shook his head. "We'd sold it already since it had started to require more upkeep than I could manage, and I was only renting until we could find something else. The buyers were very kind to let me do that, but they need to make a move on the changes. I was just told the land is being rezoned for commercial property. It seems like they need more beach chairs and towels, cups and key chains for the throngs of tourists that always seem to sit in my favorite chair at the coffee shop for three months of the year."

Besides the complete worry that Butch would be out of his home, Alice let another thought sink in: the locals felt displaced during the summer months when the tourists came into town. But their money was essential to the survival of the area. She wondered if she could have a wall of bookshelves at the ice cream shop where the locals could place their own books and newspapers, have a few chairs set aside on reserve for them... Just an idea.

"Good property is hard to find!" He lumped a pile of potato salad on a plate for Alice that was so big she could eat from it for days, and handed it to her. "There just isn't a lot out there and we're in a crunch, aren't we, Jack? I've got to find something else soon or I'm out on the streets."

"I won't leave you on the streets," Jack said quietly, peering down at his plate. He'd filled half of it with way too many vegetables and had a third spoonful ready, when he must have realized what he was doing and set the spoon back into the bowl. He still wouldn't look up.

"What will you do if you can't find somewhere to live?" she asked Butch, while filling the rest of her plate. Jack had set his plate down on the table and topped off all three of their glasses of lemonade.

"I have a spare room at my apartment in Chicago," Jack said, his voice heavy.

Butch stroked his beard thoughtfully before speaking. "You know, I don't want to sound ungrateful, because I'm not at all, but that fancy glass box you've got overlooking the city isn't exactly where I thought I'd spend my last years—I've told you that. I used up all the good years I was healthy chasing that very kind of thing, but now, I just want a small kitchen where I can bake my pies and a long front porch where I can sit and listen to the waves as they crash, just like they did the whole time I was so busy running the streets to make a million. I never made that million, but I sure missed a lot of waves. I don't want to miss any more."

"We'll figure it out," Jack said.

"This is where I want to be. Jack's right on one thing though: he and I should live closer to one another—although I don't think that's going to happen." He offered a half smile at Jack, who was now sitting next to Alice and fiddling with his potato salad, jabbing it lightly with his fork but not eating it.

Alice leaned into Jack's view, commanding his attention. "When do you go back to Chicago?" she asked, the question tearing at her heart. She'd tried to protect herself from this very feeling but, in the end, she couldn't.

He met her eyes. "A couple of weeks."

"A couple of weeks?" she said, his answer stunning her. She sat back in her chair, her fingers settling on top of her silverware. *A couple of weeks.* Yes. That was best. It was good that he was leaving sooner rather than later because this wasn't going anywhere and they were both wasting their time.

A light clatter of Jack's fork onto his plate brought her out of her reverie.

"Dad, do you mind if I talk to Alice outside for a second?"

"Not at all." Butch wiped his mouth with his napkin.

Jack scooted his chair back and stood up, holding out his hand. "Come with me," he said. "We need to talk."

She followed him out, the screen door smacking its frame as she went through it.

Jack was walking quickly, and she had to take two steps for every one of his to keep up. He marched out into the front yard and spun around, running his hand through his hair, his face crumpled in what looked like indecision.

"What's going on here?" he asked. His green eyes bored into her, his lips pressed together into a straight line, his shoulders tense. "It's like we're in the same place for just an instant and then you go cold and pull back." He took a step toward her. "Alice, you said you didn't know if you were doing the right thing. I just offered to take the shop off your hands and then everything changed between us. Why was that so bad?"

She stood there frozen, a lightning bolt moment hitting her right then and causing her to clam up: in the past, she'd have said that the right person wouldn't have offered to buy the shop, but instead would've offered to help her make the decision to open the ice cream shop; but now, as she stood in front of Jack, she realized that wasn't right either. He hadn't done *anything* wrong. It was up to *her* to make it all work, not someone else to convince her. With Sasha being sick, she'd made the last few decisions herself and she could do it just fine. She didn't need anyone helping her to figure it all out.

"Why, Alice?"

She stayed silent as she tried to get her thoughts straight.

Then, while she was still sifting through her emotions, those eyes came into view. "I'm crazy about you," Jack whispered.

Frustration bubbled up into anger. She was angry that she could never seem to be in the right place in life for a relationship to work. She could *never* get it right. And Jack was amazing. As much as she tried to tell herself otherwise, she was just as crazy about him too. She loved every single minute she spent with him. But he was going back to Chicago. "Why are you telling me all this if you're leaving in two weeks? You think that's what I want for Henry? For me? We're a nice diversion while you're here, but then you're going to leave, just like you're leaving your father. From what I hear, you're pretty good at that." Her last statement had been harsh, and she bit her lip, wishing she could retract it, but it was out there now.

"What?"

"I know the story," she said. "I was told how you left your father to run off to Chicago and become a big-shot doctor." She didn't like the idea of him in that white coat. She liked how he was right now, in this moment, even though she was so upset. She loved the way he looked at her, the way his hair fell across his forehead, the slight scruff on his face.

He rubbed his eyes in irritation, taking in a deep breath and then letting it out. "I did no such thing," he said, his jaw set.

"That's not what I heard."

"My father begged me to go. I wanted to stay here with him, but he told me that if I didn't go, all those years he'd spent away from us would mean nothing because he'd worked to give us a life, to give us something better, and going to Chicago was my chance. He'd done all he could and now it was my turn to finish it. So I went." He paced back and forth as if he were trying to keep his cool. Then he turned to her. "I went because I love him."

His last words danced in front of her, making her want to put her arms around him. "I'm sorry," she said, the anger subsiding and an immense guilt washing over her, but the frustration about the situation still lurked under her skin. "I believed it to be true because here we are, and you're telling me you have feelings for me, but you're going back to Chicago in a couple of weeks. What were you planning to do?"

"I haven't thought that far ahead yet. I hadn't exactly prepared to meet you." He shook his head, his thoughts turning inward, his eyes restless.

"Would you stay?" she asked, hoping with every beat of silence that followed that he'd say yes.

"I'm head of surgery in Chicago. I have people waiting for my return. There's nothing for me here," he said. Each thought seemed to be his own argument with some sort of inner voice, but that last statement hit her hard.

"Nothing?" she asked, the hope draining right out of her. "What about your father? What about Henry and me? We're nothing?"

"That's not what I meant," he said, trying to take her arm, but she wouldn't let him. "I was talking about work. There's nothing at the hospital for me."

"That's not what you said."

"Don't put words in my mouth, Alice. Why do you think I keep trying to see you? I'm trying to tell you that I don't have it all figured out, that you came into my life from out of nowhere and I'm scrambling to understand my next move."

She closed her eyes, remembering the young Jack who had formed her opinions about what men should be like, but it wasn't that easy, was it? She turned to him. "Maybe we're trying too hard."

He stared at her.

"You live in Chicago. Your life is there. And I live here. It's as simple as that."

His eyes narrowed. "You don't want this to work."

"What?"

"It's as if you're looking for a reason not to let me in." He paused dramatically, as though what he'd said had defined her. "You don't want it to work because you're scared."

Alice pulled back, aghast.

"You know what I think? You're terrified that what you have with someone won't be perfect, just like you were scared to death about making the right decision moving here, and then whether or not you could get the ice cream shop running. Well, I'm here to tell you that none of it will be perfect, Alice. But it'll be worth it. And you're great at it all. Henry is the most wonderful little boy—he'll be fine with this move as long as he has you; that wall of ideas that you have in the shop is incredible; and…" He broke eye contact. "You've done a number on me." He looked back up at her, a small smile on his lips. "I can't stop thinking about you." That gorgeous smile faded and he said, "You're sabotaging your own happiness. Take a look around once in a while. All that perfection you're looking for is right in front of you."

She didn't believe it. He sounded like Sasha—finding the golden glow in everything. But she was the realist, she reminded herself, and standing in that park, waiting for a man who'd never come, was the way it really was. She was just protecting herself and Henry from a similar fate.

"Are you two going to eat?" Butch's voice came slicing between them.

Alice whirled around. "Yes. We're coming in now." And without another word, she went inside. She didn't like the way the conversation was going one bit. Who was he to think he knew her inner thoughts? But the whole time she ate, Jack's assessment of her kept circling in her head.

Chapter Eighteen

Alice sat in the sand, the spray in the air from the salty sea, the foam sliding up the shore toward her, staring out at the waves. The sun was high, its yellow rays sparkling on the green-blue water, calming her.

Gramps, can you hear me? Alice said in her mind, just as a wave slammed onto the shore. *I don't know what to do. Everything is going wrong and I need a sign that I'm doing the right thing or I'm packing us up and leaving.*

She waited, watching.

A bird flew above her, its shadow on the sand, as the waves rolled over and over. A couple walked by, holding hands.

Nothing came to her, so she got up and went to be alone with her thoughts at home. Sasha had gone to a doctor's appointment to be sure that all was well now that her medicine seemed to be working. She'd been feeling markedly better, and Alice was glad for that.

She wished Sasha were home right now, though, because she was feeling pretty low. She opened the back screen door and then latched it behind her as she went inside. She'd had a handyman in to fix it and the door was as good as new. After they'd painted, she'd added new globes on the lights and she'd had the Seaside Sprinkles logo printed on a transfer to adhere to the glass door she'd shined up. She stood in the center of the glowing showroom downstairs and fought the tears.

There was a loud knock, the sound startling her. With a deep breath, she squeezed her eyes shut to clear her sadness and walked to the front, where she opened the door and greeted an old woman.

"Hello," the woman said. She was wearing a long, wide skirt, sandals, and a light cotton shirt with beading down the front, the lines on her face revealing all the time she'd spent in the sun. "I'm June Dawson." She smiled in the most comfortable way. It was so genuine and gentle that it made Alice wonder if she had a flock of grandchildren who came to visit often. Just by looking at her, Alice knew she'd be the best grandmother ever.

"Hi, Ms. Dawson. Would you like to come in?" She opened the door wider, holding it there.

"Oh, no. I was just stopping by. I wondered if you're missing something."

Was she some sort of saleswoman, about to tell her how she was missing the greatest glass cleaner on the planet or something like that?

"You see, a few days ago, I found a dog. It's the sweetest little thing. I took it right in and fed it— it didn't have a collar. I've grown so attached to it that the little guy sleeps at the foot of my bed." She smiled. "I couldn't say no with all the whimpering he was doing."

Alice's pulse was in her ears, excitement building, but she didn't want to believe it. Einstein had had a collar. Had he lost it out there by himself?

"I love him to pieces, but he's just so busy, you know. It's wearing on my old bones." She winked at Alice. "So I told a friend of mine that I'd fallen in love with this stray dog, but I was going to have to find a new owner for him. I didn't want to just give him to a shelter.

My friend said that she'd heard the ladies in the old bike shop were missing a dog. Apparently, Jack Murphy's been putting up fliers. He even put one up in my restaurant, but I hadn't noticed it."

"Restaurant?" She didn't want to ask any more about Einstein right then because she wanted to bask in the hope that June had found Henry's dog for a little while longer. If it wasn't Einstein, it was going to crush her.

"Well, I own it, but my daughter runs it; I'm too old to do all that running around. It's called Seagull's Cove. It has the best crab cake on the Outer Banks and a potato salad to die for—it's my own recipe. You should come in some time."

"Sounds really nice."

"It's pretty popular. But I don't want to jibber jabber all day about the restaurant. Come on down and see for yourself. I just stopped by because I wanted to know if the dog is yours. Would you tell me what your dog looks like?"

"He's a black Lab puppy with a tiny marking of white on his left paw, and he answers to Einstein."

June chuckled. "Well, that's the right name for him, for sure. Would you believe he's figured out how to open my cabinets to get his food? Smart little thing."

"Where is he now?" If it was true, Alice could hardly wait to see him, so relieved that he'd been loved and taken care of this whole time.

"I've got his leash around an old deck post over on the side yard in the shade, so he could run around while I talked to you. I wanted to be sure he was yours—I'm a little protective of him. Also, I'm not sure he'd sit still long enough to let us talk."

Alice's heart wanted to burst and she laughed long and hard, joy filling every bit of her. "That sounds like him." She stepped outside and moved around to the side yard. There, tied to the post, was Einstein.

His tail started wagging furiously when he saw her. Alice ran over to him, untied the leash and threw her arms around his little neck while he plastered kisses all over her face.

"Einstein," she said, letting the tears fall this time. "You scared us all to death."

He whimpered and kissed her again, as though he understood.

"Oh, I'm so glad he's yours," June said, joining them, her hands clasped together in happiness. "It looks like he sure did miss you! I'll bet he was terrified without you."

Holding Einstein's leash, Alice stood up. "I can't thank you enough for taking care of him. We've been so worried."

"I'll bet." June reached out and patted Einstein's head. "Y'all new here?" she asked, raising her hand to shield her eyes from the beating sun. "I noticed Paul's place has been empty for some time."

"Yes. He was my grandfather. We're going to try to open an ice cream shop here, but I'm not sure if it's the right location."

"Well, you won't know till you try."

Alice smiled, but she still wasn't certain it was worth trying. Einstein pawed her for more attention and she rubbed his cheeks.

"You look unsure of yourself. That's not a good sign when you're about to pour your heart and soul into a new business," June noted. "I should know. I did it with Seagull's Cove. You have to be all in."

Alice didn't say anything, and she wondered if she *was* all in. She wanted to be positive about her choice, but everything else was telling her otherwise.

"I started with a shack of a building that flooded every hurricane and barely had enough space for all the tables we needed to put in, but I didn't let it get me down, and it paid off. We added on to that shack and raised it onto stilts in 1985, and then we renovated again in 2001, and now it's standing room only all day in the waiting area and on the deck, and we're going to have to look for a new location."

Alice stopped and gaped at her, Einstein freezing too in response to her pause, her mind going back to what she'd said to Gramps just now on the beach. The hair on her arms stood up. "I know of a great location for a large restaurant," she said. "I've heard that a couple of the retailers were pulling out on the pier and they're looking for something big to take their place. It's right next door."

Consideration flooded June's face. "No one has posted the space anywhere—I've been looking," she said. "I know what's available, and I haven't heard a peep about the pier."

"It's early stages. The tenants are still there. But I spoke with the county representative and he told me they're actively looking for something to move in."

"Who'd you speak with? Was it Bill Blankenship?"

"I think that was his name."

"I'll give him a call when I get home."

"That would be amazing." The hope was back with a vengeance, and she suddenly felt like maybe this *was* right and she just hadn't been patient enough. "If Seagull's Cove moved to the pier, I'd have ice cream for everyone once they'd had dinner."

A smile spread across June's face. "Now that's the *all-in* spirit! That's exactly what it looks like." She reached over and affectionately tugged on Einstein's ear. His back leg went into convulsions trying to scratch the spot, sending sand up into the air. "It's as if it were meant to be," she said. "I mentioned needing a new space to you—a complete stranger—when I hadn't really talked it over with anyone. It's just something that's been on my mind."

"Maybe it *was* meant to be."

Einstein wriggled his way between them and nudged them both with his snout. He'd clearly made a new friend in June.

They said their goodbyes, and Alice reentered the shop with fresh eyes. Maybe, just maybe, things would work out. But she still hadn't solved the question of Grace. Grabbing the locket from the counter, where it had sat since Butch had brought it to her, Alice plopped down next to Einstein on the floor and opened it up. The photo was starting to look familiar to her now—she'd viewed it so many times. Even though the will had only had Alice's name, she felt like this shop belonged to Grace too. She just felt it.

She wondered if it was because she'd grown up with her dad and Gramps for the second half of her life. Susie and her family lived across the country, and, really, Alice had been the only girl around for a long time. She peered down at the baby's picture again, and it seemed like Grace was smiling at her. It was hard to believe that somewhere, Grace could be a woman now, going about her life, with no inclination that Alice was thinking about her. Was she still alive? Was she here? If so, where?

Alice missed Henry so much in just the short time he'd been with her dad—had someone been missing Grace that way? For how many years? She couldn't imagine being without Henry. That was why none of this made any sense at all. She couldn't wait to ask her dad about Grace, but at the same time, she was apprehensive. What if mentioning Grace caused some kind of sadness for him, or rage, or worry? She didn't want to bring about any of those feelings for her dad. She loved him so much; she'd never want to hurt him.

Indecision swam around inside her as she started to ponder whether she should even bring it up at all. She looked back down at the locket. What if she hadn't ever found it? What if it had stayed a secret? Should it remain that way?

Chapter Nineteen

"I didn't get to tell you before I left for the doctor," Sasha said as she came in, "but the showroom looks incredible. It looks like we hired an interior designer! The colors are amazing; the logo is just fantastic!"

Alice felt the fizzle of excitement, knowing that this time Sasha wasn't just being optimistic. Alice had worked her heart out and it showed. "Did you get your medicine?"

"Mm hm. Guess what else I picked up at the hospital when I went for my checkup?" Sasha said, looking very much herself this afternoon. She was puttering around their little kitchen, making herself a snack—cheese and crackers—while Einstein ran back and forth by her feet. Sasha had cried too when she'd come in and seen him, and Alice could swear he'd lifted Sasha's spirits enough to put color back in her cheeks. Sasha set the plate next to a bottle of wine and got herself a glass. It was good to see her feeling a little better.

"What? And did the doctor clear you to drink alcohol?"

There was a pop when Sasha pulled the cork loose. "So that thing that I picked up… Was a date for tomorrow night." She raised her eyebrows. "And yes. I can have alcohol. Now, want some?"

"A date?" Alice sucked her lips in for dramatic flair. *This* was the Sasha she knew: the one who could go to an appointment at a hospital, feeling awful, and manage to find a date.

"Yes!" She clapped a hand over her mouth. "He's a doctor!" Sasha twirled toward the cabinet and pulled down another glass, filling it without ever getting the go-ahead from Alice. She handed it to her.

"Oh, I wonder if he knows Jack," Alice heard herself say excitedly, before she could rein it in. She'd only been legitimately curious about whether the two doctors knew each other, but now it looked like she was ready for double dating.

Alice could see Sasha's wheels already turning as she nipped a cracker and topped it with cheese. "I don't know," she said with interest. "Why?"

"I just wondered."

"Anything new going on with Jack? You seemed to light up when you said his name." She topped another cracker with cheese and popped it into her mouth.

"Nope."

Alice had more pressing matters on her mind than Jack. She'd been dying to tell Sasha about all the things she'd missed over the last few days. Alice hadn't wanted to dump all of it on her while she was trying to recuperate, but at some point, she needed to explain everything. Right now, though, it was time to celebrate this moment with Sasha.

"Enough about Jack. I'm so happy for you! Who is this doctor and where is he taking you?"

"His name is Sam and we're just going out to dinner."

"Sam and Sasha—I like it!"

Sasha balled up her fists and shook them, doing a little dance. But then, she sobered, dropping down in the chair at the table. Alice joined her. "It's all fun and games right now, but what if things take a turn?"

"What do you mean?"

"What if things get serious? I'm scared. What if it doesn't work out?"

Alice pushed her wine glass to the center of the table and folded her arms, studying her friend. "That doesn't sound like you. You're always the optimistic one, remember? It's only a date. Take it day by day." But she knew when she said those words that sometimes there was more to it than that.

"You're right," Sasha said, grabbing her wine and her aviators. "What are we doing inside? We live at the beach! Let's go out back and soak up some sun. Einstein! Here, boy!" She patted her leg and Einstein was immediately beside her, his tail whipping back and forth as she got his leash. She hooked it to the new collar June had gotten him.

They sat down in the chairs on the patio and Einstein jumped into Alice's lap, making them laugh. He curled up, his head on its side, and closed his eyes. Alice wondered if being away from them and not knowing how to get back had been tiring for him. Had he worried about his family?

Alice took in a deep breath of briny air, the salt palpable in the sea wind. The sun was shining on the surface of the water at just the right angle to make the sparkles look orange and pink. She had so much to tell Sasha, and she was glad to finally have some time with her friend.

"I've been waiting for a chance to fill you in on an interesting story," Alice said, the moment they were settled. "Remember the boy from that summer with Gramps that I told you about? *The* boy?"

"How could I not? You've only compared every date you've ever had to that day." Sasha rolled her eyes playfully. "He's so perfect that I'm starting to wonder if you dreamed him up. Is he even real?"

"Oh, yes. He's real all right. You'll never believe who that boy turned out to be…"

Sasha's eyes grew round behind her sunglasses. "Nooo." She clapped a hand over her gaping mouth. By her reaction, Alice could tell that Sasha knew exactly who it was.

Alice nodded. "Yep. It's Jack."

"You didn't even have to tell me—I knew it! So Jack is your dream guy…" Sasha's mouth slowly formed a grin, her words loaded with give-him-a-chance messages.

Alice wasn't even going to approach that topic right now. "Wait," she said. "There's more. I found something of Gramps's. A locket with two baby photos inside. One of the pictures is of me and the other is someone else. Apparently, Gramps told Jack that the two photos inside the locket were of his grandchildren, but I showed Aunt Claire and the second baby isn't Susie."

"Sooo, who could it be then?" Sasha said, catching on.

"Someone named Grace. That's what Gramps told Jack."

"But you don't know how you're related?" Sasha's face lit up suddenly. "It could be someone famous! You could have a famous cousin no one ever knew about! Or! What if she's the best person you've ever met and we can invite her to parties?" Then Sasha's expression dropped, her eyes flicking back and forth as she processed this news further. "What if she has twenty-five cats and fifteen children, and she and her husband want you to babysit? You're allergic to cats."

Alice laughed, so happy to have the Sasha she knew back. "We're getting ahead of ourselves. I haven't found her yet. But I *did* find a note from Gramps saying he'd like to leave the bike shop to both of us. *Both* of us," she repeated for emphasis. "Me and Grace. Even though it seems like he'd changed his mind by the time he drew up his will, I'm struggling to know how to proceed when I've got someone out there I don't know and possibly the unfulfilled wishes of my grandfather."

Sasha sat quietly, undoubtedly digesting all this.

"Have you talked to your dad? Does he know who she is?"

Alice shook her head. "I tried to call him, but he's busy with Henry. I plan to talk to him in person. Aunt Claire doesn't know a thing about the girl in the locket, so Dad *must* know. If Grace isn't Claire's child—and I'm praying Gramps didn't have some sort of secret affair—then the only other person in the family she could belong to is Dad." Just saying it out loud gave her a shiver despite the heat.

"You might have a sister?"

"I can't imagine…" Alice couldn't even say it. It would mean that her parents had deceived her, held this from her. Or at least her father had. Had her mother known or was this the result of some sordid affair? The idea was too overwhelming to accept. "No matter how we're related, if she's family—and Gramps was sure enough that she was to write that letter—then I need to find her."

This didn't just affect Alice; it changed everything for Sasha as well. If they found Grace, and brought her in on their plans, she might have a totally different vision for this place—or she might want something else altogether.

Einstein had rolled over onto his back, his legs twitching in his sleep, the sun on the patio clearly relaxing him.

"I agree that you need to find her, but I don't think you need to include her in your inheritance, Alice. She can't be very close to your grandfather if you've never even heard of her."

But Alice couldn't deny that Gramps had wanted to leave the bike shop to this person. Even if he had left it to Alice in the end. "I'm going to wait until Dad brings Henry back and talk to him about her then. What if it's a sensitive topic? What if Grace passed away or something? It's best to wait until I'm with him."

"Good idea. I can keep Henry busy if you need me. You could make your father-daughter cups of coffee like you do."

Melly walked around the corner, halting their conversation, an enormous grin on her face. "I heard about Sam," she said, with no introductions. "You two move in and scoop up all the eligible doctors!" She plopped down into the chair beside Alice, her hair pulled back into a ponytail, her camera around her neck. "This view makes the hardest day seem like nothing. The ocean just swallows up whatever is eating at you." She lifted the camera to her face and twisted the zoom, snapping a picture. Then she pulled the wide strap over her head and set the camera down on the table.

Alice thought back to the sadness in Melly's eyes when they'd first met. It was as though being with people had helped her in some way. "My gramps used to think the ocean could solve his problems." She dared not mention that sometimes she didn't believe it, although the possibility of Seagull's Cove coming to the pier and Einstein being returned certainly made her wonder.

Alice squinted her eyes at Melly playfully. "You look extra happy today." It was good to see her worry over being let go subsiding briefly.

"I am extra happy," she said, pressing her lips together as if something were going to burst from them. "I spent the last few hours taking photos of the wild horses in Corolla and having a cocktail—just because! Even before that, this morning, I saw the county putting up a billboard. I talked to a few people at work about it; there's going to be a concert on the beach right here in a few weeks. They're going to use the pier as a venue since it'll be empty. The stores will have all pulled out by then, and instead of having it sit vacant, they're putting in concessions and offering the public bathrooms up there." She leaned forward dramatically, causing Einstein to snort and flip over, ears raised, eyes focused on her. "Top bands will be there."

"Sounds fun!" Sasha said, her smile pushing up her aviators and her wine glass nearly empty. "And great for business!" She turned to Alice. "Think we can be ready?"

Alice broke into a huge grin, so excited to hear this news. A soft opening before a major concert might be exactly what they needed. "I've just ordered the ice cream ingredients, and it should all be here in a few days. Let's make it happen!"

Chapter Twenty

Sasha had been much more herself as the night wore on, but she'd gone to bed early last night while Alice stayed up to finish some work. The more Alice allowed herself to ease into the idea that she could do this, the more confident she became in her choices.

Last night, she'd emailed a local wine and candy shop in a nearby village to see if they could make their chocolates smaller, to be used as ice cream toppings exclusively at Seaside Sprinkles, alongside a display of chocolates in their regular size and a glossy sign with directions to their shop. They were thrilled, offering her an assortment of specialty chocolates to try. She'd just picked them up this morning.

She'd decided to go local with everything, and this morning she'd even found a couple of gorgeous wooden chairs with a space at the back of each one, where she could attach small chalkboard signs and write the names of frequenting residents, so they'd always have *their* seats on reserve. She'd already written Butch's name on one of them. She planned to ask him if he'd like to have the birds he'd carved painted in bright colors and hung from her ceiling.

The ideas wall had been taken down, and in its place she'd put a large, white bookshelf, where she'd stacked a few of her favorite books and a chalkboard sign that told people they were welcome to leave their reading material here until next time. She'd had the local artist she'd worked with on the logo make up a jar full of hand-painted bookmarks for sale, in case the regulars had left theirs at home.

While Sasha had gone to pick up a few things at the store, Alice had driven to June's restaurant, Seagull's Cove, and told them about the plans for the pier, giving them Bill Blankenship's number at the county office. Before she'd left, she'd asked if they had any large pickle jars they were throwing out. They gave her an enormous one. She'd brought it back, washed it out, and put a sign on it that read, "Save the Pier! Ideas and donations welcome." She'd also gotten the addresses of three non-profit organizations that might be able to help, since the pier was a historical landmark.

She was just sitting down for a break when the new bells on the door jingled and Jack walked through. He glanced over at Einstein, who was chewing a bone in his bed, and then he gave Alice that gorgeous smile of his. "I had to come right over when I heard Einstein had been returned—you didn't say anything."

Alice stood up.

"I ran into June in town," he said, nearing her. "She told me she'd had Einstein the whole time."

"Yep! I'm sorry I didn't tell you." It was so good to see him.

He turned away from her to look around. "You've outdone yourself here! It looks amazing."

"Thanks," she beamed. "I was thinking of asking your dad to hang his birds from the ceiling. I thought I could sell them to raise funds for the pier, if he would let me. Do you think he would?"

"We could ask him." He moved closer to her, his scent settling in the air between them, making it difficult for her to focus. He leaned down and stroked Einstein's head.

"We?"

He righted himself and looked into her eyes. "I came to see Einstein, yes. But I came to see you too." He had that irresistible expression on his face, like he'd had when they'd first met and he'd sat her down on the bench to listen. "Look, I'm here for two more weeks. Why don't we just enjoy them? Go out with me."

She bit her lip, considering. Could her heart take it when he left if she allowed herself to see him?

"The other day, you spoke as if the moment I go back to Chicago, it's the end of something. But it doesn't have to be."

He'd been right when he'd told her she was scared. She was terrified of getting hurt. Just seeing him now made her miss him already and he hadn't even left yet.

"Stop trying to control everything and just let fate decide."

Fate.

"You know what? You're right," she said, suddenly getting an idea. She walked over to the counter and pushed the box of chocolates toward him, opening the lid. "You said I get to choose the next bet, right?" She wasn't letting him get off as easily this time, with his little game of darts.

He eyed her suspiciously before peering down at the massive array of little chocolate balls and clusters from the local candy shop, all settled comfortably in their paper shells.

"You pick a flavor of your choice. Then, we check these chocolates and if that flavor is in the center of any of them, I'll go out with you."

He leaned over the box, inspecting them.

"What will it be: vanilla? Raspberry? Peanut butter?" She knew she had him here. There was no way for this bet to be fixed. He couldn't have any inclination as to what was inside the chocolates. She didn't even know herself. It would be a complete surprise—fate.

"You've got yourself a bet." He picked one up and smelled it, then set it back down. Then he carried the box over to one of the small tables that had replaced the old one she and Sasha had been using, and took a seat in Butch's chair, grinning at the nameplate.

Alice sat down across from him.

"Toffee," he said with certainty.

"That's your guess?"

"Yep."

"So you think that somewhere in here, there's a toffee-flavored filling."

He shrugged. "Why not? It's a popular flavor." He picked up one of the chocolates and took a bite, chewing and then swallowing. "Found it! First try."

"Let me see," she said, disbelieving. "That doesn't look like toffee."

He held out the rest of the chocolate, the inside sliding out. "Taste for yourself."

Not wanting to make a mess, she leaned in and took the bite, her lips touching his fingers. He seemed to notice, meeting her eyes.

She swallowed it down. "That's walnut."

The corner of his mouth went up in amusement. "That's not walnut. It's like a toffee cream."

"You didn't say toffee cream. Toffee is usually crunchy. You have to find a crunchy one."

"You're changing the rules," he teased, a playful look in his eyes.

"I am not! You said toffee."

He rolled his eyes with a huff of laughter and pinched another chocolate, taking a bite. He wrinkled his nose. "Strawberry."

"Oh, yum! I love strawberry. I'll eat it; give it here."

Einstein stretched and walked over, looking back and forth between them as they sat across from each other, the box of chocolates in the center of the small table.

"Apparently, Einstein likes strawberry too," Jack said with a grin, as he reached over to give her the other half of the candy.

She took it with her fingers this time, and popped it into her mouth. "Definitely strawberry," she said, the rich flavor filling her mouth.

Jack pointed to the one in the middle of the box. It was flat and rectangular. "This one is definitely toffee," he said, picking it up and scrutinizing it. He broke it in half. "Argh," he said, outwardly disappointed. "Cookie center." He handed her half.

They continued until they had half the box finished off, their bellies aching. There must have been forty chocolates in there when she'd brought it home. Still no toffee.

"I don't feel well," she admitted, the richness still invading her senses even though she'd swallowed the last bite ages ago. She wanted to drink some water, but the idea of putting anything else in her stomach made her feel queasy. "I think I need to lie down."

"Mmm," he said, looking just as miserable as she did. He put the lid on the box and stood up, tucking it under his arm. "Come with me." He led her to the front door. "I know what will make us feel better. We need a breather. But I won't be defeated. We can finish the bet in a little while."

She grabbed her house keys, locked up, and got in his car. He pulled away from the shop, the windows down, the salty breeze warm against her skin. She closed her eyes, surrendering completely to the feeling of summer, of the happiness she felt, of the present—not the future or the past, just now.

After a drive, she found herself at Butch's. "Dad's gone out to help someone build a barn, but we can ask him about his birds when he gets back." He turned off the engine and grabbed the chocolates. "Let's put these in the fridge so they don't melt in this heat, and then I've got something to show you out back."

They dropped the chocolates off inside and went to the backyard, a lush spot of grass under a canopy of trees. In the shade, hanging from two of the oaks, was a giant hammock with built-in pillows. Jack held it steady and motioned for her to get on. "You said you wanted to lie down."

She clambered up on it, the thick braids of rope swinging back and forth underneath her as she got comfortable. Jack climbed on beside her, the motion steadying it. He crossed his legs at the ankle and clasped his hands behind his head, but the hammock wobbled. He straightened an arm to keep the weight distributed as she sat up just a bit in response to the shaking, and when she relaxed again, his arm was behind her, supporting her neck. Their bodies were close, the sun sparkling through the trees, a light breeze sailing over them—it all made her forget about her stomach ache.

"This is nice," he said, turning carefully on his side to face her. One more arm around her and they'd be embracing. His head lay on the pillow as he looked at her, not saying anything else.

"I don't know how you do it," she said with a grin.

He waited for an explanation.

"You never found any toffee!" she laughed. "Yet here we are, together, on a hammock in your dad's back yard."

He huffed out a few chuckles, fondness in his eyes. "It took a lot of chocolate to get you here," he said with a sideways grin. "I was only giving you a place to lie down while we wait to ask Dad if we can have his birds." He flashed an amused look at her and then lay flat, both of them looking up at the sky.

"Stop thinking," he said unexpectedly. "Just let yourself enjoy this."

She smiled, knowing exactly what he meant.

Alice didn't remember going up to bed. Had she taken her makeup off? Confusion weaved its way through her mind as she emerged from sleep. It was warm, a little too warm, but still nice. And breezy—had Sasha opened a window? Then suddenly, her eyes snapped open and, without moving her head, she shifted her eyes to her left where she saw Jack dozing beside her. They'd fallen asleep on the hammock.

Every nerve in her body was taking stock of his position. He was on his side again, one arm draped over her, the other behind her neck, their legs intertwined. A gentle tickle from his breath caressed her face and, if she inhaled, she could smell his clean, spicy, woody scent. He was completely relaxed, that big smile of his replaced by a peaceful expression. She noticed the small lines around his eyes that could only be made from laughing, and lying there beside him was so perfect that a tiny jolt of panic shot through her, making her want to get up before she started thinking about the fact that he wasn't going to be around a lot longer. But instead, she stayed, unwilling to give up this moment.

How long had they been asleep? Her phone was in the back pocket of her shorts, and she didn't want to disturb him by trying to get it out. She also couldn't admit to herself that she didn't want him to move a muscle. There was something that made her feel complete, watching him sleep.

Where would they be in a few weeks' time if she kept letting this kind of thing happen? He was going to break her heart; there was no denying that. Because, in the end, he *had* to go back to Chicago and she didn't want to have a long-distance relationship. Things were so early on that they'd lose touch and she'd be left, just like she had been that summer so long ago: comparing everyone she met to this moment, to this man. And nothing would ever compare.

Alice had made a couple of decisions in her life where she knew that, once she'd made them, there would be no going back. The first one was having Henry; the second was deciding, with her acceptance letter in hand, not to enroll in the four-year college program that she knew she could've done well in. This was the third. She was about to do something completely out of character. For the first time in her life, she wasn't thinking this through, she wasn't concerned about what would happen next, and she was acting on her emotions instead of reason.

She rolled over toward Jack, her heart knocking around in her chest. He inhaled deeply, her movement disturbing his sleep. She wriggled one hand under his arm and the other between him and the hammock, and wrapped him in a hug, their faces close together. He opened his eyes, groggy, a grin forming as he focused on her. Without allowing herself to consider anything but him—his face her only focus because she might not go through with it otherwise—she leaned in and gently pressed her lips to his.

His eyes opened completely, and he pulled back just a bit. When he did, she could tell he sensed the tentativeness in her decision. He raised a hand and stroked her arm, his gaze swallowing her. Then, he leaned in again and kissed her softly, as if allowing her one more chance to make the choice. She closed her eyes and kissed him back. In response, Jack pulled her into his body, his mouth moving on hers, his hands now at her back. The feel of his breath, the taste of salt on his lips from the air outside—it all felt like complete perfection, as if they'd been made to fit together; and only now did she realize that she hadn't felt whole all these years—not until now.

She didn't want to consider what they would do in the months to come. All she cared about was having this second with him, feeling his embrace, and knowing that right here, right now, she was perfectly happy.

"Looks like I have a few more birds in the woods," Butch said, after clearing his throat. "I've found a couple of love birds."

They both jumped, nearly turning the hammock over. Jack stopped Alice from toppling to the ground, steadying the wobbling hammock by placing one foot down while Alice frantically untangled herself from his other leg. She was glad for the diversion; no one would notice the fire in her cheeks.

When she finally made eye contact with Butch, she could see the friendliness on his face, and it made her feel a little better.

"Speaking of birds," Jack said, placing both feet on the ground and standing up. He reached out a hand to help Alice out of the hammock. "Alice would like to talk to you about yours."

Butch's forehead wrinkled with interest. "Oh? Well, come on in. I've made another pie and I can't eat it by myself. It's chocolate."

Both Alice and Jack looked at each other and laughed.

Chapter Twenty-One

Alice had been frantically working on the marketing for Butch's birds, to bring awareness about the pier to the patrons of Seaside Sprinkles. Butch had been thrilled with the idea, so happy his work could do something wonderful for the community and have a part in saving a landmark so dear to his own son's heart.

She had been glad to throw herself into this project, to avoid thinking about how much she missed Henry. She hadn't been away from him this long before and she couldn't wait for him to come home. But she knew being with her dad was good for Henry. She was happy to have such a positive male role model in his life. She just wished they could all live a bit closer. This traveling back and forth to see each other was going to be difficult, and while she'd known that going in, actually living it was harder than she'd expected.

She'd just finished showing Sasha her ideas and she'd hit save on her computer document when Melly walked in. She'd come over this afternoon, her nose bright red, her eyes bloodshot.

"I have the date they're letting us all go," she said to them both, her lip trembling.

Sasha walked over and put a supportive arm around her new friend.

"I heard it'll be in three weeks. I don't know what I'm going to do after that."

Einstein was pushing his ball around the floor while Melly talked to Alice and Sasha. His tags jingled, the ball thumping along the planks of wood. Melly put her face in her hands and let herself cry.

Sasha handed her a tissue from across the counter.

Melly looked up. "Thank you," she said, with a hiccup. She wiped her eyes. And then blew her nose. "They're supposed to tell us all tomorrow."

"They can't find any money to keep you?" Alice was pouring glasses of iced tea for the three of them. She couldn't believe they'd hire Melly, only to fire her months later. It seemed so unfair.

"They're stretched thinner financially than they'd anticipated. Some of the nurses were upset that they had enough funds to cover Jack Murphy and his research, but they were wrong about him. Did you know that he's doing it for free? He's using all his vacation time to help. And that favor he owed his friend was a high school bet over a football game that he never even had to repay." She sniffled and took a sip of her drink, the changed subject causing her tears to subside a bit. "One of the nurses told me about it. She said that if they'd had to pay for him, they wouldn't have been able to afford him."

"He's serious about his bets," Sasha said with a laugh, lightening the mood briefly.

Alice sat quietly, drinking her tea and taking that fact in. So even if Jack wanted to stay, even if she could convince him, the hospital didn't have enough money to keep him on the staff. He was the head of neurosurgery at one of the largest hospitals on this side of the country. How could he ever make the same living at a small hospital on these barrier islands? He couldn't. She thought back to their moment on the hammock, how he'd held her hand while they ate chocolate pie just to be polite to Butch, their tummies still aching from all the candy they'd had during their bet, and Jack's excitement as they talked about putting Butch's birds in Seaside Sprinkles.

She'd had that feeling she'd always been chasing: like the universe had been with her in that moment, and that somehow, some way, it would all work out. But Melly was a perfect example of how it might not work out. She'd gotten the job she'd wanted, moved to her rainy-day place, the place she'd always hoped to be, and look at what was happening. She was about to lose it all. That could happen to Alice. And now she was in a real dilemma because she'd fallen for Jack. Not just fallen for him. She'd never met another human being who could make her feel like she did when she was with him.

"Look at her," she heard Sasha saying, and when she came to, Sasha was grinning. "One mention of Jack and she's all starry-eyed. Hello-o! Earth to Alice. You with us?"

"I'm with you," she said, rolling her eyes playfully to hide her contemplations. Then she directed her focus at Melly. "So what are you going to do?" she asked.

"I have no idea," Melly said, shaking her head. She looked completely dejected. "But talking to you two is helping. I feel so much better just having you all to hear me. Sometimes, even if nothing can change, it's so valuable just to know that you have a person to listen, you know?"

"I totally get that," Sasha said, hopping up onto the counter and crossing her legs underneath her. "I don't know where I'd be without Alice." She offered a warm look at her friend. "And now I have you too, Melly. I'm so glad you're here."

"Me too."

* *

"I'm going out with Sam tonight," Sasha said, just before she'd told Alice she needed to start getting ready. They'd spent the rest of the afternoon after Melly left talking about Seaside Sprinkles. Alice had described Butch's wooden birds to Sasha and told her what she planned to do with them. She'd called and asked him if they could auction them off to raise money for the pier, the idea coming to Alice as she'd discussed it with Sasha.

Alice had created cards on organic paper with brown lettering telling the story of the "Wooden Birds of the Outer Banks," describing how they were born in the forest, whittled by hand, and each bird had its own wish for the buyer inscribed on the card—it had taken her ages to think of them all. She'd bought a spool of twine for the tags and a ream of tissue paper to wrap them up when it was time to transport them to the shop.

Sasha had excitedly told her as her arms moved in the air, "We could market them like this: unique artwork, limited quantities, a collaboration of local artists. We could even say that Butch has come out of retirement just for this event. That's true—he is in retirement and he's just now selling his art…"

It sounded like a great idea.

"Yes! We could make it an event, bringing people in just for the auction. What if we advertised it as The Confectionery Auction: sharing the love of dessert and fine art? We could ask the wine and candy shop to donate one-of-a-kind desserts for the auction as well. They seemed really nice when I spoke to them, and with their love of community, I'm sure they'd be in. We might even be able to pull in more local artists," Alice said, before turning her attention to Sasha, suddenly taking stock of her friend's expression. She wasn't all excited and bouncy like she'd just been. "You look nervous." Alice observed the uncertainty in her eyes. She'd been so busy brainstorming that she hadn't noticed until now that something else was on Sasha's mind.

"It might be too soon after the divorce… the date," Sasha admitted, completely changing the subject. "Am I ready? What do I do? Am I supposed to kiss him or anything tonight? Sorry. I didn't mean to freak out, but I kind of am."

Alice found Sasha's apprehension endearing. "You don't *have* to do anything that you don't want to do. Just see how it goes and if you're in the position to kiss him *and* you want to, then go for it! But you might just have dinner and drinks and call it a night."

Sasha nodded, but her worry was still evident. Then she offered Alice a giant smile. "Your auction idea is awesome. I just got side tracked because I'm so out of practice with all this."

"You'll be great! You always are."

"Will you help me find what to wear?" Sasha grabbed Alice's arm and started up the steps. "So, tell me," she said, more relaxed now, as they reached the top. She dropped Alice's arm and faced her. "You've made me feel much better about going out with a new man," she said with a grin. "Now, let's talk about yours. What was that look all about when Melly mentioned Jack earlier? Something was going through your head, I could tell."

Alice walked over to the area of the closet where Sasha had started to unpack, and flicked through a few flowy shirts. She pulled out the light yellow one with the fringe on the bottom before turning around, unsure of where to begin.

"What?" Sasha whined. "*Tell me.*" She took the shirt from Alice, her mouth turned down and unsure, shook her head and put it back into the closet.

Alice didn't want to say it out loud, but Sasha always told her just how it was—no sugarcoating—so it might be nice to hear her thoughts. She grabbed the black V-neck and held it out to her friend. "I think I've fallen in love with Jack."

Sasha's eyes widened, a look of warning in them at the same time as she took the shirt from Alice. It hung at her side as she ignored it, still staring at Alice.

"I tried not to." Alice flopped down on Sasha's bed and let out a sigh.

Sasha joined her, crossing her feet at the ankle, the V-neck in a wad on her lap. "I don't blame you. He's a great guy, Alice. And you deserve someone like him." The way she said the words, it was clear that she understood the dilemma and could feel Alice's anguish over it.

Alice dropped her head into her hands and breathed into them in frustration. "I have no idea what to do. I was hoping you could help me find an answer."

Sasha put her arm around Alice. "I don't have one. Unless you move there or he moves here, there's nothing either of you can do." She twisted on the bed to face Alice. "Would you want to live in Chicago?"

"Leave Gramps's memories and all the wonderful things we've created here to live in some high-rise in a busy city? No way. And Jack can't move here. There's no work for him. You heard Melly—they wouldn't be able to pay him." She rubbed her face. "And then when I think about it, Sash, what happens when we go back to real life? I'm sure his work schedule is insane. I'd probably never see him. And what about when we open Seaside Sprinkles? We'll be working every single day of the week as late as nine o'clock at night, until we make enough money to hire someone else to help out. I don't know how I'll have time myself for a relationship."

"Whoa, whoa, whoa. Slow down. You're overthinking it."

"I'm not. I'm being realistic."

"The only part of your argument that's proven true is the fact that you two live far apart. If you're working until nine o'clock, you know he'll be here right by your side. And if he's working, you'll be there for him the minute he gets home. You're playing into your fears. You don't think I'm scared to death to take the next step after Landon? You think I feel ready to put on something nice and go out with a guy I've only just met? But you told me to just see what happens. How are you so different from me? Because I don't think you are."

"What about Henry?"

"I'm not saying you have to involve Henry in all of this yet. Just enjoy yourself. You're always thinking about some big plan, but maybe you should just live in the moment, go with it."

Alice had heard that a lot lately, and she'd tried, she really had. But that just wasn't who she was. Her chest ached with what she was about to say. Talking to Sasha hadn't made it any better; it had only made it clearer. "If there isn't even a possibility for a future then I'd only get my heart broken—and Henry's. I knew this going in and I tried to convince myself that I was strong enough to deal with whatever happens, but for me and Jack, it's different. My heart is already breaking and he hasn't even left yet." Her head was starting to throb so she squeezed her eyes shut to clear it. "But you know what?" She stood up and grabbed Sasha's hands, pulling her off the bed, and pushing all thoughts of Jack away, ignoring the fact that her chest felt like it had a boulder on it. "There *is* a chance for you and Sam. He lives here, he makes you smile already, and he asked you out! So let's get you ready, Missy!"

Chapter Twenty-Two

Sasha came padding into the kitchen the next morning, squinting, her hair a mess of tangles, her eyeliner down her face. She opened one eye at Alice in gratitude as Alice handed her a cup of coffee. Alice had already gotten ready for the day and had even finished a little work for Seaside Sprinkles.

"Good night?" Alice said with interest, trying not to give away her smile until Sasha was completely coherent. From the look of her, Sasha had had a great night. And judging by her love-stricken sigh, it looked like she was smitten. Alice wiped down the counter and joined her friend at the table. "Did you enjoy yourself then?"

Sasha grunted and wrapped both hands around her cup, lifting it to her lips. She closed her eyes and breathed in, her chest rising as if the coffee would give her magical strength at the first sip. The chair made a screech on the floor, and Sasha grimaced. She sat down next to Alice with a thud, the warm morning wind coming in through the open window at the back of the shop.

"I feel like I've been hit by a truck," Sasha finally said, her voice raspy, but the words coming through the most contented smile.

Alice could lecture her about how she should take it easy with the partying until she was 100 percent well, but she knew it would do no good. It was at least worth mentioning, though. "You shouldn't be running your body down like that. You're not totally well yet."

"I couldn't help it," she croaked, twisting toward Alice. "Sam took me to a beach bar that had live music till one in the morning. There were cocktails and lots of beach dancing… It was so much fun."

"Anything else?" Alice nudged her playfully.

Sasha finally opened her eyes all the way, an enormous smile spreading over her face. "He kissed me."

Alice clapped a hand over her mouth and gawked with surprise from behind her fingers.

"I didn't have to think about anything. He took my drink and set it on the railing of the boardwalk leading to the bar. Then, he swept me up in his arms and kissed me! It was the best kiss I've ever had." She sighed and took another drink of her coffee. "It was so good that I didn't have time to worry about anything."

"Better than Bennie Coleman in tenth grade?"

Sasha had talked about him for months after he'd kissed her on a street corner outside the movie theater.

"Oh gosh, yes!" Sasha giggled.

"So will you see him again?"

"Um, I think so," she said, wagging her head up and down with a look that was more excited than she'd been for quite a while. She leaned on her elbow. "Is Henry coming home today?"

"Yes!" Alice nearly shrieked. She was so happy to see him. She'd missed him terribly. "But first I'm going to run over to Butch's to talk to him about having his birds painted by that artist we've used. I think she'd make them look amazing. We could sell them for twenty-five dollars, and she's only taking five dollars each for her supplies. The rest from the auction we can donate to the pier. I also thought we could include a flier with directions for donating larger sums. The birds could raise awareness about the project, but we can do more to get higher amounts in."

"Brilliant idea!"

Alice's tires ground against the gravel as she pulled into the drive at Butch's house the next morning. His pickup truck was parked out front, the back full of empty boxes. When she got out of her car, he was standing on the porch to greet her, hands in the pockets of his overalls, a smile showing under that burly beard of his.

"Morning!" he said, his voice bellowing out toward her.

"Morning, Butch!" Alice grabbed the ream of tissue paper and the bag of tags she'd created and shut her car door. "What are all the boxes there?"

Butch's eyebrows raised and he let out a huff of air. "Freight boxes—I got them all from the local grocer before he threw them out. We'll grab a few for the birds. The rest are for me to put my things in when I move."

Alice climbed the three porch steps to face him. "Did Jack find you a new place to live?" Wouldn't that be wonderful? She hoped Jack had uncovered someplace amazing where Butch could spend his days making those birds of his and relaxing.

"Yep. He sure did." He eyed the bag of tags and then turned toward the door. "Come on inside." Butch let her in first, following behind her.

"That's wonderful!" Alice said, looking over her shoulder at him as she headed into the small kitchen and took a seat in front of about a hundred birds, all brightly painted. She could just imagine the little country kitchen where Butch would have pies cooling in the breeze from the ocean coming through the window.

She dropped the tags and tissue and picked one up, so thrilled to see what the artist had done. "Where's the new house?" she asked, peering at the blue wing on one of the birds.

"Chicago."

She looked up.

"But you said…"

"Yeah, I know what I said." His lips were pursed, defeat in his eyes. He reached into the bag Alice had brought and pulled out one of the tags, smiling as he read it. Then, his smile dropped. "There isn't anything here for rent at the moment and nothing worth buying. And the more I think about it, the more I realize that I'd give up all this to be closer to Jack. In the end, it's memories of my son that will carry me."

Alice thought about her own father and how far away from each other they were now. She knew what Butch meant about making memories. They didn't even have to be big memories to be important. Alice remembered the day her father had gotten a new sprinkler to attach to the hose. He had a bare spot in the back yard that he'd seeded and needed to water. Just to keep Henry busy, her father had asked him to help test it to make sure it worked. He'd turned it on in the grass, the sprinkler heads sending wild, circular streams of water into the air, soaking them both. Instead of ducking and running, her father had started to dance, jumping over the spray, and running into it. Henry had doubled over laughing, his clothes completely drenched. He still talked about that day whenever they went to the home improvement store. Now that they lived so far from each other, their memories would be limited, and Alice wasn't so sure she was comfortable with that.

So Butch had a point. But, while he'd be close to his son, would Jack be working too much to see him? Would he leave Butch alone in that apartment, where Butch didn't really want to be?

"But…" Alice remembered what he'd said about listening to the waves and baking his pies. She was willing to bet that he'd spent his whole life clean-shaven, hair combed, shaking the hands of strangers, bustling by shops and restaurants with no time to spend in them. She looked at those overalls he had on, that beard he'd been growing for quite some time, and she knew that he was ready to slow down—he'd said so himself. "Jack must know that's not what you want."

Butch offered a knowing smile. "Of course he does. But what's he to do?" With a cough, as if to clear the air, he said, "Don't fret over me. I'll be fine. Let's get these birds packed up so you can get them on display. I'm excited to see what you do with them."

Alice tried to disregard the guilt and worry she had for Butch, focusing on the bird in her hand. She set it down carefully and pulled out the first tag. "This one says, 'The ocean will give you answers whenever you're ready to ask.'"

Butch smiled, but it didn't reach his eyes.

"That was something my gramps always told me." Funny how much more complicated it was than that.

Sasha gave Alice an affectionate pat on the shoulder. Alice had been peeking out the front window since she'd gotten home from Butch's. She'd given Einstein a bath and even tied a big blue ribbon around his neck. She couldn't wait to see Henry. When her father pulled into the front drive, Alice went zooming out the door to greet them.

"Mom!" Henry called out, as he pushed open the car door and jumped onto the gravel. He ran, throwing his arms around her once he got to her. "I did so much with Grandpa Frank! We took a monster truck ride! And we went fishing! And guess what! We went to a fair and ate cotton candy and I had a caramel apple—I've never had one of those. Have you?" He didn't even let her answer, barely taking a breath. "Grandpa Frank let me stay up late! We watched movies and we slept in our sleeping bags!"

Alice's father stepped up beside Henry, giving Alice a hug.

"Oh my gosh!" she finally cut in. "It sounds like you had a blast. Well, the fun isn't over quite yet."

That was enough to quiet Henry.

"Go see what's inside."

Henry bolted into the house, and Alice laughed when she heard Henry's squeal as he saw Einstein. Through the front door window, she could see Henry as he nearly tackled Einstein, the puppy kissing his face relentlessly. They rolled around on the floor together, Einstein's joyful whimpers so loud she could hear them through the door. Henry came up for breath and Einstein jumped up and kissed him again, nudging his hand to request more affection. Henry threw his arms around the puppy's neck, burying his face in his fur.

"I had a ball with Henry," her father said, his eyes, too, on Henry and his dog. "But I don't know how you keep up with him day in and day out." He chuckled. "My back is killing me."

"Well, I don't sleep in sleeping bags every night, and eat junk, and stay up late." She winked at him to let him know she was only teasing. "He'll remember that for the rest of his life." As she said it, the memories of her visits to Gramps came into her mind. She wondered if Gramps had been as sore and tired after she'd left as her father was now. If he had been, he'd have never let on that he was.

"Mind if I soak in some of this glorious sunshine and fresh air and stay a while? You can show me all the things you've done with the place. I can't wait to hear all about it now that Henry isn't hurrying me out the door." He offered another smile.

"Why don't you stay over tonight? I really want to spend some time with Henry right now—I'm sure he wants to get into the ocean— but you can relax on the patio and then tonight we could hang out." That would give her the perfect opportunity to discuss Grace with him.

"Hang out?" The idea clearly delighted him and she could tell he was considering it. "Let me think... I have a doctor's appointment tomorrow afternoon. And I haven't packed for a night away."

"You can leave first thing in the morning. And Stop & Shop down the road has toothbrushes and T-shirts. I don't mind doing laundry if you need me to."

"You've sold me. Hanging out it is!"

"Awesome! I'm so excited! I'll just see what Henry wants to do. Let's go in and you can make yourself comfortable."

When they entered the shop, Alice's father was visibly astounded as he finally had a real chance to take in all the changes. She left him, head tilted back, eyes roaming the space, greeting Sasha while her friend told him about their plans. Alice walked over to Henry. He was in the corner on the floor, Einstein in his lap, his arms still around the puppy. They'd definitely missed each other.

"Where was he?" Henry said, burying his face in Einstein's fur once more.

"A lady named June found him and took care of him for us. The reason we couldn't find him was because he was all warm and snuggly in her house. She even bought him a collar."

Henry slipped his finger under the collar to inspect it before giving Einstein another hug. "I missed him so much."

"I know. I've fixed the door so he can't get out again, but he's been by my side ever since he came back, so I don't know if he'd run off anyway. I think he knows what happened."

Einstein looked up at her, his tongue hanging out of his mouth in happiness.

"Want to go outside and get into the waves?" she asked, kneeling down beside them and stroking Einstein. The puppy nudged her hand and whined.

"I will in a little while," Henry said. "I just want to see Einstein right now. I thought he was lost and we'd never find him."

Alice kissed the top of Henry's head. "Well, Grandpa Frank and I will be out on the patio whenever you're ready. Just put Einstein in the crate before you come out, okay?"

"Okay." He looked up at her, his eyes big, complete contentment on his face. It was so good to have him home. She couldn't wait to tuck him into bed tonight, once he'd settled down and the house was quiet, so she could hear all about his time with her dad. His little voice, telling her his stories, would be music to her ears.

Alice went back over to her father and Sasha. "We've started hanging those birds, but we've got a ton more to do. They're a fundraiser to increase resources for the pier. We're going to auction them off."

"Did you hear it's closing?" Sasha said, grabbing a bird from the box and tying a tag to its wing.

"No, I hadn't. That's shocking. It's been around for at least a hundred years in one form or another."

"I know," Alice said. "And we need it for business. I'm scrambling for ideas to save it."

"Sometimes it just takes time to put things right, you know?" Alice's father said.

She nodded, still thinking. Had she done enough? Would Seaside Sprinkles be a success? Would people invest in the pier and bring the area back to its bustling glory? Only time would tell.

"Wanna go outside?" he asked.

She snapped out of her worries and turned her attention to him. "Yes! Actually, I have something I'd like to show you. Why don't you go on outside and get comfortable? I'll make us some iced tea and meet you out there."

"I'm heading into town to see Sam," Sasha said. "I won't be long." She winked at Alice, her eyebrows dancing up and down, making Alice laugh.

While Alice's father went outside, she grabbed the locket from the counter, slowing down to open it. She needed a minute more with this little stranger before she heard her story. She was certain her father would have answers because he was the only one left to ask, and she needed a second to prepare herself. Would he tell her something life-changing? Would he know where Grace was? Would he be upset when she asked him? She closed it and slipped it into her pocket. Then she poured them both two brimming iced teas and dropped a lemon wedge on the top.

Once she got to the patio, she handed him a glass and sat down. Her mind was going a hundred miles an hour as she prepared herself for what she wanted to ask about Grace. It hadn't really hit her until this moment, but she was about to ask her father if he had another daughter. What if he'd fathered another child with someone else? What if he'd been unfaithful to her mother? What if something had happened to Grace and Alice was about to bring back terribly painful memories?

"Thank you, kindly," her father said, holding his glass up as if he were toasting something. He tipped it up to his lips carefully, and she realized she'd filled it too high, her mind on Grace. He swallowed his sip slowly and then said, "It's a scorcher today, isn't it?"

She couldn't think about anything but the mysterious Grace.

He swirled his drink around, the ice clinking in the sweating glass. It was so hot that the moment she'd walked outside with the drinks, condensation had formed on the outside of them, cooling her fingers. But the heat didn't bother her right now—she barely noticed it. Her own glass began to wobble with her shaking hands, so she set it down on the table and pushed her fingers between her knees to keep them steady.

"The summer's just getting started," she managed.

Henry opened the door, his swim trunks on and a towel over his shoulder. It was the big blue one he always used to dry off after he spent the day catching waves. He grabbed his boogie board, which was leaning against the building. "I'm going into the ocean!" he said, oblivious to their conversation. "Einstein's in his crate, Mom."

"Okay, honey."

Henry ran down over the dune.

"Hey, I have something I want to show you." The words gushed out as Henry broke the tension, and before she could second-guess her decision to bring it up. Alice reached into her pocket and pulled out the locket, handing it to him. "I was wondering… do you… by chance…" She took in a steadying breath. "Do you remember anyone by the name of Grace?" she asked, praying he'd give her an answer that explained the situation easily. Could it all just be some sort of a misunderstanding?

Her father's face suddenly went white as a ghost, his glass tipping in his hand, and her fears were confirmed. The last thing she wanted was to upset him—he'd been the one person who'd been there every single minute for her after her mother had died, in her darkest hours, and she didn't want to put any unnecessary pressure on him. His iced tea started to spill.

"Careful!" she said, reaching for the drink. Startled, he looked down at it, straightening it up before the tea poured into his lap. He put the glass down and, with trembling fingers, tried to open the locket. His breathing had sped up, two creases now between his eyes as his burly fingers tried unsuccessfully to unfasten it. Finally, Alice reached over and pried it open with her fingernail. "Are you okay?"

He was silent.

"Who is that?" she nearly whispered, tapping the photo of the mystery baby.

He didn't answer. He just stared at the photo, his lips trembling in an odd way that she hadn't seen since her mother's funeral. "Grace," he said in a whisper, his eyes filling with tears.

For a moment, she didn't say anything, waiting for him to manage whatever it was that was obviously affecting him—it looked like a hundred different thoughts on his face. His hand continued to shake, the open locket in his palm. He looked out at the ocean, his expression frantic, and she wondered if he was looking for answers there like Gramps had always taught them to do.

"Who is that?" she pressed—calmly, to let him know it was okay to tell her.

He finally looked over, meeting her eyes. "Your sister."

Chapter Twenty-Three

Alice looked back down at the locket in her father's hand, confusion wreaking havoc in her head. So many questions were pelting her at once. Her entire life, she'd wanted a sister, someone she could confide in, someone who shared all the same memories and genetics, who responded to things like she would because they were raised the same way.

But it was clear that this sister would be different. Whoever she was.

An unexpected pulse of anger shot through her, as Alice wondered why her father hadn't told her the truth before. And he was only telling her now because he'd been cornered. What if she hadn't found the locket? Would he have ever told her she had a sister? Why hadn't her mother ever said anything?

"Where is she?" Alice asked, her whole body trembling, overwhelmed. Even more questions had surfaced, but this one seemed like the most important, so she asked it first.

"I don't know." Alice's father set the locket on the table and ran his hands over his face.

"She's your daughter? Is she Mom's too?"

"Yes." He closed his eyes, a tear escaping down his cheek.

Alice looked out at the ocean, but all she saw was Henry. She thought about how many Christmases and Thanksgivings she'd spent with Aunt Claire and Uncle George. How she and her cousin Susie had grown up together, shared birthdays together… Did Grace have a family? How many years had Henry missed with his own aunt?

"I need answers, Dad." She deserved to know the whole story. And she wanted to hear it right now. She couldn't live for another minute without finding out where this lost member of her family was. She was out there somewhere, and Alice wanted to get every bit of information she could from her father before she set out to find her.

Her father traced the rim of his glass, and it looked as though he were holding it for support, the ice tinkling with the quivering of his hands. Alice reached over, her own hands shaking terribly, and tried to steady them. He looked up at her gratefully and she could tell by his eyes that he was ready to tell her.

"Your mom and I were so young—only seventeen. We were babies ourselves. We didn't know how to raise a child." He looked out over the ocean and she followed his gaze past Henry this time, the vast expanse of blue pushing and pulling, as unsettled as Alice's heart. "We came here to your gramps's and lived for the nine months so no one would know, because we just didn't think we could deal with revisiting what we were about to do throughout our lives. I couldn't handle anyone bringing it up or showing me pity. Your grandma wasn't doing well, and Gramps was wrapped up in her heart problems, spending long hours at the hospital with her. It was quite a difficult period before they'd managed to get her stable. At that time, it was touch and go—we had no idea that she'd be all right and eventually be able to help us raise a little girl. And we knew we'd need help. We were still growing up ourselves.

"It was a secret your mother and I had to bear alone. Grace was born, and we decided adoption would be the best way to go. We went to the hospital, and after eight hours of labor, we kissed Grace and watched two strangers take her away."

His eyes filled with tears, his lips wobbling. Alice had never seen her father so vulnerable. The strong man who had carried her through her mother's death, who'd helped her with every obstacle she'd had in life, wasn't as resilient today. Her heart broke for him.

"It was the hardest moment of my life. And your mother's."

Alice had only been nineteen when she'd had Henry. Just two years older. Her parents had rallied around her. But she knew that even though Grandma had been okay through her childhood, she'd been frail, and Alice couldn't imagine the demands a new baby would've put on her heart—all the sleep deprivation, and the ups and downs of caring for a new life.

She remembered that day in the hospital when she'd held Henry in her arms for the first time. She thought about what it would feel like to just give him away, never seeing his little eyes open and look up at her, never feeling his tiny fingers as they wrapped themselves around hers, never hearing his soft breathing as he lay on her chest. The lump in her throat got bigger and she had to blink away her tears.

"I kept Henry," she said, barely able to get the words out, wishing they'd have found a way to do the same, and knowing her parents and grandparents were faced with an unthinkable decision.

He nodded. "You have always been an old soul. Your mother and I weren't nearly as mature as you were at that age. You've been amazing with Henry. But I don't know if we'd have been as great as you are." He wound his fingers with hers and squeezed. "We felt like this time we could do it. If you needed us, we were there. And you were amazing. You always have been."

"Why didn't you ever tell me?" She felt betrayed by their silence. Even Gramps, who'd been the closest person to her, had known and hadn't said a word. No one had. "Why didn't anyone tell me?"

Henry dove into the water, throwing himself onto his board, his arms paddling furiously, his belly pressed against it, as he maneuvered himself to the crest of a wave. It bubbled and gurgled beneath him, sending him sliding up onto the sand. Alice looked back at her dad.

"Why? Why didn't you tell me?" she repeated, realizing her father hadn't answered. She understood that her parents hadn't wanted to revisit that pain but surely she had a right to know?

"Your mother and I talked about it all the time. But in the end, we decided she hadn't belonged to us, really. Grace belonged to another family; we just brought her into the world for them. We needed to let them have their little girl with no strings attached. Your mother would cry, thinking about what it would be like for anyone to come into our lives and disrupt what we had with you, and she couldn't bring herself to do that to Grace. We both loved Grace enough to let her belong to her family without our interference. In the end, we decided to give her the gift of happiness."

"But what if Grace had wanted to know? What if she'd wanted to know *us*?"

Tears spilled over his eyes and he let them fall. "Then that would be up to her parents to tell her. It isn't my place. It never has been."

"I don't agree."

The locket sat open on the table, both babies looking back at her: she and her sister. That locket was the only way the two of them had ever been together and now she felt a hole in her life that she wished had been filled. She thought again how she'd always yearned for a sister—was it because she'd had one and was missing her, and some cosmic force in the back of her mind had always told her that?

"Gramps left a letter. He was going to leave the bike shop to both Grace and me. I don't know why he changed his mind at the end, but I can't let it go that he originally wanted us both to have it."

She could tell in his face that he already knew this information, making her feel even more left out of things.

"I told him not to leave it to Grace. I explained it the same way I just explained it to you. She belongs to someone else."

"But you're not giving her a choice in the matter!" Frustration was causing her voice to rise and she was glad for the charging surf and the constant wind to drown out her volume. "*You're* deciding for her. Because that's what makes you feel better about the whole thing."

She bit her lip, wishing she hadn't said that last sentence. She hadn't meant it that way. Her mother and father had made an honorable decision, and Grace probably had a much better life because of it. She was letting her anger over not having a choice dictate her words.

"I'm sorry." Alice hung her head. "That was awful of me. I just meant that—"

"We knew this day might come. Your mother and I were very worried about the decision we made not to tell anyone. We were down here, had the baby—even your Aunt Claire and Uncle George didn't know anything had happened—and then we went back to our regular lives. Your mom and I went off to college, and after, we got married. Then, when we were financially able, we planned our little family and had you. We were scared about whether our decision not to tell you, in particular, was the right one. But in the end, we decided together that we couldn't second-guess ourselves. We'd made a choice to move on and, while we missed Grace every single day, and we both ached for her, we had to move forward as if our choice were the only choice. Because if we didn't, we'd both go crazy. We weren't withholding it from everyone. We were simply carving out the two separate families that had now been created: ours and Grace's."

"Do you know anything about her at all? Where she is? Who her adoptive parents are? Anything?"

"We met them just once in the hospital but asked not to know their names."

"Do you ever wonder if she feels abandoned by you?"

"I pray that she is adored by her family and doesn't even consider that feeling. That would be my hope for her. Although, I love her so much and in my heart, I've never abandoned her. I've wondered about her childhood, about her high school years, whether she went to college…" He picked up the locket again and stroked the baby's face, tears resurfacing. "It's easy to say now that we should've done this or could've done that, but every single minute of our lives after giving her up, we thought about what we'd decided. I woke up in a cold sweat some nights, thinking about her, praying I'd done the right thing. And there were times your mother broke down and feared she'd made the wrong decision." He closed the locket and looked out at Henry. "What got us through those nights was the memory of the tears in Grace's new parents' eyes, and the smiles that nearly split their faces when they looked at her."

The more her father explained, the more her anger and hurt subsided, and she knew that she, too, had to trust her parents' decision. And she also knew they hadn't made it lightly. "I'm sorry I snapped at you," she said. "I should've known that you always make good choices. You've never steered me wrong. What you and Mom did took so much courage and you did the right thing. I believe it."

"Thank you," he said, squeezing her hand. "I'm glad you know now. Where did you find this locket, anyway? It was your mother's."

"Oh, I thought it belonged to Grandma. It was in Gramps's trunk."

"When your mother died, the pain of losing her intensified my anxiety over leaving Grace and not ever knowing her, and every time I saw the locket, I felt it, so I gave it to your grandma."

"Did Mom wear it?"

"Every day. Under her clothes."

Now that she thought about it, Alice did remember seeing that delicate gold chain at the neck of her mother's shirts. She'd always had it on, but it hadn't occurred to Alice that it was anything more than just her favorite necklace.

Her father cleared his throat, emotion surfacing again. "Just before she died, she gave it to me and said not to bury her with it. She wanted me to save it, but she never told me what to do with it. I thought it was so odd that she didn't want to take it with her in the end. But now I wonder if she had some sort of sense of all this now. She hated keeping the truth from you after Henry was born, but we'd decided that either way—whichever direction we chose to go—it would be life-changing. It was best to just keep things as simple as possible. We didn't know how Grace's parents would feel about her family tracking her down; I have no idea if they even told her she was adopted."

"Maybe it's best not to try to find her then," she said, wishing there could be some other way. She wanted so badly to know her sister. With a deep breath, she looked out at the endless ocean for those answers that never seemed to come.

Chapter Twenty-Four

Alice spent the entire evening with her father and Henry, riding in the waves, building sandcastles, and basking in the sun, only going inside right before bedtime when night finally made its appearance. Henry had fallen into bed and stroked Einstein until they were both fast asleep together. She'd peered down at him, his arm around his puppy, the two of them completely content. Unable to bring herself to wake up Einstein and put him in the crate, she did a quick puppy-proof of the room and left him in Henry's bed. Einstein had spent a long time away from his boy, and Henry had spent too many days without his dog. They needed to be together tonight.

They were still asleep this morning when her father gave Sasha a kiss and said goodbye, before he and Alice took a moment together on the front porch. They sat side by side on the step, the coastal breeze gentle this morning, the heat heavy. It was already bright and sunny, birds flying overhead, a few tourists walking down the road to the public beach access, surfboards under their arms. Her dad had his legs stretched out, his heels in the sand of the walkway, his fingers spread along the step, and the paper cup of coffee and egg sandwich she'd made wrapped up beside him.

"I missed you," Alice said, putting a hand on his.

He turned his hand over and clasped it around Alice's. "I'm not so sure about this drive every time I need to see you and Henry." He had a smile on his face, obviously glad Alice was doing what she was doing with the shop, but his words were serious.

"I know. But once we get settled, you can come and stay for weeks at a time." She beamed at him, the idea of it so wonderful that she could feel the excitement bubbling up inside.

Today felt like the first day of her future. She'd slept like a rock last night, her worries about Grace subsiding for the moment, the sound of the ocean through the open window lulling her into a deep sleep. She wasn't sure why, but she felt like she'd find her. Somehow. And, while she wanted to mention her sister to her dad this morning, she didn't. She'd leave things where they were right now and focus on what she could control. Finding that locket and finally talking to her dad had made her feel like her gramps, her grandma, and her mom were all up there rooting for them, wishing them the best, and cheering them on.

"Well," her dad said, dropping her hand and standing up, the sun causing him to squint as he looked at her. "I'd better head out toward home before the tourists fill up the bypass. They'll all be checking out and heading home in an hour or so. You know how Sundays get."

She smiled again at him, her happiness coming from being able to see him, to be near him, and to share her feelings with him like she always had.

"Give Henry lots of hugs from his Grandpa Frank."

"I will."

Then, armed with the coffee and the sandwich, he set off.

Alice went in and quietly got Einstein up, walked him, and then spent the next hour telling Sasha all about Grace.

"Do you think you'll search for her?" Sasha, appearing much more rested than she had after her last date with Sam, was cooking a late breakfast, pouring her egg mixture into the same pan Alice had used earlier.

"Probably not," she said, trying to hide her disappointment. She wasn't going to let it get her down today. If they were meant to find each other, they would. She had to believe that. She took a glass of orange juice to one of the café tables and dropped down into a chair. "It just doesn't seem like I should. Even though I'd love to know who she is. What if she wonders about me?"

"Or has no idea you exist." Sasha scraped back and forth in the pan with her spatula, mixing the eggs. "I know she'd want to know you, though. You're so much fun!"

"Haha. Thanks." Alice tipped her glass and looked down into the yellow liquid, the pulp swirling around. Then she took a sip.

There was a creak on the floorboards and Henry came into the kitchen, his white-blond hair sticking up in every possible direction, his eyes still sleepy. He'd had a great time with his Grandpa Frank, and by the way he'd slept in, it was clear that Alice's father had run him to the point of exhaustion. She remembered visits like that with Gramps.

"Morning, sleepy head!" she said.

Einstein ran over to him, jumping up and putting his paws on Henry's chest, nearly knocking him over, the puppy's tail wagging feverishly as his back claws tapped the hardwoods. Henry hugged him back and the two of them came over to the table, Henry sitting beside Alice and Einstein settling on the floor.

"Want some eggs?" Sasha called from the stove, where she was still scrambling.

"Yes, please," Henry said.

Einstein barked.

"Not for you," Sasha teased the dog. "But if you're nice, your mom might get you a treat from the jar."

Einstein barked again and this time, Melly appeared in the room. "Morning!" she said. "I used the hide-a-key you told me about." On their movie night, Alice had thanked her, telling her what a great friend she was already. They'd divulged the location of the hide-a-key in case she ever needed it and told her she was welcome anytime. She had her camera with her, her hair pulled up into a wispy bun, a light slick of gloss on her lips.

"Did you see the sign on the pier? I was out taking photos of the surf when I noticed it," Melly said, smiling.

Alice had walked Einstein up the beach the other direction from the pier, so she hadn't even looked in that direction. She abandoned her orange juice and stood up to see. Henry stayed with Einstein as Alice followed Melly down to the lot in front of the shop.

Tied to the pier was an enormous banner. With a gasp, she flew back in to tell Sasha, taking the stairs two at a time and leaving the door open for Melly to follow.

"Sasha! There's a sign on the pier! It says, 'Seagull's Cove will be opening in its new location! Coming soon!'" She ran over to her friend, hugging her, nearly knocking the spatula from her hands and making her laugh.

"That's amazing!" Sasha said.

Then Alice let the excitement settle as she sat down at the table. She could feel it was a good day. "We aren't out of the woods, though. It's a great start, for sure. But it isn't a guarantee that the pier will succeed. The aquarium was pretty big, and yet it still didn't bring in enough revenue."

Melly, who'd made herself at home next to Alice, turned her camera around, showing Alice a close-up of her and Sasha as she had thrown her arms around her and hugged her just now. The shot looked like some sort of movie poster. Melly wrinkled her nose with a smile and turned it back around to view it again. "I'll get it to you later."

Sasha turned off the stove and came over to join them, setting a plate of eggs in front of Henry and then another for herself. "Yes, but it's a sign!" she said. "Things will work out! You have to open yourself up to it and *believe* it! And we'll raise so much money for it that it will be better than it has ever been!"

Alice giggled, covering her mouth in excitement, allowing Sasha's optimism to take hold. She wasn't sure what had come over her today, but she felt great.

Sasha picked up Melly's camera and looked at the photo she'd taken of them. "If you're always taking pictures, how will you ever get any of yourself? We need you in the shot." She held the camera out to her friend.

Melly smiled, clearly happy to be included. She took the camera and stood up, setting it across from them on the counter and hitting a few buttons. Then she went back to the table, stood between Sasha and Alice, and put her arms around them as the camera started to beep.

"Say cheese!" she said with a laugh.

The camera snapped, capturing the three of them—grinning, arms around each other—new and old friends.

Melly clapped her hands, clearly thrilled by everything. "I'm so happy for you two!" she said. "I had to come tell you as soon as I saw the sign."

"I'm glad you did!" Sasha said. "Want some breakfast?"

"No, I've already had some, thanks. I was up early today. I had an appointment with a real estate agent."

"For?" Alice asked.

"I'm going to have to sell my cottage or at least rent it out. I won't be able to pay the mortgage once I don't have a job." She turned her head toward the open window, the breeze getting just a little too warm to keep it open anymore. But the sound of the tide was so calming that Alice had left it open regardless.

"But you love that cottage. It's your rainy-day cottage," Sasha said, a mouthful of scrambled egg on her fork.

"I know." Tears surfaced, but Melly blinked them away, clearly to avoid putting a dampener on the moment. "I just don't know what else to do," she said, forcing a smile. "This is where I want to be. I don't want to live anywhere else." She took in a deep breath and let it out. "That was why I was at the beach taking photos. It's my favorite thing to do. It relaxes me. And even if I have to move, I'll always have those pictures to remind me of how great it is here."

The thought occurred to Alice that Butch could rent or even buy Melly's cottage, but she didn't mention it. Getting Melly a tenant or buyer would solve the problem of paying the mortgage, but it wouldn't fix the fact that she would have to leave, and by her tears, it was clear she didn't want to. Alice needed to think it through before mentioning the idea.

Alice had been weighing the pros and cons as they all sat on the beach together after breakfast, while Henry alternated between building a large trench, filling it with seawater, and playing in the waves. They'd been quiet, sunning themselves and enjoying the day, until Melly had gone home to get ready for her shift, leaving just Sasha and Alice.

Having Butch across the street would give him a place to live very close to where Jack had wanted to make a forever home for him.

Alice and Sasha would have a wonderful neighbor, because Butch was amazing, and she might get to see Jack when he visited. But on the other hand, did she want to see Jack? What if he came to visit years from now and he brought a girlfriend or a wife—could she handle that? And then there was Melly. She didn't want her friend to leave. Where would she go? Alice worried she'd lose touch with her.

"Mom," Henry said. "There's a boy over there!" He pointed down the shore. "Can I go down and say hello?"

The boy looked about Henry's age, lanky with fine brown hair, playing outside of a cottage a few doors down. It was the cottage with a flag on the deck that pictured the Bodie Island Lighthouse against a bright blue background. She'd noticed the cottage before; it was covered in light yellow shingles with white trim, and a wooden sign above the front door said Beachin' It. The boy was digging a hole in the sand and filling it with water, running back and forth to the breaking waves with an orange bucket just like Henry had done.

"Of course you can say hello!"

Without another word, Henry dropped his boogie board at Alice's feet and ran down the beach, arms pumping, his eagerness to meet someone his age clear.

"Look at him," Alice said to Sasha. "He's so excited! Oh, I hope it's a resident and not a vacationer. I'd love it if he could make a friend."

Sasha straightened her aviators to get a better view of the two boys. "He will, Alice. Just give him time. He hasn't started school yet."

"I don't want him to have to wait for school. That's still months away. I want him to have someone to play with this summer." She looked down the beach again. Henry was squatting next to the boy, talking, helping him dig. The sight filled her with happiness.

"I get that, though. I like meeting people around us. I don't want Melly to leave. It's nice having a friend across the street. And I really like her."

"Me too." Alice brushed the sand off her leg where the wind had blown it onto her skin. "And she seems so broken up about it. Imagine putting all this work in, only to be forced out of our home. Maybe it's because we met her here, but I can't imagine her living anywhere but in the Outer Banks. With us. And Melly wants to stay so badly." She couldn't help but feel frustrated with the hospital for bringing two wonderful people into her life, only to have them both taken away. But she knew she was just trying to blame someone. Things happen that are simply beyond anyone's control. The key was picking up the pieces and moving forward. Even when she felt sometimes like she couldn't.

Alice looked out at their little slice of paradise, the lapping waves, the bright sun, the cobalt blue sky above them. A seagull swooped down to the water and then soared back up. She knew exactly how Melly felt. She wondered what the purpose in it all was. Why had Melly been able to make all those plans—working here and buying the cottage—if she wasn't meant to stay? Why had Alice and Sasha become friends with Melly? For that matter, why had Alice reconnected with Jack after all these years? Would it have been better to have never met either of them? That didn't seem right either. Was it all so Butch could have a place to retire? Perhaps…

"I was going to suggest that Jack get in touch with her to rent her cottage for Butch." As she said it, the idea was bittersweet.

Sasha didn't respond, and Alice wondered if she was thinking the same thing. Sasha, too, had said how wonderful it was to have met Melly. They'd all just fallen in together, like old friends.

Henry and the little boy ran up to their chairs. "Mom, this is Simon," Henry said. "He lives in that cottage right there!" He pointed to the yellow bungalow just behind the sea oats. "He's five too!"

"That's wonderful, Henry! Hi, Simon."

"Hello," the boy said.

His skin was bronze from all the sun he'd clearly had, and his green eyes looked like crystals against it. She couldn't believe they hadn't run into him before now.

"Can Henry keep digging with me?"

"Of course! Just stay where I can see you, okay, Henry?"

"Okay!" Henry grabbed Simon's arm and they ran back down the beach, leaving Alice with her thoughts once more.

Chapter Twenty-Five

"I wonder what Jack's up to," Alice said cautiously to Sasha as she pulled a baseball cap over her ponytail. "I texted that I wanted to talk to him about moving Butch to Chicago, and he asked me if I could clear my schedule and be ready to go with Henry and Einstein in an hour." She wasn't entirely sure she wanted to involve Henry in meeting Jack today. She knew it was because Henry would fall for Jack just like she had, and in the end, when it was time for Jack to leave, he'd be heartbroken. She wanted to protect him from that feeling. But Sasha had her last checkup today to make sure the medication was working and her blood pressure was okay, and Sam had asked her to lunch after, so Alice hadn't wanted to ask if she'd watch Henry for her.

Sasha offered an excited look. "What has the wonderful and gorgeous Jack got in store for you two? I love surprises."

"We're both to wear our swimsuits."

"Sounds like a good time! I can't wait to hear all about it when you get home!"

Alice finished rounding up Einstein and Henry just as Jack pulled up in Butch's old pickup truck. It had one long bench across the front, so when Alice opened the door, she let Henry and Einstein get in first. Once she'd climbed inside and shut them all in, she looked over at Jack.

He gave her that same crooked grin she'd seen during the darts game. The old truck engine groaned as he pulled out onto Beach Road. Alice threw a hand out the window to Sasha and off they went.

"Where are you taking us?" she asked, leaning around Henry and Einstein.

"It's a surprise! Just enjoy the ride." Jack turned up the radio, beach tunes sailing through the air as the warm wind forced its way through the open windows, blowing around them. Einstein crawled across her, settling in her lap, and rested his head on the open window. Henry was buckled in the center seat between them and Alice noticed the admiration in Henry's eyes when he looked at Jack, making her uneasy. Unable to change the situation, she looked away at the beach as it slipped past them, trying to enjoy the ride.

They exited the bypass onto a narrow road that led to a small inlet. With the slower speed, the hot air crept in and Einstein started panting. Despite that, he seemed so happy to be with them. When they got to the beach, with a bump, Jack pulled the truck onto the sand. "Unbuckle your belt and hop on my lap, Henry. You can drive us." He pointed down the beach. It was secluded, not a soul in sight, a few pelicans finding their meal and then settling in the tall grass at the edge.

Henry searched his mother's face for permission.

"Go ahead," she said.

Henry climbed onto Jack's lap, taking the wheel as it jiggled, Alice putting her arm in front of Einstein to settle him. Jack shifted gears and showed Henry how to maneuver around the dips in the sand. Alice tried to commit every single image to memory so that once Jack was gone, on those cold, lonely winter nights, she could remember this. She took in Henry's smile and uncertainty; the way

Jack's hands were on the seat on either side of him to allow Henry to steer, his foot gently pressing the gas pedal; the orange glare from the sun on the windshield; the tilt of Jack's head, and the softness of his voice as he guided her son. Einstein had crawled across her lap again and was resting quietly in the spot where Henry had sat, and, in that moment, it was as if the world had aligned, all the worries out of her head, and she could just be present right then, right there.

Jack adjusted the rearview mirror, tilting it lower. "Look at you! You're driving!" he said. "Take us down the beach to that dock, okay?" At the end of the shore, there was a small pier with a boat tied to it. The gentle waves of the sound kissed the edge of it, the water sparkling in the sunlight.

"Okay," Henry said, as he concentrated on the wheel.

Jack eased off the gas to allow Henry to get a good handle on the steering while they bumped along toward their stopping point. Henry's little hands gripped the wheel tightly, his shoulders relaxing as the truck sailed over the sand.

"Turn slightly…" Jack directed as they neared the edge of the water. Henry did as he was told.

"To the right. That's it. Just like that… Okay, now hold the wheel still." He pressed on the brakes with a gentle motion until they coasted to a stop. "Great driving!" he said, shifting the old truck into park.

Alice couldn't help but think how easily this type of living came to Jack, even though he'd spent his adult life in a city high-rise. He was so composed and careful with her son, easing Henry's nerves and making him feel comfortable. It was clear that being a doctor who worked with children had given him quite the skill in calming them, because every time Henry was with him, her son seemed as relaxed as he was with his own family.

Jack opened the door and set Henry onto the sand, hopping out behind him and grabbing Einstein's leash, coaxing him out his side of the truck. He walked around with the dog and opened Alice's door for her.

She could see the boat at the dock more clearly now. This one was more like the kind she was used to: a fishing schooner with one seat for the driver and a small bench at the back. The captain waved from the dock and Jack returned his greeting.

"Are you all ready to find some seashells?" he called out to them.

Henry looked up at Alice and she shrugged. "I don't know any more than you do," she said. "You'll have to ask Jack."

Jack tousled Henry's hair as they headed toward the boat. He was walking Einstein, and Alice tried not to think about how perfect her view was: the three of them in silhouette, like the happy ending of a movie. "This is Captain Lenny," he said. "He's going to take us out on the sound today."

Alice had wonderful memories of the sound, the stretch of peaceful water between the barrier islands of the Outer Banks and the mainland. While Gramps had assured her that there were places where the lagoon could reach twelve feet deep or more, it seemed like she could walk for miles and the water would never get above her waist. While various parts of this body of water had different names, she knew this one well: the Roanoke Sound. She and Gramps had done lots of fishing here.

"All grownups wear a life vest," Captain Lenny said, handing one to Henry with a wink. "The kids are on their own." He threw a thumb over to Alice and Jack. "I'll assist you with buckling it if you need help; just let me know." Then he stepped into the boat, the small vessel rocking with his weight, and held out a hand to Alice. "Ladies first."

She took hold of him, climbing in and steadying herself with the pole that held the small awning over the captain's seat. Then she reached out to help Henry aboard, but Jack was already lifting him in, having handed Einstein's leash to the captain. Once everyone was in the boat and seated on the bench at the back, Einstein comfortably on a cushion on the vessel's floor, Captain Lenny fired up the motor and started backing out. Within minutes, they were sailing the clear waters of the Roanoke Sound, the sun high in the blue sky above them. The wind picked up with their speed, and Einstein turned his snout toward the airstream, his ears looking as though they were pinned back.

Out of habit, Alice closed her eyes. She always used to do that when Gramps got the boat going—it made her feel like she was flying. The salty smell in the air, the spray of the water misting her from the side of the boat, the warm wind—it all took her back, and if she opened her eyes right now, she would almost swear that Gramps was driving. The only thing that told her otherwise was the absence of his voice. He would tell her the history of the area, the science of the water and the animals in it, and he'd answer her questions.

But just as she thought about that, Captain Lenny spoke. "We're headed to an uninhabited bit of land called Seashell Island." His voice sailed into her ears, making her open her eyes. The captain was still looking forward, talking while he steered the schooner, the vessel bobbing heavily as he maneuvered around choppy waters from another passing boat. "I say 'uninhabited' but there's plenty of life there, just not any pesky humans." The motor slowed as they entered a calmer area, and the captain patted the open spot on the bench where he was sitting. "Mr. Henry," he called over his shoulder. "Would you like to come up front with me? I'm going to let you pick the best part of the island to dock."

Henry's eyes rounded with excitement while he walked to the front of the boat, swaying as it rocked.

Once Henry was with Captain Lenny, Jack scooted closer to Alice. "Hi," he said, like he'd just approached her. He broke out into that gorgeous smile that could make her lose all her rational thought. "I hadn't even said hi yet." Einstein shifted on his cushion. "It's so good to see you."

The affection on his face made her all fluttery.

Jack sat back and put his arm around her, and she wished that they could sit just like that for the rest of the day.

Henry and Captain Lenny pulled the boat to a stop on the shore of the flat island, its surface covered in sea grass with the exception of the sandy beaches. Henry grabbed Einstein's leash.

"I suggest leaving your shoes on the boat," Captain Lenny said. He kicked off an old battered pair of sandals. They all followed suit and climbed out together.

Alice took Jack's hand as her feet hit the soft shore beneath her, and he let her go once she was steady. But within the silky sand, she could feel sharp protrusions. She bent down to look through the crystal-clear water to see what they were. "Look at all the seashells," she said, breathless. Through the water, and scattered around her toes, were shells in pinks, whites, pearl-colored, purple… "There are so many," she said.

"Welcome to Seashell Island," Captain Lenny said with a smile. "Now, I'm going to take Henry and his puppy down the sand a bit. You two are welcome to come with us if you'd like to hear the history of shells in the area and how they all got here." He handed Henry an old bucket. "You'll need this."

As Henry, Einstein, and the captain walked in front of them, Jack looked down at Alice. "You wanted to tell me something about Chicago?" he asked.

"Yes." Alice reached down and picked up a shell, its swirling purple and white pattern like a piece of stained glass. She rubbed it with her thumb. "I'm sure you already know that the nurses that were just hired at the hospital are being let go."

Jack nodded, somber. "Yes. In the defense of the hospital, they were told at interview that their positions could be temporary."

She didn't want to get into it, and it wasn't her place anyway. "Well, because of the cuts, Melly has to rent her cottage, or eventually sell it. Butch wouldn't be happy in Chicago... Melly's house might be perfect for him."

Consideration flooded Jack's face, and it was so clear to her in that moment how good he was. He wanted to do the right thing for his father. "Yes," he said. Then he grinned at her. "That would also mean that I'd be able to see you when I came to visit."

She'd already thought about that. A lot. But even so, the words pelted her: *when he came to visit.* Without warning, tears pricked her eyes. She looked out at Henry, breaking eye contact. Henry squatted down, his hand in the water, retrieving a shell. Einstein was on the end of the leash; Captain Lenny obviously had a good handle on him. Einstein was sniffing the shore like crazy before he stopped, lifting his paw in the hunting position. She blinked her tears away. By Jack's comment, he definitely wasn't even trying to figure out how to stay. And she couldn't expect him to. But she'd dated enough people to know that guys like Jack don't come around very often, and because of that, he'd ruined every other guy's chance because now, without a doubt, she'd compare them to him—not the teenage him, but the man he'd become.

She felt his hold on her hands, his face coming into focus.

"What is it?" His brows knitted together, the concern showing in the creases on his forehead.

"I don't want you to visit," she managed, knowing she'd picked the wrong words. She was too upset to form the whole sentence she'd wanted.

He started at her, obviously confused.

"I want you to *stay*." Her voice broke on the last word and she turned toward the water to calm herself down. "I know you can't." She didn't look at him; it was too hard.

He squeezed her hand affectionately, giving her the courage to look at him.

"There's no work for me at this hospital. Your life is in the Outer Banks. I'm scrambling for the right move, here. It's all happened so fast."

Einstein splashed in the water, making Henry laugh. Captain Lenny held out a shell and started telling Henry about it.

"Maybe it just wasn't meant to be… I often feel that," she said, "when I realize that I'm pushing too hard to make something happen." Her mind fluttered back to Matt and she squeezed her eyes shut. "I think it would be better if we didn't prolong the inevitable." She'd known she was going to get hurt and by the way her heart was breaking, she was aware that the hurt was now upon her. "You and Butch should contact Melly. It's a great place. And if you want to stop in for ice cream, we'll always be open for you."

"I wish I had an answer," Jack said, lips pursed, eyes on the sand, ignoring her last comment. "I don't right now. But it won't stop me from trying."

"The answer is: you go back to Chicago and I stay here. It's that simple."

He looked out ahead of them silently and she knew that was all they could do.

Chapter Twenty-Six

The ride back to the shop had flown by. With the salty warmth on their cheeks and the lull of the music on the radio, the old truck's engine humming, Alice's thoughts were heavy and constant, and when she'd looked up they were home.

Clearly getting back to her old self, and fueled by the obvious excitement she had after having a really wonderful time with Sam, Sasha had already found Gramps's tall ladders and set them up against the old whitewashed siding of the shop, with some of the large containers of paint lined up beside them. After years in the harsh coastal elements, the place was in need of a fresh coat, so they'd bought gallons upon gallons of white paint and, with Alice's budget getting slimmer by the minute, decided this was something they could do on their own. The interior painting had gone so well, Alice knew she could handle this. But as her eyes roamed the surface of that little fishing shack, it didn't look so little. It would take them days if not weeks to finish with just the two of them.

"Are you having some painting done?" Jack said, killing the engine and leaning toward the windshield to view Sasha's preparations.

Einstein sat up from his spot on the seat, looking around with tired eyes. He was worn out.

"Sasha and I are going to paint the house," she said.

"And me!" Henry piped up, reaching over Alice and unlatching the door. He crawled across her lap and hopped out, taking Einstein with him. "Sasha!" he said, as he ran to the doorway where she stood, Einstein bounding along beside him. "Look what I got!" Captain Lenny had asked that they throw back all the shells they found, some of them housing hermit crabs that had crawled along their hands. But he told Henry to find one empty shell that he wanted to keep as a memento.

"Sasha shouldn't be climbing high ladders in this heat yet," Jack noted, sitting back against the truck's bench seat and turning toward her. "And you can't possibly reach the roofline from that ladder."

"We'll figure it out," Alice said nonchalantly, not wanting to admit that they just didn't have enough money to hire someone, nor did they have the time to wait for a crew to get out there. She needed to get it done.

"Dad has a taller ladder." He inched forward and tipped his head up again to examine the roofline before looking cautiously at her. "I could help you paint."

She could see his uncertainty as he offered and she knew he was thinking the same thing she was: should they spend any more time together? But the fact that he had offered to help revealed his decision. "Don't you have research to do?" she asked, more so to give him one more chance to back out.

"I stayed late last night," he said with a smile. "And I've told you not to worry about me. I can get my work done. I wouldn't have offered otherwise."

If she were honest with herself, she didn't really need the help, but she just wanted to hold on to this day, even this moment, a little longer. She'd had such a wonderful time with him that she wanted to push the heartbreak away until later. Because she knew that the minute he drove away, that would be the end, and the ache in her chest would set in. She decided not to think about it, indulging herself in those green eyes instead.

"Can you imagine how straight my paint line is?" he said with a smirk, taking her hand and turning it over. He set his on top of hers, stilling all movement in her fingers with steady, purposeful effort. She imagined all the things he could do with those hands… He met her eyes as if his thoughts had moved right along with hers. "Give me twenty minutes. I'll be back with the ladder."

"I'll start on this side with Henry painting the bottom boards," Sasha said, wearing an old T-shirt that was way too big for her. Alice smiled to herself, wondering if it was Landon's and she planned to get paint all over it to spite him. That would be just like Sasha. "You and Jack take the top on the other side."

Jack had brought Butch's ladder and leaned it against the south side of the house next to Gramps's shorter ladder. They'd filled the paint buckets, and he'd climbed each ladder to hang them from the hooks by the top riser. The sun was relentless, beating down on Alice as they climbed up together.

"Brush," he said, as if he were handing her a medical instrument, reaching out to give it to her. He'd refused to let her carry anything with her to the top of the ladder.

"Thank you."

Alice took in the strength of his arms, the roundness of his chest, the way his lips moved into a slightly pursed position as he concentrated while he painted beside her. He was so familiar now, so much a part of this place and who she was here, that she didn't want to think about the days ahead without him. She dipped her brush into the paint, the gray bristles dripping with white, and dragged it along the wood, making the old paint look more dingy against the freshness of the new.

"I'm so happy for you, you know," Jack said, facing the house, his brush moving in perfect strokes along the siding. "You've done a phenomenal job. Everything looks amazing."

She was thankful for his praise, but she still wasn't convinced that she'd done enough. "Now we just have to get the people to come," she said. "June Dawson is opening Seagull's Cove on the pier—I'm excited about that. The popularity of the restaurant should help business."

"I'd heard," he said with obvious hopefulness.

He could be so upset with the fact that Butch couldn't live here, but he wasn't. He was genuinely delighted for Alice; she could sense it. That was just the kind of person Jack was. He wanted the best for everyone.

"I spoke to June about it," he said, and she had to swim out of her thoughts. "Her daughter's running it now, but she had a hand in deciding the location. She's a great woman—I've known her for years."

Alice was happy to hear that, because if Jack thought she was great, then she knew she really was. From what she'd seen of June already, she liked her. She hoped June would pop in when she was down this way; Einstein would certainly like to see her.

"You'll do just fine here," he said. "I wish I could be around longer to help in the beginning months. But June will be a wonderful mentor. She knows her stuff."

"That's an added benefit of having her nearby."

"Yes."

Jack fell into silence. He dragged his brush along one of the planks, that smile shifting to a look of contemplation. Was sadness taking over his thoughts already? She didn't want him to think about not being here, about leaving. Not yet.

Jack and Alice were still painting in the dark of night, their side of the shop illuminated by the lights from the pier. Neither of them had articulated exactly why they'd kept going after Sasha and Henry had gone in to have dinner, Sasha offering to help Henry to bed so they could finish. But Alice knew why she'd continued, her arm aching from the long hours: because she didn't want the day to end. If she thought about it, she'd start to panic, so she just kept painting.

Jack had brought a change of clothes in the truck so he wouldn't get paint on the seats when he went home, but it was so late—and he wanted to be at the hospital very early the next morning—that it made more sense to just sleep on this side of town instead of driving all the way inland to Butch's. Alice had lost her resolve. She had completely fallen for Jack Murphy and when he'd asked if he could crash on her couch, against every rational thought she had, she'd said yes.

He'd showered at Alice's and settled on the sofa upstairs. Sasha had turned in already, giving them some time alone. After taking her own shower, Alice had just checked on Henry, who was fast asleep, when she joined him.

"You smell like me," she said with a giggle.

His thick hair was wet and combed. He leaned back onto the sofa, his shoulders relaxed, a content look on his face. "I used your shampoo," he admitted with a grin.

He looked tired, and if he was half as exhausted as she was, they had a problem because the sofa looked a little shorter than he was and he'd never fit there.

"What are you thinking about?" he asked, putting his arm behind her and scooting closer.

"You don't fit on this sofa."

His head tilted adorably as he tried to make sense of her comment. It only took a second before she could see his mind whirring, his gaze moving down the hallway toward her room.

That feeling started to creep in again: the panic. Because she knew she wanted to have him with her, to have his arms around her, to wake up to his face in the morning. "I can fit on the sofa," she said, trying to squash any ideas he might be having, as well as her own.

"I'd never take your bed from you. Plus, I might as well push through till morning. I'm wide awake." He yawned, making them both laugh.

Her mind wandered again to what it would be like to fall asleep beside him in the darkness. She wondered where he'd rest his hands, how they'd fit together, the steadiness of his breathing as he lay beside her. There was no way she was sharing her bed with anyone while Henry was around to witness it. She swallowed, trying to rein her thoughts in.

The truth was that she used to imagine what it might be like to spend every day with someone like Jack, to fall asleep at night with him and open her eyes to her perfect person, the one she'd spend her whole life with. She'd try to fit the person she was dating into that picture and it was a little like putting the wrong puzzle piece into place, bending the edges, pushing too hard to make it fit. But with Jack, she could picture it so easily: rolling over in the morning to that smile, those green eyes crinkling at the edges, his arms wrapping around her; sitting together at the breakfast table while he read the paper and she poured cereal for Henry, Einstein at his feet; kissing him goodbye before he left for work. The ease of being with him hit her right then and she let her smile fade away, a pain in her chest taking the place of her thoughts.

"What are we doing?" she asked point blank, standing up. Suddenly, she wanted to run, to get out of there, but it was her place, so she felt trapped, the fear of losing him overwhelming her.

The gravity of the situation washed over his face as he caught on to her change in mood instantly, making her wonder if he had been anticipating the question. He looked down at his hands, the hands that held all the wisdom in the world on an operating table. "We're just being."

"And what happens when we can't 'just be' anymore? What happens when you leave? I keep asking it and we keep pretending that it doesn't matter, but Jack, every minute I spend with you makes that day harder for me."

He nodded. After a long silence, he stood up, and she could tell he felt the same way. "What do you want to do, Alice?"

She didn't want to say it because all she wished for right then was to have him hold her all night, but she knew that wouldn't make things any better. "I think you should go home." She said the words kindly and kept her emotions in check. This was enough. "I mean it this time. Please don't try to sweet talk me into another visit or one more day out. If you care about my feelings, then respect them. Because I don't have the strength to stay away from you on my own."

The hurt she felt, the ache, the loss of something big—it all showed on Jack's face. But she stood her ground because if he stayed, she knew she'd change her mind about asking him to leave her alone. It took all her will to get the words out. When she didn't say anything more, Jack looked down at the floor and nodded to himself. With sadness in his eyes, he took her hand, his fingers lightly intertwining with hers. She closed her eyes and slowly pulled away before the tears came.

When she opened them, she could see how much he wanted to stay, but it was also clear that he wanted to give her what she was asking for. So without another word, he left.

Chapter Twenty-Seven

It had been a week since that night on the sofa when Alice had asked Jack not to see her again. He'd kept his promise, but he had tried to text her, and she'd asked if he wouldn't. It was just too difficult. After that, he'd gone silent.

As the days went by, she'd thought about him, though. What surprised her was that the image that came to mind most often was of him in his white lab coat. Only recently did she realize why she didn't like seeing him dressed like that: all the greats keep going in life, always moving forward; they don't settle down. And Jack was one of the greats. He wouldn't return to the town where he grew up because he was still moving forward and that life was far behind him; he'd already lived it. He needed the next big challenge to make him whole; that thrill of adventure. That was who he was. Seeing him in his work environment reminded her of that fact.

During all her free moments, Alice had thrown herself into getting the shop ready, trying to keep her mind off losing him, because if she paused to really think about the days ahead without him, she could hardly manage. She hadn't even stopped for so much as a cup of coffee. She'd helped Melly with her packing. Her new friend had decided to stay with her parents until she could find a place to live. And when she wasn't helping Melly, Alice had ridden the waves with Henry, flown his new kite together, taken long walks with him and Einstein on the beach; and then, when he'd gone to play with Simon, she and Sasha had started planning: posters, website design, inventory—whatever she could do. She did the same thing after Henry and Sasha had gone to bed because the nights were the hardest. That was when all the thoughts and what-ifs crept in.

Sasha had only asked a few times, but Alice knew that her friend could sense her emotions about Jack leaving, so Sasha didn't press her when she changed the subject. She just worked right alongside her, showing her support through her effort to get the shop running.

So, that afternoon, when she saw Jack come around the corner of the shop, she had to remind herself to breathe. She set down the hose she'd been using to water the new plants and turned off the spigot, straightening herself and lifting her chin to keep from crumbling into his arms.

"I wanted to say goodbye before I left," Jack said, that smile of his she loved so much absent, replaced by apprehension. He stayed where he was. She saw the unhappiness in his eyes; he looked so tired, like he hadn't been sleeping well. Just seeing him like that made her want to burst into tears.

Why had he come? She couldn't do this. It was too hard.

He stepped toward her, and took her hand. His gaze swallowed her and he seemed as though he were asking permission to kiss her goodbye, but she wouldn't be able to cope if he did, so she moved away from him, letting go of his hand. Like he always seemed to do, he read her body language perfectly, nodding so subtly that she could hardly tell, but she knew that he'd decided he didn't want to push her. He was always trying to make her happy and this was his last effort.

"I'll see you." He stood there for a second, grief washing over his features despite his obvious attempt to keep his expression casual. It looked like he didn't want to leave. Inside she was screaming for him to stay, but she remained silent because if she made a sound, the tears would come hard and fast and she wouldn't know how to turn them off. Then, slowly, he started to back away, his eyes not leaving hers, every part of her body trembling more with every step he took.

He turned around, his back swelling with his breath, and he cleared his throat, still walking—it made her wonder if his emotion had gotten the better of him. She could understand because it was taking all her iron will to keep herself from calling out to him, from crying in his arms, and telling him not to go. Her lips quivering, her eyes now brimming with tears, she stood there while he opened the door to his car.

She couldn't watch any longer, so she turned around and walked over the dune to the beach, her legs barely able to carry her. She focused on every step as she moved further down the beach. She went all the way to the surf, her heart shattered, tears now streaming down her face, wishing he'd have just left without seeing her but knowing he never would've. She focused on the sea. She didn't try to look for answers there anymore—there weren't any.

She felt like she had a boulder on her chest, and she was taking in large gulps of briny air to keep herself from heaving with sorrow. Alice knew that she was able to live without Jack. She could live her life and raise Henry all by herself. But she wouldn't be truly happy without him. Jack made her feel complete.

As she contemplated this, behind her, she heard a soft pounding on the sand coming closer and closer, causing her to spin around. Jack was running toward her at full speed, his green eyes clamped onto hers. He came to a jolting stop in front of her, sheer determination on his face, those eyes more intense than she'd ever seen them. He slid his hands onto her face, running them up through the back of her hair, pulling her to him. But he didn't have to work very hard at all because she was moving into him like they'd been pushed together by a magnetic force. She grabbed onto him as if he could save her from all her emotion, and every muscle in her body released when his lips moved on hers, the softness of them combined with the energy of that moment making her more vulnerable than she'd ever been before.

With those strong arms around her, his breath mixing with hers, their entire past flashed in her mind: the young green eyes that first landed on her that day so long ago, their teenage hands side by side on the pier as he inched his towards hers, the slightly shy look he'd given her just before walking off down the road, throwing up a hand to her and Gramps; the way his smile had come into view in front of the apples the day she'd first arrived, the sweetness on his face as he'd listened to her on that bench; the moment their lips had touched when she'd caught the fish… All the memories came faster than she could process them, his lips moving urgently on hers as if he remembered them all too. How would she live without him?

Their kiss finally slowed and he pressed his forehead to hers. "Come to Chicago," he whispered. "Please."

She shook her head, but she could tell he already knew. He placed his hand on her shattered heart and closed his eyes.

"Okay. I'll go." He kissed her forehead, his lips lingering on her skin. And then, he was gone.

Alice hadn't slept at all last night. She'd been scrambling for anything that could bring Jack back, but she knew that there was nothing. He didn't have work here, and he had to work. It was pretty clear to her that Jack was supplementing Butch's income with his involvement in renting or buying a home and he needed to make that money. And if he stayed, would he even be happy here?

At the end of the day, when Alice hadn't been in the picture, he'd chosen to live in the city, and she wondered if he'd miss the fast-paced environment. Or had he only gone for his father? She'd never know because she wasn't going to have any long conversations with Jack Murphy anymore. She needed to make a clean break so she could give her heart time to heal. She didn't even want to think about whether or not that could actually happen. Right now, it didn't feel like it would. He'd always be that what-if in her life, that beacon of happiness that she hadn't followed. She wasn't thinking about any of that today, though, because she was heading over to have a goodbye breakfast with Melly.

Melly was leaving for her parents' tomorrow and Butch would be moving in by the end of next week. With Einstein in his crate, Henry over at Simon's house for a play date, and Simon's mother equipped with Alice's number should she have any questions, Alice picked up the present she'd gotten her friend and called upstairs to Sasha.

"Sash! Ready to go over to Melly's?"

They'd been quiet getting ready this morning as they shared the bathroom mirror, both of them trying not to be too emotional about their friend leaving. Melly's moving was going to leave a hole that even someone as wonderful as Butch wouldn't be able to fill.

Sasha came downstairs holding a brightly wrapped package and linked arms with Alice. Then, gifts in hand, they crossed the street to Melly's. Melly had tears in her eyes when she opened the door, and Alice felt the change in the air by the absence of the starfish wreath that used to hang in the place of a doorknocker.

Melly waved her hands in the air frantically, her tears coming faster. "Oh! I knew I couldn't do it without crying," she said, smiling as she opened the door wider. "I made sure to have extra tissue boxes today because I'm never going to make it through this."

With heavy hearts, they all went inside. The beautiful beach interior was now a sea of boxes, the floors dusty, the lighting harsh, all the lamps packed, leaving only the bright sunshine coming through the windows and the fluorescent kitchen light that ran along the ceiling in the open area between the counters and the living space on the other side. Alice set her gift down and climbed up on one of the barstools, grabbing a tissue just in case.

Melly gave Alice a hug—or rather, she plastered her with one, her arms squeezing Alice as if she were holding on for dear life. Then she did the same to Sasha. Sasha, as she always did when something was bothering her, went into chatty, smiley mode, thrusting her gift into Melly's hands and talking a mile a minute about how she'd spent weeks trying to find something perfect. The gift was wrapped in mint green paper with little palm trees printed on it, and a giant bow tied around the middle.

Melly set it on the counter. "Wait," she said with a sniffle. "I have something for the two of you." She left the room and returned, carrying a large, flat gift, wrapped in blue paper with little fishes on it and tied with twine. "This is for the both of you," she said, setting it on the bar between Sasha and Alice.

Sasha pulled the end of the twine, untying it and gently pulling it free. She set it aside and slipped her finger under the paper at one end, unfastening the tape that held it all together. With a tug, she pulled out a large picture frame, turning it around so both she and Alice could view it.

Alice swallowed, trying to keep her emotion at bay. It was the picture of the three of them, smiling, happy, the pastel colors of the shop behind them. They couldn't have predicted this moment when Melly had set the camera out and taken the photo, but now it seemed like Melly had given them the perfect gift. The three of them looked radiant, laughing, their cheeks tanned from the sun, the light coming in behind them like a ray of hope.

"This is so good, it could be a print ad for the shop," Sasha said, running a finger under her nose as if she had an itch, but Alice knew she, too, was trying to hold it together.

Alice pulled the frame closer to her, tilting it to get the glare off the glass so she could get a better look at her lovely friends. "It would go so well above the counter on the back wall so it's the first thing everyone sees when they come in."

"Maybe you can stay," Sasha said, that chattiness coming back again. "You could be a photographer. Do portraits for people on the beach? Or you could take marketing photos for people. You should start a portfolio…"

Melly grinned at that. "Maybe one day," she said.

"This is amazing," Alice said, still looking at the photo.

Melly bit her lip, obviously trying not to cry as well. "I love taking photos because they make such great memories and we just never know when we'll need them. I have a copy of that myself to take with me."

"I got something for you too!" Sasha said, sliding her palm-tree-wrapped gift toward Melly: her attempt at keeping her emotion in check. If any of them spent too long thinking about it, they wouldn't get through this.

Slowly and carefully, Melly picked it up, looking down at it for a second as if she didn't want to open it, as if she wanted time to slow down. She tugged on the ribbon until it fell loose and then opened one end. She slid the box out to reveal a handmade, fabric-covered photo album.

"For your photos," Sasha said, finally showing her emotion. She cleared her throat and smiled, tears sliding down her cheeks. She wiped them away with the back of her hand, her eyes blinking too much while she forced a smile.

Melly ran her hand delicately over the album cover. It was a beachy plaid colored with shades of apricot, and sea-foam greens, sandy browns and sea-oat tans. Melly set it down and put her face in her hands, and she started to sob. Her reaction to the gift seemed overly sentimental, and Alice wondered what was going through her mind. While they were all sad, Melly looked positively heartbroken, so much so that it was alarming to Alice. Melly's face was crumpled, her chest heaving, and she was barely able to catch her breath.

"This is the *perfect* gift," she finally managed, after the worst had subsided. "I know just what photo to begin with," she said, standing up and grabbing her bag. "I take it with me everywhere. It's the photo that started this whole journey for me."

Her face looked so forlorn that Alice was actually concerned for her friend. The pain was so visible that Alice just knew she was about to share whatever it was that had lurked there the whole time they'd known her. There had been more to her past, and Melly was finally going to tell them. Alice took in a breath to steady herself for whatever support her friend might need.

"Let's have a seat together on the sofa." Melly grabbed an envelope and came back over, setting it in her lap. "I've never told anyone this story before, but I've never had any friends as true as you two. Would you like to hear what really brought me to the Outer Banks?"

Alice couldn't think of any reasons better than a new job, distance from her ex-husband, and a beautiful location, but she did remember her earlier exchange with Sasha and she wondered again if there was more to the story with her ex-husband. She couldn't wait to hear; she felt so fortunate to have this last moment to support her friend. It was clear that Melly needed Alice and Sasha.

Sasha leaned in and patted Melly's knee, urging her to confide in them.

"The bike shop you all bought—it belonged to a man."

Alice felt the confusion on her face. Of course it belonged to a man. But it occurred to her that she'd never told Melly about him. How did Melly know that? Had Gramps made another little friend? She didn't remember meeting any young girls over her summers with Gramps, like when she'd met Jack. Had Melly rented a bike from him? Had he shared something with her? But Melly didn't grow up here… Alice's mind was going a hundred miles an hour trying to figure it out before Melly could tell them. Would Melly know something about Gramps that Alice needed to know? Suddenly she wanted to hear this story more than anything in the world. Her pulse racing in her ears, she listened.

Melly pulled a photo from the envelope and set it on her lap, facing them. The edges were worn, the finish faded. Alice held her breath, only becoming more confused by the photo in Melly's possession. It was Gramps—younger—in black and white. He was on the pier, holding a fish, a proud smile on his lips like she'd seen him hundreds of times. How had Melly gotten this photo and why would this have brought her here? Alice tried to swallow but her mouth was bone dry.

"My mother gave me this photo," Melly said, looking down at it. "She told me it was of a man in the Outer Banks. He owned a bike shop, and he was the kindest man she'd ever met."

With that one description of Gramps, Alice knew Melly's story was true. But how had he known Melly's mother? Alice spread her fingers on her thighs, her hands cold and sweaty as she awaited more explanation. She'd felt so close to Melly from the very beginning. Had Gramps initiated some sort of connection between the two of them? The room was completely quiet except for Alice's thoughts and the sound of the ocean coming through the window. Sasha caught Alice's eye. She looked riveted by what Melly had said, only making Alice's curiosity more unbearable.

Melly broke the silence again. "He'd shown up at my mother's doorstep one day, and he told her that no one in his family knew he'd come, but he wanted to see me. I was about five. My mom was terrified at first of this stranger, but then she remembered him from the day she adopted me. He had been there with my birth parents. He told her he was my grandfather."

Alice could literally feel the blood drain from her face. Her whole body started to shake. She wanted to say something, do something, but she was frozen, her mind taking all this in.

"You see, my mother, like me, couldn't have children—which we had a little chuckle over because we aren't blood relatives; but it was as if we were meant to be together."

Tears sprang to Alice's eyes, a wave of relief for her own parents washing over her. They'd been right. They'd been so right. Melly's parents were good and they'd been everything Alice's own parents had wanted for their first daughter. Melly was wonderful—it seemed as though she'd had a great relationship with her parents—and just as Alice had always wanted in a sister, they got along brilliantly. As she looked at Melly, really looked at her, it occurred to her that Melly had no idea to whom she was telling this story. But Alice's need to hear it in full kept her silent.

"You were adopted," she said, in the form of a statement. That was all she could get out before the silence took over again. She was in awe of the person in front of her. They'd spent all those days together completely unaware…

"My parents have never hidden the fact that I was adopted, and they told me my birth parents were amazing people, that they loved me so much, they knew my mom and dad would be the best for me. My mom told me about the talk she'd had with them in the hospital just before I was born and how perfect they were. And she told me about the man in the bike shop—my grandfather." Her eyes dropped down to the photo. "I've known about him for quite a while. I've had this picture since my tenth birthday, but I only recently felt like I had the courage to find him.

"I came here, hoping to meet him, and I was disappointed to find the shop had been sold. But I met you two instead, so I feel like it was meant to be." She smiled, the photo now unsteady in her hands.

"I prayed to learn more about where I came from. Not because I needed more family—mine was wonderful. But because I felt in my bones like I was missing something great." She shook her head. Alice took stock of the oval shape of Melly's face, the curve of her nose—both like Alice's father's and her own.

Sasha's eyes were the size of saucers, as she silently pressed Alice to say something, but she still couldn't find the words when she looked at her sister. She noticed the thin curve of her lips, like her mother's, and now she couldn't believe she hadn't spotted the resemblance before. It was practically glaring now. Melly's hair was thick, like her grandma's, her height similar to Gramps's…

"I don't know where he is now; that was my only lead. But my mom told me how much he adored this area and I just wanted to be near him. I've never felt different from anyone else growing up. I've had the best life. But there's this small part of me that felt a tiny void without the rest of my family present. He was my family. And I set out to tell him that. But I was too late and he'd gone."

Alice had put her hands over her mouth to stifle the total disbelief that something this wonderful could be true. She was staring right into the face of her sister. The sister she'd always wanted. The sister she'd missed so many years with. Tears were hot in her eyes, her breathing shallow.

She'd asked the sea—Gramps—to tell her if she'd made the right decision coming here, and this moment, this one moment, was worth anything else that had happened. It didn't matter whether Seaside Sprinkles was a success or the pier made it or *anything*—she had found her sister! Melly had been right here all along.

Melly must have read her face because she, too, had stopped talking and was now looking at Alice as if she'd just seen her, curiosity all over her face. The two of them hadn't even realized that Sasha was gone. They were both lost in thought.

Melly was the first to speak again: "I almost asked what had happened to the man at the bike shop that day when I first met you, but I figured you wouldn't know…" They both stared at each other, hope in Melly's eyes. Alice knew it was hope because she'd had that kind of hope before—the hope for something meant for her. "Do you? Do you know what happened to him?"

Finally, Alice spoke, taking Gramps's photo with a wobbly hand, feeling lightheaded. "Yes, I know what happened to him," she said, working to fill her lungs with breath so she could finish the explanation. "This is my gramps."

Melly's eyes were wide now, tears rolling down her cheeks. Alice wondered if she could see what Alice had seen, if she recognized her own eyes in Alice's, the similarities in their faces. Melly's bottom lip was quivering, and she was clearly robbed of her voice just like Alice had been. But it didn't matter. She didn't have to speak for Alice to know what she felt. Because Alice felt it too. Two only children now had each other.

"We're sisters," Alice said, the word rolling off her tongue and sounding so right, yet foreign at the same time. How had she missed this? How had she spent so much time with Melly and not felt it? Because now it was so clear to her, so obvious that she couldn't *not* see it. "But Gramps called you Grace."

Melly smiled. "That was the name given to me at the hospital, but my parents changed my name. They called me Melissa Grace St. James."

"Mm." That made Alice smile, her vision blurred with emotion. She put her arms around Melly, the two of them holding each other, both of them crying tears of joy. Everything was all coming together now. When they'd finally let go of one another, Alice said, "I can tell you all about your other family—our family."

Sasha suddenly came back in, out of breath, having obviously sprinted back to the shop. She handed the locket to Melly and then slid a small, folded piece of paper discreetly into Alice's hand as Melly's focus was on the locket. Alice knew what the paper was: it was Gramps's letter, stating that both girls should have the shop. Alice knew her friend well, and what she was saying with that gesture was to include Melly, to ask her to be a part of Seaside Sprinkles, just as Gramps had intended.

Melly got up to get another tissue and Sasha leaned over quickly and whispered, "There's enough room upstairs for three of us. We can squeeze her in."

Alice didn't need time to think about it. She knew that Jack was already paying well over the mortgage rate to rent the cottage for

Butch—Melly had asked Alice to tell Jack that it was too much, but he'd insisted on paying a good price. Melly had enough income from the rent that if she wanted to stay, she could probably swing it. And, in time, if they could make a go of Seaside Sprinkles, they'd have enough to pay her a salary.

Melly came back, her eyes still on the locket. "This is us," she whispered. "Together." She grabbed Alice's hands, laughing and crying at the same time.

Finding her was so amazing that Alice felt as though her heart would burst. Giggling through her tears, she said, "I have so much to tell you that I don't even know where to begin. I have the answers to all your questions."

"I can't wait to hear them!" Melly laughed. "I have so many questions that we could stay up all night talking. For days!" Then she held Alice's gaze. "Just when we found each other, we're being pulled apart again."

Alice nodded. Then, the hope she'd lost so many times swelled in her chest and she knew that this time, it wouldn't leave her. "I have an idea," she said, thinking of all the possibilities before them. "I want to discuss it with you, but I need to be sure I have it all worked out." She didn't want to raise Melly's hopes only to have the plan not work out. "Give me just a little time and then I'll tell you all about it."

Chapter Twenty-Eight

It had been two weeks since Jack had left. Alice had forced herself not to think about him—as much as she'd practiced keeping him off her mind, she wasn't getting any better at it. She just tried to keep her focus on Seaside Sprinkles.

The machines were gleaming, the toppings bar was brimming with local candies and chocolates, and the ceiling was a flock of brightly colored birds. The Donation Station was complete: a small shelf anchored to the wall, with a stool and a bright yellow-and-white striped cushion below. On the shelf was Alice's laptop, covered in local bumper stickers and open to their website, where patrons could donate to the pier. On the other side of the old showroom, across a sea of white tables and chairs, there was a brightly painted bookshelf. Sasha had filled it with books from the second-hand shop and all the chairs saved for the locals were scattered around it. Alice couldn't bring herself to change the one she'd labeled "Jack" in a moment of weakness. Perhaps it had been her last surge of optimism. Now it just felt like stupidity.

The only time she talked about Jack was when Henry mentioned him. He said he missed him. She'd just been honest and told him she did too, and that Jack would be back to visit because his dad was living in Melly's cottage right across Beach Road.

The concert Melly had mentioned a few weeks ago, Coastal Tortuga Jam, was being held tonight. Alice had sent out invitations to all her friends and family, inviting them to the show and the grand opening that she and Sasha had planned. She'd thought long and hard about whether or not to send an invitation to Jack, because she knew how difficult it would be for both of them, but she couldn't exclude him. She wanted him there to celebrate. A few days ago, she'd received his reply card, with a little note telling her that he had other commitments, but he wished her all the success in the world. She'd studied his handwriting, revisiting it all day, the card folded in her back pocket. She kept it with her just so she could feel close to him. It was a double-edged sword: if he'd said he could come, she'd only be sad when he left again, and she didn't think she could cope with him leaving a second time. But seeing that he wasn't coming had been disappointing, her hopes dashed.

She decided to put all her emotional energy into her family. Alice knew that she and Melly had a long road ahead of them: Alice still had to think of the best way to tell Henry he had an aunt, and she knew she had to tell her father she'd found her sister. Would Melly's family want that for her? Would they accept Alice and her father into their lives? Would her own family accept Melly? She'd discussed it all with Melly, the two of them unified in their worries, but, in the end, this could only be a good thing—she could just feel it. This was what Gramps would've wanted. Right?

Alice would start answering those questions tonight. Her father was coming for the grand opening, and it would be here that he would come face to face with his first-born. She'd already prepared Melly, and they'd decided to hold off until after everyone else had left, so he could hear the news in the presence of just his immediate family.

Melly couldn't wait to meet him. "I came looking for one man and I found a whole family," she'd said, barely able to contain herself at the thought of meeting her biological father. Alice had extended an invitation to Melly to stay the night with them at the shop when she'd come back from her parents' house for the opening of Seaside Sprinkles. Alice had told her she could stay as long as she liked.

Alice, Sasha, Melly, and Henry stood in the space that used to be the bicycle showroom. It was an explosion of pinks, blues, greens, and whites, all the glass in the windows gleaming, the logos looking so professional. The tables were filled with helium balloons in complementary colors; shiny cellophane gift bags full of ice cream-shaped cookies and chocolates from the local confectioner, tied with curly ribbon, were piled on their surfaces. The framed photo of the three women that Melly had taken was hung above the counter, just like Alice had said she would. The other photos Melly had taken of the old shop had been framed in white and they lined the wall by the door.

The ice cream flavors lined the inside of the glass-topped counters; bright white spoons jutted invitingly out of every topping container on the bar in the center of the room. They had caramel sauce, hot fudge, whipped cream, and even a container of red velvet sauce for the cream cheese ice cream they'd made specially for this day.

"We did it," Sasha said to Alice, shaking her head in awe at the transformation. Gramps's shabby little beach bike shop was a vibrant, cheerful new space.

Melly pinched the top of one of the gift bags and held it up to view its contents. Then she gingerly put it back in its place. "I can't believe how much you've done in such a short time! You're gonna have so much business, you won't be able to serve them all—I can feel it!"

"I hope you're right! If so, we'll need all hands on deck," Alice said. She threw a look over to Sasha, and Sasha nodded. "Melly, can we go upstairs for a second? I'd like to show you something." She knew that Sasha could greet any early visitors. Alice and Sasha had talked a lot about this in the last week, and she knew it was the perfect time to bring Melly in on it.

Alice led the way to the top loft area.

"I still can't get over how pretty it is up here," Melly said, her head swiveling from one end of the room to the other. She'd really liked the new interior when she'd arrived this morning.

Einstein perked up in his crate. He'd had a bath and was waiting for his ice cream cone-patterned ribbon to be tied to his neck with a pink leash for opening night.

"Glad you like it! Sasha and I have a lot more planned for up here. Maybe you'll be able to give us a few ideas," Alice said, threading her fingers through Einstein's crate and wriggling them. He batted at them with his paw, his tail thumping the inside of the crate. Alice sat down on the sofa and pulled the folded piece of paper from her pocket, where it had been all day. All morning, she'd put her hand in her pocket, grabbing hold of it off and on as she prepared for the opening, thinking through whether or not inviting Melly to co-own and help run the shop would work. She and Sasha had talked it over and as long as they made enough money for the three of them to live on, they agreed it would be just fine to bring her aboard.

Melly joined Alice on the sofa.

"I have something to show you and then a question to ask." She opened the paper, pressing it flat against her leg.

"What is it?" Melly turned her attention to the document in Alice's hands as she wriggled up beside her to get a better view of the writing.

Through the open window, the band was doing sound checks. A gigantic stage had been erected during the day—Henry had watched it all from the patio, mesmerized by it. Lights went up, makeshift crowd fences were put in place, and enormous speakers were brought in. Alice could hear the mics being tested, giving the whole atmosphere a boost of anticipation.

"Well, I have a bomb to drop on you."

Melly looked at her curiously.

"When Gramps passed away, he left me his shop. But originally, he willed it to both you and me." She held out the letter for Melly to read properly and she watched her sister's eyes scan Gramps's words.

Melly's eyes widened, her mouth falling open just slightly before she snapped it closed. She looked up. "That's crazy."

"Not so crazy. He was your grandfather too."

"But I didn't do anything to deserve an inheritance."

Alice grinned, her thoughts on the man who would offer free bike rides every Christmas and Easter, the man who did bicycle and roller skate tune-ups for anyone under eighteen and stroller repairs for free, the man who donated all his profits on the fourth of July to the local volunteer fire department.

"That was Gramps. He was just like that." She could almost feel him there with them now. Alice knew he'd be delighted to see how well they got along.

"I was thinking—and Sasha is also on board with this—would you like to run Seaside Sprinkles with us? We have room for you up here." She got up and took Melly down the hall to a small room they had filled with boxes. "You'd have to downsize considerably, but we could make it work."

Melly stared at her, her eyes restless, clearly taking in this new proposition. She walked over to the window overlooking the beach.

Alice took a step toward her, peering out the window, the crowds beginning to dot the sand, the sound checks still going on. The announcer was practicing now. When Melly turned around, her eyes were glassy with emotion. "It's a wonderful offer," she said. "But I would hate to impose on your dream. I just feel like you deserve it all."

"So do you. Maybe this is why you came here. You wanted to find Gramps and you did. Things just went a little differently than you'd planned." She looked Melly in the eye—those familiar eyes. "I want you to stay. I need my sister here."

Melly broke out into a wide grin and threw her arms around Alice. "Okay!" she said, excitement bubbling up in her voice. "I'd love to!"

Alice laughed, hugging her sister. "Then we'd better get downstairs! We have work to do and you start tonight!"

Alice was delighted with the number of people who'd driven hours just to come to the opening of Seaside Sprinkles. Even parents of her childhood friends had shown up. The place was packed—standing room only—everyone eating ice cream, nibbling their opening day cookies among the balloons, and lining up to log in donations for the pier at the computer. They'd nearly sold out of the most popular three flavors, and the toppings containers had to be refilled so many times she'd lost count. People were chatting, laughing, enjoying themselves while they walked around sampling treats from a few trays Alice and Sasha had made up earlier.

Einstein was popular with the kids: they all took turns walking him around the shop and petting him. His tail hadn't stopped wagging since the doors first opened. He'd been so good, the crowds keeping him too busy to try to get the candy on the table. Sasha had put out a special bowl full of dog treats just for him.

There were so many people stopping her to talk that Alice could hardly get around to everyone. Some had wanted to reminisce about the bike shop, telling her old memories they'd had with Gramps. Others grabbed her arm to wish her congratulations and tell her how great a job she'd done. She'd smiled, talked to them, offered them different flavors of ice cream to try, but it wasn't until she saw one particular friendly face that a warm happiness washed over her. She couldn't deny the elation that filled her when she saw Butch. She hadn't met up with him since before Jack had left, and just seeing his smile and that white beard brought back all those wonderful days she'd had with him and his son.

"I found my chair," he said with obvious delight, pulling it out so he could view his name on the plate. "I can't wait to use it this summer." His gaze flickered to the chair labeled "Jack," but he didn't mention it. He just smiled at her instead.

"Bring me that wonderful pie of yours and I'll trade you for ice cream." She drew him in for a hug. "I'm so happy you came."

"I wouldn't miss it for the world."

"Are you going to the concert?"

"Oh, no. This old man is going to take his ice cream and head home. But I want to catch up later once everything settles down, okay?"

"Okay." She wanted to ask about Jack, but she didn't. She wanted to know how he was, what he'd been up to. But it would only make her emotional, and she needed to think happy thoughts today for her launch. This was a great day and things were going so well for her. She needed to enjoy that and try not to dwell on how much she missed him. She pushed away the fear that once things settled down—when she didn't have the opening and all that had happened with Melly to busy her mind, and she fell into the quiet routine of life—the pain of losing him would hit her at full force and she'd struggle to recover.

The concert was getting started, the music thumping its way into the shop. When the door opened, the smell of outdoor grills and beer filled the air. The static sound of the ocean against the music had a buzzing effect, the atmosphere positively electric. As everyone headed out to the beach, Alice said goodbye to Butch, made sure Henry was by her side, and found her father through the crowd as they exited the shop. She locked up and grabbed her dad's hand. He smiled down at her, then tickled Henry's sides, making him laugh, clearly energized by the surroundings.

It wasn't the time to introduce them properly, but she wanted Melly and her father to share this memory together. The live music, the warm air, and the excitement of the crowd were something they didn't get to experience right outside the back door of the shop every day. This was a once-in-a-lifetime event, and Alice could already tell it would be one of her fondest memories. She took her father over to where Melly was standing. Sasha found them too, after putting Einstein in his crate. The puppy was exhausted from all the attention and the crowd outside was so massive that they'd decided to keep him safely at home.

Sasha took Henry's hand and found a place among the concertgoers.

"I want you to meet my friend," Alice said to her dad, linking arms with Melly. "This is Melly St. James. Melly, this is my father, Frank."

"Oh, hello, Melly," her father said politely, his voice raised to project it over the guitars that were squealing as the band got going. "It's nice to meet you."

"Melly's going to work here at the shop with us." Alice turned to Melly, and, because she knew, she could see the reaction in Melly's face at being there with him, but she was hiding it well, clearly knowing that their reunion would be a sweet one.

"It's *so* nice to meet you," she said loudly, giving each of the words significance when she said them, her gaze sweeping his face, back and forth. Alice wished Melly could've met their mother too, but her mom and Gramps were probably smiling down on them right now.

They found their places in the sand, squeezing their way through people to be next to Sasha and Henry, just as the band was kicking up, the cheers louder than the crashing waves. Alice looked out at the ocean, thinking now how it had given her more answers than she'd given it credit for. It had brought her to Melly, offered her a place where she could remember Gramps, and a home for her and Henry. She had been given more than so many people had, which was why she felt guilty even looking at the ocean, because she silently wished she could have had something great with Jack. She missed him so much, and she just didn't feel like this day was complete without him.

Indulgently, she wanted to send the ocean one more wish, hoping it would give her answers, and knowing in her heart that she was asking too much. But, as she looked out at the waves, her wish on her lips, she was interrupted by June.

"There she is!" June called out. "There's my girl!" She sent a heartfelt smile over to Alice while she pushed through the crowd to get closer.

A young woman walked beside June, smiling at Alice as if she knew her.

When they reached her, June said, "This is my daughter, Emma. She opened the new Seagull's Cove site for me."

"Oh, hello," Alice said over the roar of the crowd, shaking her hand.

"The new space is fantastic," Emma said. "I'm so glad you suggested it to Mom."

It was difficult to hear, Emma having to nearly scream the words, so they couldn't talk too long.

"We're going back into the restaurant," June said. "Lots to do before we open! But promise me, when you get tired of all this noise you'll come in!"

"Okay, I will!"

"Promise?" June raised her eyebrows, commanding Alice's full attention.

"I promise."

Chapter Twenty-Nine

That evening, they'd all come back from the concert just before it had finished, to prepare for anyone who might be stopping by for ice cream after the show. Henry had taken a seat in one of the chairs next to his Grandpa Frank, and Sasha had gone upstairs to give the family a moment together before they frantically filled the toppings containers, replenished the bowls, spoons and napkins, and wiped down the tables. Right now, however, they were all planning to settle at one of the tables together—the whole little family.

This was it. It was time.

"Dad?" Alice said, setting the bowls of ice cream she'd scooped for them on the table and sitting down next to Melly, holding her hand while the music outside continued to play, muffled by the closed windows. Melly smiled, her demeanor anxious with anticipation, her focus on her birth father, as Henry picked up his spoon and dipped it into his ice cream. "Melly and I want to share something with you and Henry."

"Oh?" Her dad sat up, curiosity showing as he looked at the two of them.

Melly glanced over to Alice to ask if she could speak first and Alice nodded. "Alice didn't tell you my whole name when I first met you," she said. "It's Melissa Grace." She waited; it was clear that she had him thinking by the way his eyes grew round. "Grace."

Frank turned to Alice for confirmation. Alice couldn't help but smile, her lips starting to wobble, the tears coming faster than she had anticipated. "She had a picture of Gramps," she said, breathless. "She moved here to find him, but she found us instead. We waited to tell you when we could all be alone together."

With a jagged breath, her dad clapped his hands over his mouth, his eyes brimming with tears and disbelief, as he studied the face of his daughter.

"It's really her, Dad. Look. She has your eyes."

Frank slumped forward, grabbing the hands of both girls and putting them to his lips, sobbing into them.

"Why's Grandpa Frank crying?" Henry asked.

Alice squeezed her dad's hands while she answered her son. "Because for a long time, he's wanted to see Melly and now he has. Melly is my sister, but another family adopted her and took care of her until she was a grownup." She knew there would be more questions, and she'd have to think hard about the answers, but for now that satisfied Henry.

Henry put his spoon down and walked over to Melly, sitting next to her, his little feet swinging above the paint-splattered hardwoods that they'd lacquered with high gloss. "Does this mean you get to have Christmas with us?"

"Yep!" she said, with a laugh and then a sniffle. "I'll have two Christmases: one with my other family and one with yours."

"That's lucky," he said, undoubtedly thinking this over.

She laughed. "Yes. Yes, it is very lucky."

* *

Alice had gone up and gotten Sasha, they'd served customers all night until they finally closed and then, together, they'd opened a bottle of champagne, toasting their success and the new beginnings that started tonight. Melly and her dad hadn't stopped talking the entire time, the champagne making their conversation even more fluid, their laughter rising into the air like bubbles. They'd talked about everything: Melly's and Alice's childhoods; a little story that Melly's adoptive mother had told her must have been because of her genetics—apparently, Melly was the only one in the family who loved jazz music, and her mother remembered it playing in Gramps's car when he'd stopped by that day so long ago. Her dad had told Melly about her birth mother, about their decision to give her to her adoptive parents, and how much they'd missed her.

Alice had asked her dad to stay the night, knowing that he and Melly might still be there talking in the wee hours of the morning. Alice, too, had a lot of catching up to do with Melly—she had so many questions for her new sister. But she knew that they had all the time they'd need, and she couldn't be happier for that gift.

"Oh!" Alice said suddenly, remembering her promise to June. She went over to the door and opened it to look at the restaurant windows at the end of the pier. They were all still bright. "I know it's late, but I promised June I'd come by after the concert."

"It *is* really late," Sasha said. "You could probably go tomorrow."

"She made me promise. I'll just run over there quickly. I'd feel awful telling her I'd come by and then not showing. I'll let her know she doesn't have to entertain me, that I just popped by for a quick second, and we can catch up tomorrow. I'm sure she saw how busy we were and she'd understand."

Alice set her champagne down and slipped her shoes back on. "I'll be right back." She left them all filling their glasses again.

The pier was still lit up under the black sky that was like a bowl of stars, the darkness completely hiding the ocean. Alice wouldn't even know it was there, except for its roar as the waves came tumbling onto the sand below her. The restaurant windows were open when she got to the door and tugged on the large brass handles.

"Hello?" she called inside, noting the doors were unlocked, so they couldn't have all gone home yet. She walked in and stood in the empty space that would soon be their dining room. It was a large expanse, with gleaming wooden floors and high ceilings, and she was willing to bet that, in the light of day, every window would offer an amazing view of the Atlantic.

"You made it!" June said, coming in, her shoes clacking, sending an echo through the room.

She went over to a stack of chairs on the far wall and pulled two down, dragging them to the center where Alice stood. "Have a chat with me." She shifted one of the chairs toward Alice, the leg squealing as it made contact with the floor.

"Oh, I only came by to see the place since I promised. I know it's late and I wouldn't want to keep you…"

"I know. I've been waiting forever. Have a seat. I have some news."

News? Alice sat down across from June, not asking any questions, though her curiosity was getting the better of her. She placed her hands in her lap, her eyes on June.

"The good news is my daughter Emma is pregnant."

"Oh, wow!" Alice said, scooting forward and leaning on her knees to share in June's excitement. "Congratulations. That's wonderful." She had no doubt that June would be the very best grandmother.

Obviously proud of that news, June looked elated. "Thank you. We're thrilled. It was a surprise for us all." She was talking with her hands, her eyebrows bouncing up and down.

Then June pressed her lips together, and Alice wondered, by the look on her face, if there was more to the story than she'd divulged. There was something else behind her smile.

"Emma was running the restaurant and we've just moved to this new building. The baby has changed the game. Emma doesn't want to run it full time anymore."

Her face became serious, causing Alice to sit up straight, already wondering about the fate of Seagull's Cove.

"She'd always said that when she had a baby, she wanted to stop working and raise her children. I'm ready to retire, and I know what goes into running this place. I don't have the energy anymore."

Oh, no. If the restaurant closed, the pier wouldn't survive and Seaside Sprinkles would definitely feel the blow of that. Alice wished she'd listened to Sasha and waited to come over until tomorrow. She would've liked to have at least one night of happiness, but now all her fears were sliding back in. They'd come so far, only to fall now.

"I've sold the restaurant, Alice," June said, pulling her from her worry.

Sold it?

That's not closing it. That could work.

This was an unexpected development. She knew the dangers of changing management. Seagull's Cove might not survive if the new owner didn't keep up June's high level of performance. It meant the door hadn't shut entirely; although it certainly didn't ease Alice's mind a whole lot.

"Do you think it will be as successful under new management?" she asked, all this new information, mixed with the champagne, giving her a throbbing sensation at her temples.

"Will you wait right here for a quick second?" June said. "I'll go get the new owner."

It was late. Alice was tired. Did she have to do this now?

She looked up when June returned, but it wasn't June.

It was Jack.

"Hey," he said with that crooked grin. "I hear you have some questions about the new management." He walked over toward her while he spoke and she wanted to throw her arms around him, but she didn't trust the situation yet. She needed to find out what was going on. He couldn't have…

"What do you know about running a restaurant?" she asked, overwhelmed by his presence, but trying her best to keep her cool.

He broke into an enormous smile that sent her heart pounding. "Absolutely nothing." He chuckled, his gaze never leaving hers. "But June's going to show me the ropes." He reached her, looking down at her, his scent making it hard to focus. She swallowed to avoid breathing in large gulps of it like she wanted to do.

"You'll work all hours," she worried aloud, keeping herself composed, still not believing it completely.

Jack pursed his lips in contemplation, his smile returning. "I'm used to that."

"You'll be exhausted at the end of the night."

He took the last step closer to her. "I can just walk across to Dad's if I'm that tired. I'll have things there."

"And where will you live?"

"With him."

"So you just gave up your regular job to run a restaurant?"

He smiled down at her. "I know someone else who did something similar."

"You're crazy."

"Maybe. But if that's the case, then you are too." He leaned toward her, that cottony, spicy scent now assaulting her. "Remember that day when you first got here and you didn't think you'd made the right choice? I thought about that a lot. Moving here makes no sense for me career-wise. There's no place for me full time at the hospital here, although I do plan to help out now and then. I'm leaving the best team of surgeons in Chicago that I know.

"Everything about working here is wrong. But what did I tell you that day? I said if you make the wrong decision, you just have to try a little harder to turn it into the right one. I didn't become a doctor for me; I did it for my dad. It's all I know how to do, but I'm ready for the next challenge. And I had all the motivation in the world because you are so right for me. I didn't care what I had to do, because all I knew was that I needed to be with you, and if that meant coming home, then I had to figure it out. I love it here. I love *you*."

He put his hands on her waist and drew her close, their faces inches apart. "The minute June mentioned it to me, I knew it was right. I wanted to tell you what I was doing, but I didn't want to get your hopes up, only to have something fall through. I had to wait for just the right time to tell you."

"You could've come for my opening," she said, the idea suddenly hitting her.

"I didn't want what we had to work through to take away from your day."

"But I could've danced with you at the concert," she teased, finally allowing herself to smile at him.

"We'll have the rest of our lives to dance."

Jack raised his hands to her face and gently pulled her toward him. Then, he pressed his mouth to hers, the sweet taste of summer on his lips, the sound of the ocean and all its answers crashing behind them.

Two Years Later

The pier was empty except for Alice. She leaned on the very back railing of it, facing the waves, thinking of Gramps. This was where she had always come for answers: the sea. That beautiful coastal wind blew against the white chiffon of her dress as her newly manicured fingers gripped the old wood, which had been draped in magnolia garlands. The diamond that Jack had slipped on her finger after he'd hidden it in one of Butch's birds shone, as she thought about the words he'd engraved on the band: "Let's make you and me an us."

The rows of white chairs behind her had been full of her loved ones today. Melly had brought a brand-new date to Alice and Jack's wedding, and she'd giggled all day long. He'd made her laugh, spun her around in the sunshine on the makeshift dance floor, her rose-colored bridesmaid's dress fanning out around her just before he'd drawn her in for a kiss. He was a chef who'd moved to the Outer Banks to work at Jack's restaurant. According to Melly, Steven's crab bisque was to die for. Sasha agreed. She and Sam had tried it the night they'd introduced Melly to Steven. He happened to be Sam's cousin, so they'd set Melly and Steven up for their first meeting as a double date with Sasha and Sam. The four of them had had a blast.

A lot had happened for Sasha and Sam in the last two years. They'd eloped last year on the beach with Alice and Melly their only witnesses. Sasha had said she'd never been happier in her life, and Alice couldn't hide her smile when she'd had to get the seamstress to loosen the stitches in the waist of Sasha's bridesmaid dress at their last fitting. Her friend had sat her down, tears in her eyes, and told her that the doctors said this pregnancy was moving along just perfectly, and if she was really still, she could feel her little girl move in her belly. Sam had been beside himself with excitement when he'd found out, and he'd completely furnished a small room as a nursery, having a local artist paint a seashell mural in pinks and creams to surprise Sasha. When she saw it for the first time, he'd kneeled down in front of her and spoken into her belly, telling their little girl he'd do anything for her and her mother.

The pier behind Alice was littered in confetti, the tables along the sides full of champagne glasses, Sasha and Melly's bridesmaid bouquets left on top. The white satin bow that Einstein had worn for the ceremony was draped on a chair. Seagull's Cove had outdone itself with the food for the reception. This day had been their day—hers and Jack's. And now, after everyone had gone, Sasha having taken Henry home next door, Alice looked out at her world.

The last truck had pulled away yesterday, the remodel of Seaside Sprinkles finished. The shop had been a hit right off the bat, and here Alice was, two years later, staring at the place where Gramps's old fishing shack-turned-bike shop had been. The shack was still there, or its bones were—she'd made the builders keep the original frame—but now there was an addition off the back with an enormous covered patio with paddle fans and outdoor lighting strung along the ceiling; there were bright pots of geraniums and pink umbrellas at white tables for overflow when the indoor room got full. Although that would be a little more difficult now that the room was three times its original size.

They'd also renovated the top floor into a suite for Alice, Jack and Henry, with small bungalows added to the property, each one with its own kitchen, living room, bedroom and bath. There was a bungalow for everyone: Melly, Sasha and Sam, Butch—and even Henry's Grandpa Frank, who'd sold his home in Richmond and moved the minute he'd found out he could. When they'd gotten so busy they could hardly manage, Melly had sold her cottage across the street and invested all the profits in Seaside Sprinkles. With her contribution and a further outlay from Jack, they were able to achieve exactly what they wanted.

Each bungalow had its own double doors that led out onto a porch facing the beach, with pebble paths between them lined with wildflowers. The ceilings were high, the spaces modern, with brand-new appliances and lighting, and they were all painted that bright beachy white, making them appear bigger than they were, like Gramps had originally done.

Alice turned back to the ocean. So many times she'd looked to the Atlantic for answers, and only now did she really hear the words Gramps had spoken: "When you need to know the answers to life, you turn to the sea. It gives you the calm you need to filter through the static in your head, until you can hear the answers loud and clear." She'd had to filter a lot of static first, but now, she could hear, and she knew that there was nothing but happiness ahead of her.

While Melly had decided to stay in the Outer Banks and live with Alice, they'd all met Melly's adoptive family, and her mother and father were absolutely wonderful people. They fit in perfectly with Alice's family, and they'd spent the last two Christmases together as one group. This year, Melly had suggested that everyone spend the holiday in the

Outer Banks, and she, Alice and Sasha had already started planning the festivities even though it was still summer. They'd squeeze everyone into the main house, light fires in the fireplaces, and fill the tables with food and wine, cakes and Christmas cookies. Alice could hardly wait.

The ocean seemed to reflect her mood, the tide gentle and quiet today. As the breeze blew the wisps of curls from her up-do around her face, she felt two strong arms encircle her and Jack's lips on her bare shoulder.

"Here you are," he said. He'd followed Sasha back to the house to make sure Henry was settled in the new space. Sasha had offered to go alone, but Henry had insisted that Jack take him; they were inseparable. Jack had even signed up to be the baseball coach for Henry's little league team.

Alice leaned into Jack, closing her eyes and remembering the first moment she'd encountered those arms. It was right at the forefront of her mind because only a few hours earlier, she'd burst into laughter when she and Jack entered Seagull's Cove as man and wife to the applause of their friends and family, and she realized that Jack had planned an extra table full of apples as a display by the cake. Each one had been carved perfectly with their initials.

"Well, Mrs. Murphy, let's go take a look at our house," Jack said, his lips near her ear as he stood behind her, looking over from the pier to the front porch that wrapped around the entire building. There were rocking chairs and plants, porch swings and little tables. It was dreamy and bright, and she couldn't wait to see her family fill its space.

Without warning, he swept her up into his arms, causing her to squeal. "I'm carrying you across the threshold."

Still giggling, she wrapped her arms around his neck. "It's a long way to the house," she warned.

"I do four days a week at the gym! I've told you this!" He buried his head in her neck, tickling her with kisses and making her laugh again.

Then he set off on a sprint down the pier, past the place where they'd sat catching fish with Gramps that day so long ago, down the steps where she'd watched him walk home that first day she'd met him as a girl, across the front of Seaside Sprinkles where he'd first found out the building belonged to her, and all the way up to their room where they would make new memories for the rest of their lives.

A Letter from Jenny Hale

I'm delighted you grabbed yourself a copy of *The Summer Hideaway*. I hope it made you feel so summery that you couldn't wait to slip on those sunglasses and put your toes in the sand!

If this was the first time you've read one of my summer books, I have plenty more for you! Have a look at my other titles to keep the coastal breeze blowing: *The Summer House*, *Summer at Oyster Bay*, *Summer by the Sea*, and *A Barefoot Summer*.

If you did enjoy *The Summer Hideaway* I'd love it if you'd write a review. Getting feedback from readers is so exciting, and it also helps to persuade other readers to pick up one of my books for the first time.

I do hope you pick up more books by me so I can share my stories with you. And if after reading all my books, you're craving even more happy endings, I can drop you an email when my next one is out. You can **sign up here**:

www.bookouture.com/jenny-hale

I won't share your email with anyone else, and I'll only email you when a new book is released.

Until next time!

Jenny

Find me on:

author/show/7201437.Jenny_Hale

jennyhaleauthor

@jhaleauthor

jhaleauthor

www.itsjennyhale.com

Acknowledgments

This book is possible as a result of years of support from great folks. A gigantic thank you to two amazing people for their patience and attention, while I embarked on this journey and as I continue: Oliver Rhodes and Natasha Harding—I am forever grateful for you both; without the two of you, I would not be where I am in this business today. Oliver, I thank you for the potential you saw in me, and the time you spent on the process to get me here. Natasha, you are the absolute best with your encouragement and team approach. I'm so thankful for you. To the fantastic team at Bookouture who have made this an experience I will never forget, thank you so very much. To all those outside of my publisher—Axelrod-Ett Productions, Nina Weinman, and so many more who continue to lift me higher in other media—thank you.

To my wonderful friends—Patty, Tia, and Adrienne, who read all my texts and corresponding emoticons during every step I made along the way—I am so grateful for your humor and excitement. The book groups who graciously had me visit and talked stories with me over the years, I send you all big hugs. Kathleen, the martinis and video book club rank up at the top! To those early readers, you are my army of good vibes; your kind words fuel me as I start every project.

And last of all, a heartfelt thank you must go out to my husband, Justin, and my kids, who I drag along to tours, landmarks, and historical sites every vacation while I squeeze in research and inspiration for that next novel that's simmering away in my crazy brain. They have taken SUVs on the beach, climbed lighthouses, toured Christmas lights on historical homes, and had many other adventures so that I could get that reality into my scenes to bring the readers better stories. They are an amazing support and my whole world.

empty of Gramps's bikes, and put her hands on her hips. Even with the new sense of purpose that had taken over her, it still stung a little to see the bike shop without Gramps. There was a part of her that didn't want to touch a thing and then another part that knew Gramps would be delighted to see what she could do with the place. Her eyes fell on the glass front door, where Gramps would always be standing waiting for her. It felt like he should be there now, smiling, asking if he could help her bring her things inside. It was as if he'd just vanished and she couldn't get used to it.

The coastal wind rippled her T-shirt, temporarily relieving the humidity. The waves were big today—good for surfing, but bad for fishing, she immediately thought. The sun and surf would bring out all the early tourists, scaring the fish further out to sea. Over the dune, she could already make out a few multicolored umbrellas dotting the shoreline. She let her gaze roam to the pier beside them, its towering legs sprawled into the tide, its body reaching out 754 feet over the ocean, as Gramps had told her. A few people were walking down it, and others sat in rocking chairs provided by the small shops at the entrance, but it was quiet today.

An airplane flew over, its thunderous engine commanding her attention. It was one of those familiar propeller planes that hugged the coast, a banner trailing behind it with an advertisement for the early tourists. It crossed between her and the sun, blocking the penetrating rays for an instant. Alice shielded her eyes and squinted up at the text promoting an all-you-can-eat seafood buffet. The tourists always seemed to like that: getting their hard-earned money's worth after they'd traveled miles and miles to soak up the sun for a week.

It was also those people who rented bikes from Gramps so they could pop around to the souvenir and trinket shops. They didn't know anything about the man at the bike shop; how kind Gramps was, how much he gave of himself, how he had even repaired beach cruisers for two elderly women—Olive and Maple, his friends who lived in town. They brought him breakfast: egg sandwiches on buttermilk biscuits the size of Alice's fist, and little fritters with okra inside. They biked well into their eighties, their pastel beach cruisers sporting little baskets on the front where they'd hold their brown bags of food, folded over once and in a perfect line so as not to crush the contents.

Occasionally, in the afternoons, they'd stop by and ask Gramps to check their tires. He'd fill them up with air, free of charge. Olive and Maple were sweeter than the lemonade sorbet they were known for, and that was saying something. Alice wondered if Gramps was with them now, handing out Mason jars of iced tea while they all sat in their heavenly rockers up there in the land that, at the church Gramps took her to on Sundays, was promised to all who believe.

"I want to get into that water already," Sasha said, stepping up next to her. Her nose was still a little red, but behind her sunglasses it was difficult to tell if she was emotional again. It wasn't the right time to press her, though. Her friend's dark hair was pulled up into a ponytail, her aviators reflecting the pier. "It's gorgeous today, so warm already. Maybe we can unpack a few boxes—just enough—and spend the rest of the day on the beach. I'm beat from loading the trailer this morning."

Alice didn't want to think about how tired she was. If she let the exhaustion set in, she'd be asleep the moment she slowed down, and they still had unpacking to do. Six in the morning had come early for her today; she'd spent a good five hours finishing up the packing of the trailer the night before, staying up way too late, so she was beat before she'd even made the drive to the Outer Banks.

"I want to go swimming too!" Henry said, walking over with Einstein, who'd found a piece of driftwood and had it in his mouth,